CW01649864

…NS

Tanya smiled sexily at Adrian [illegible] low light from the bedside lamp as she began to strip. Slowly she slid the black silk dress down her voluptuous body, her skin shimmering in the soft reflected light. Now she was naked but for a half-cup bra which barely concealed her overflowing breasts and matching cream panties cut high on her gleaming hips.

'What are you waiting for?' she said, reaching behind her to unfasten her bra. 'Come in and close the door.'

And as her big white breasts tumbled free, Adrian did as he was told . . .

Also available from Headline Delta

Kiss of Death
The Phallus of Osiris
Empire of Lust
Citizen Juliette
Amateur Nights
Amateur Days
Bianca
Compulsion
Two Weeks in May
The Downfall of Danielle
Exposed
Indecent
Fondle in Flagrante
Fondle on Top
Fondle All Over
Hot Pursuit
High Jinks Hall
Lust on the Loose
Maid
Passion in Paradise
Reluctant Lust
The Wife-Watcher Letters
Amorous Appetites
Hotel D'Amour
My Duty, My Desire
Sinderella
The Story of Honey O
Three Women
Total Abandon
Wild Abandon

Ultimate Vibrations

Jeff Charles

HEADLINE
DELTA

Copyright © 1997 Potiphar Productions

The right of Jeff Charles to be identified as the Author of the Work has been asserted by him in accordance with the Copyright, Designs and Patents Act 1988.

First published in 1997
by HEADLINE BOOK PUBLISHING

A HEADLINE DELTA paperback

10 9 8 7 6 5 4 3 2

All rights reserved. No part of this publication may be reproduced, stored in a retrieval system, or transmitted, in any form or by any means without the prior written permission of the publisher, nor be otherwise circulated in any form of binding or cover other than that in which it is published and without a similar condition being imposed on the subsequent purchaser.

All characters in this publication are fictitious and any resemblance to real persons, living or dead, is purely coincidental.

ISBN 0 7452 5449 4

Typeset by Palimpsest Book Production Limited,
Polmont, Stirlingshire
Printed and bound in Great Britain by
Mackays of Chatham PLC, Chatham, Kent

HEADLINE BOOK PUBLISHING
A division of Hodder Headline PLC
338 Euston Road,
London NW1 3BH

This is for Noel Amos,
a jolly good sport and a jolly good sort

Auld nature swears, the lovely dears
  Her noblest work she classes, O
Her prentice han' she tried on man
  An' then she made the lassies, O!

Robert Burns [1759–1796]

CHAPTER ONE

When Saturday Comes

Adrian Klein and his friend, Simon Byrne, added their voices to the collective groan of disapproval that rang round Craven Cottage as the Fulham centre-forward skied the ball over the bar from three yards out with the goalkeeper flat on his back and no Manchester City defender within tackling distance.

Trembling with rage, Adrian shot up out of his seat and yelled out: 'Wake up, Horne, you stupid wanker!'

Then he suddenly remembered that, since the start of the season, a plump middle-aged lady had been sitting behind him at every home game. Adrian's cheeks flushed with embarrassment as he turned and apologised profusely for his outburst.

'That's all right, dear,' she said with a hoarse chuckle. 'I couldn't have put it better myself.'

The Fulham faithful began to chant to the tune of *Jingle Bells*:

Garry Horne, Garry Horne
Garry, Garry Horne;
When he gets the ball
He does fuck all,
Garry, Garry Horne

Simon Byrne pretended to be shocked at the raucous singing and complained: 'Tsk, tsk, I know it's 1968 and we're living in the Permissive Society, but there's no need for that sort of language.'

'At least they aren't spoiling for a fight with the Manchester fans,' replied Adrian mildly. 'Not that you can talk. Look at that novel your firm published last week, what was it called now? *Locked Into Midnight*. It made those old Hank Janson stories we all used to sneak out of school to buy look like Noddy in Toyland.'

'That's freedom of expression, without which the literary world would grind to a halt,' laughed Simon, who had entered the world of books as a junior editor with an educational publisher after leaving University. Now he had progressed to the position of editorial director of Herald Books, a brash new paperback house which specialised in racy fiction and kiss-and-tell biographies of popular TV and film stars.

Adrian opened his mouth to speak but his words were drowned by a yell of delight from the small knot of Manchester City supporters on the terraces behind the home team's goal, as the hapless Fulham centre-half nodded the ball past his own goalkeeper. That put their team three-one up with less than ten minutes to play.

'I don't know why we bother to turn up here week after week,' said Adrian in disgust. 'Every season we fork out fifty quid for season tickets and all we get is bloody aggravation. I mean, it's only two years ago that I was at Wembley watching Bobby Moore lift the World Cup. Frankly, I'd rather watch a game on Hampstead Heath than this load of rubbish.'

'Be fair, they've had a lot of injuries this season and Jimmy Hill hit the post twice in the first half,' argued Simon, but Adrian continued to mutter fiercely to himself. He buried his face in his hands as the City outside right danced through a hesitant Fulham defence to score a fourth and put the result beyond further doubt.

'Come on, I've seen enough,' urged Adrian as he rose from his seat. Simon shrugged and followed his friend up the stairs where they joined the steady trickle of despondent Fulham fans who were already making their way towards the exit.

'So that's the afternoon gone for a Burton,' muttered Simon as they trudged down Stevenage Road towards his car. Then he brightened up and said: 'On the other hand, it's still Saturday night in Swinging London and I'll even forgive Garry Horne for missing that open goal if I score myself tonight! What exactly are we doing, by the way?'

Adrian shrugged his shoulders. 'Whatever you like, old mate. Do you fancy a film and then popping into Crazy Kate's for a bite afterwards?'

'That's okay as far as it goes. I wouldn't mind seeing *The Night They Raided Minsky's* at the Plaza, all the papers gave it good reviews and Britt Ekland's in it,' nodded Simon thoughtfully. 'But here's a much better idea – why don't you ring up two gorgeous dollybirds to come over to your pad for dinner and then the four of us can fuck ourselves silly all night? You can say that I'll drive them to St John's Wood and back home in the morning – or I'll even pay for a minicab if they've come from out of town!'

'Yup, that's a much better idea, Mr Byrne,' answered Adrian with heavy sarcasm. 'There's a telephone box on the corner and I'll call them right now. All I need from you are these girls' telephone numbers.'

Simon threw out his arms and exclaimed: 'Bloody hell, Ade, you're one of the top theatrical agents in London. You spend all your time with stars of stage and screen. I would have thought there must be hundreds of girls who would do anything to be handled by Adrian Klein of the Rose and Griffin agency – and I do mean handled!'

'If only,' sighed Adrian as they reached Simon's red MGB sports car. 'Unfortunately, it doesn't work like that. Look, my job is to put forward the names of artistes we represent to impresarios like Lou Baum and Dickie Segal – they're the lucky ones with casting couches in their offices because they're the guys who can make or break a performer.

'Not that I'm saying that girls have to fuck their way to the top, especially where Lou and Dickie are concerned,' he added hastily, for these two gentlemen owned three commercial television channels between them as well as a substantial number of theatres all over the country. Like all other agents, Adrian Klein needed to keep on friendly terms with such powerful showbiz moguls.

But his friend was unconvinced by this explanation. 'Come off it, Ade. Is Dickie Segal going to sue *Private Eye* about the story they printed about how he got the nickname of "Nipper"? And only the other day you were moaning to me how you can never get to see your boss after five o'clock because that's the time he closets himself in his office with his new secretary.'

'That's different! Teddy Dixon's a randy old goat and I bet there are plenty like him in publishing,' said Adrian defensively as they climbed into the car. 'Like you and your art editor chap, for example.'

Simon shook his head and grumbled: 'Chance would be a fine thing! I only see the rough proofs of the paperback jackets and, in any case, Gerard's a raving woofter, which is just as well otherwise he'd be walking around with a hard-on all day. He spends all his time interviewing pretty young models and looking at pictures of luscious nudes.

'Anyhow, was there any truth in that *Private Eye* piece? It said that Dickie Segal's chums call him 'Nipper' because years ago whilst an exotic dancer called Peaches was sucking him off, the chair he was sitting on overbalanced and the girl was so startled she nipped his knob much harder than usual and left poor old Dickie with a badly bruised prick.'

'That's the tale which has been going around ever since I came into the business,' agreed Adrian with a grin. 'Only I was told that the stripper's name was Cherry Ripe and she was supposed to have the biggest pair of tits this side of Watford, but I doubt if either Dickie or Cherry will bother to sue!'

Simon gave a low chuckle as he started the car and weaved his way through the crowd towards Hammersmith Broadway. 'At least he got a blow-job which is more than I've had since I've came back from holiday last month,' he sighed.

Adrian looked at him in some surprise. 'Didn't you drive down to the South of France with what's-her-name, Sharon?' He recalled the red-headed secretary in the publicity department whom he had seen Simon with at the Bull and Bush a couple of months previously. 'I could have sworn you told me that Sharon was a good shag but she wasn't really keen on giving you a gobble.'

'Right on both counts, Ade,' smirked Simon. The memory of a fun-filled holiday caused a happy smile to play about his lips. 'I haven't had a chance to tell you about what happened in St Tropez, have I?'

'No, and perhaps you'd better not because I'll only be jealous. It's all right for some to go swanning off to hob-nob with the jet-set. I had to spend most of August schlapping round the country from one seaside town to another checking out how our artistes are getting on in their summer shows. Thank goodness they're all doing very well but I was living out of a bloody suitcase, never staying anywhere for more than three days.'

'Don't tell me you didn't get your leg over now and then,' leered Simon, swinging out to pass a shiny black Ford Anglia driven by an elderly man who, despite the warm September afternoon, was bundled up in an overcoat and was wearing an old-fashioned trilby hat.

'Stupid old git,' commented Simon irritably as he slowed down to a halt behind a gleaming new Bentley at the red traffic light a hundred yards ahead. 'There's only one thing worse being caught behind an old duffer in a hat and coat and that's if he's smoking a pipe. Then you might as well pull up and take a nap for ten minutes because it's odds-on you'll catch him up again ten minutes later.'

'Don't be so impatient, you'll be just the same in forty years' time,' Adrian advised him. He peered through the front window at the elegant car in front of them. Then he tapped Simon on the arm and went on: 'Never mind about the old farts clogging up the roads, I recognise the fellow driving that swanky silver Bentley. It's Angelo Calabro of *La Miraggio*.

You and I are both in the wrong game, Simon. It's obvious we should go into the night-club business.'

Adrian was familiar with the owner and staff of *La Miraggio*, a fashionable night club just off Berkeley Square and only a stone's throw away from the Dover Street offices of the Rose and Griffin theatrical agency. The head of the agency – and Adrian's boss – was Teddy Dixon. He and Angelo Calabro soon became firm friends after striking a mutually beneficial deal by which Rose and Griffin booked all the artistes for the club's cabaret and in return used *La Miraggio* for entertaining celebrities and American wheelers and dealers.

And more often than not when the long-suffering Mrs Dixon went to Bournemouth for a few days to visit her sister, Teddy popped a bottle of champagne with one of Angelo's sultry hostesses whilst he scrutinised the performance of a comedian or singer recently taken on by Rose and Griffin. The agency used the cabaret to see how their latest signings performed in an intimate, sophisticated environment. Inevitably, after having a few words with whoever he had come to see, Teddy took the girl back either to her flat or to his own luxurious house in Hampstead Garden Suburb. Funnily enough, he never paid anything for these extra services out of his own pocket as the girl's charges were automatically added to the hostess fee on his bill.

Simon gave a grunt of assent and when he pulled up alongside the Bentley at the next set of traffic lights, Adrian rolled down his window and shouted: 'Hi there, Signor Calabro, *come sta*?'

The stocky driver of the Bentley turned and flashed back a wide smile when he saw who had called out to him. '*Va bene, grazie*, Adrian,' he called back. 'Will I see you at the club tonight? That new young singer, Diane Daniels, will be coming in with the Rolling Stones after her concert at the Albert Hall. Play your cards right and I'll introduce you to her, she might be in the market for a new British agent.'

Adrian shot a quick look at Simon who instantly nodded his head and gave a cheery thumbs-up sign. 'It might be a bit pricey,' warned Adrian but Simon shrugged. 'I'll be able to bung something on expenses,' he said. 'After all, I can always say I wanted to sound out Diane Daniels about whether she might front a book for us. How about you?'

'Could be a bit tricky for me to get away with a scam like that as Teddy Dixon's been looking hard at our budgets since we lost Alan Brooke to a big American outfit. But I daresay he won't quibble too much about me spending twenty quid on chatting up a pop star like Diane.' He turned back to ask Angelo if he could have a table for two at eleven o'clock.

'I'll see you boys later,' responded the night-club owner and when the lights turned green he signalled to them to carry on and pass him. Adrian waved a goodbye as Simon accelerated and pulled away from Signor Calabro's expensive vehicle.

'Things are going our way, I can feel it in my water,' crowed Simon happily. He bombed through Wellington Road at sixty miles an hour before parking the MG in an empty bay in the large block of luxury flats where Adrian had lived for the past twelve months. 'See, there was even a place to park. So what about a quick cup of tea and then I'll go back to my place and change into my best pick-up gear. Mark my words, with any luck we'll both get our ends away tonight.'

'Let's hope you're right,' remarked Adrian and five minutes later, whilst they were munching through a packet of shortbread biscuits, Simon offered to tell him about his holiday with Sharon in St Tropez.

'Oh yes, you mentioned something about that earlier,' said Adrian with a wan smile. 'You must have had a damned good time or you wouldn't be dying to tell me all the lurid details. As I said to you in the car, the only pussy I ever saw last month was a fat marmalade tabby which belonged to my landlady in Scarborough. But carry on, it's nice to know that your mate is getting his oats even if you aren't.'

'You're too kind, Mr Klein,' commented Simon. He nudged Adrian in the ribs as he continued; 'Although I still think you pull more birds than any other player in the Hampstead Hotspurs, the team which Ladbroke's have made odds-on favourites to win the North West London Sunday Soccer League this season.'

Adrian gave a short laugh. 'Oh, don't be too sure about that. If we do manage to pull later on, I can't see us giving our best tomorrow morning. Mind you, if I had to choose between scoring with a bird this evening or scoring a hat trick for the Hotspurs tomorrow—'

'You'd go for glory on the football field,' teased his chum. Adrian picked up his mug of tea and answered: 'Of course, and I know you would do the same, especially after having over-exercised your old man on holiday with Sharon, you jammy bugger!'

'*Touché, mon brave*,' smiled Simon. 'Now, just for that, I'll make you feel really randy by telling you exactly what happened in St Tropez. In fact, the fun and games began even before we arrived there. Things didn't go too well at first because I'd booked an early ferry from Dover and though the crossing wasn't rough, Sharon had developed a splitting headache by the time we left Calais. Anyhow, she slept most of the way down south and I only stopped for petrol until about five o'clock when we were about twenty miles north of Lyons and I pulled off the main road to look for somewhere to stay the night.

'Luckily I found a very pleasant little hotel in a village called Thoissey. Actually, it was more of a guest-house, but I pointed out to Sharon that there was a British Ford Zephyr in the car park. "Well, if they can put us up, at least you'll have someone to talk to tonight," she said as we walked through into the lobby. "All I want to do tonight is to get to bed and sleep off this lousy headache."

'Fortunately there was one room left and after unpacking, we ate a light supper and Sharon immediately retired upstairs to bed. However, I stayed downstairs and walked into the bar where I introduced myself to the other English couple who were already knocking back large brandies. Their names were Freddie and Clare Norrice and although Freddie must have been in his late thirties or even early forties, Clare couldn't have been more than thirty and was a real stunner. Not only did she have fine silky hair, so blonde that it was almost white, but she also had dazzling blue eyes, a pretty face and a sumptuous figure with large breasts and a nice peachy bum. I don't mind admitting that I was already getting a hard-on by the time I sat down opposite her and ordered myself a cognac. Believe me, Ade, it was no surprise to hear that Clare used to be a showroom model. She had married Freddie last year after a whirlwind romance.

'"Talk about being swept off my feet," she explained with a friendly smile. "I walked into Freddie's factory in the afternoon and by midnight we were dancing at the Stork Club after having a lovely dinner at Le Gavroche."

'Anyhow, Freddie bought us another round of drinks and then he stood up and said: "You two young people must excuse me, but it's been a long day, I'm going up to bed." Funnily enough, at the time I thought he exchanged a curious look with his wife which I assumed was an unspoken request for Clare to join him, but she simply offered up her face for him to kiss and said: "All right, darling, I shan't be too long."

'Then she turned to me and added: "We're in room twenty-three, Simon. Aren't you on the second floor too?"

'"Yes, actually my girl friend and I are next door to you in number twenty-four," I said in all innocence, little dreaming of what was in her mind. I stood up and shook hands with Freddie who toddled upstairs leaving Clare and I alone in the bar. We only stayed for another half hour or so and I could hardly take my eyes off her gorgeous body as we chatted away.

'Then, whilst I was gabbling on about some new film I'd just seen, I felt Clare's toes brush my ankle. At first I thought she was just finding somewhere comfortable to rest her foot for she was sitting there with a sweet innocent look on her face like butter wouldn't melt in her mouth. But when Clare moved her foot further up my leg, I completely lost my train of thought and just sat there tongue-tied as she finished her drink and said softly: "Simon, don't you think we should turn in now? It's getting rather late and I presume you'll also want to make an early start tomorrow morning."

'"Yes, of course," I mumbled. Hastily swigging down the rest of my drink, I hauled myself up and followed her out of the bar and up the stairs to the second floor where she stopped outside her bedroom door and gave me a gentle kiss on the cheek. "It was so nice meeting you tonight, I hope we'll meet again. Freddie and I are staying in Cannes for the next week but we haven't made any reservations after that so perhaps we'll motor across to St Tropez." "That would be wonderful," I gulped and then pressed my lips against the soft skin of her face as I fumbled for my key.

'"Good night then," she smiled as I opened the door and tip-toed in. Now there was a street lamp below the window of our room so I could undress without putting on the light and waking up Sharon who was tucked up fast asleep under the covers. Anyhow, I quickly pulled off my clothes and I was just about to slip into bed when I heard the floorboards creaking outside on the landing and I saw the door handle slowly being pulled down. I realised that I had forgotten to lock the door behind me and, thinking that this nocturnal visitor might be a sneak thief on the prowl, I slipped on my dressing gown and padded over to the door. Then I wrenched it open and nearly fainted from shock when I saw who was there.'

Simon paused for dramatic effect and Adrian sighed: 'All right, don't tell me, I'll guess it was this guy Freddie demanding to know if you and his lovely wife were having it away in your bedroom.'

'Good try, Ade, but no cigar,' grinned Simon cheerfully. 'Although Freddie comes into the story a little later. No, it was none other than Clare standing in the doorway, wearing a very short transparent pink nightie. Her figure was silhouetted against the light and it was clear that she wasn't wearing anything underneath! My God, how that light showed to perfection the beautiful curves of her breasts, her shapely legs and the dark triangle of pussy hair between her thighs.

'"Hi, Simon, sorry if I startled you, but I've just seen a picture of me in this month's *Vogue* which I thought you might want to see," she whispered. I nodded as I gently propelled her out back onto the landing. I closed the door behind us and said: "I'd like nothing better, but won't we disturb Freddie?"

'Clare shook her head and took hold of my hand as we walked the few steps to their room. I wrapped my dressing gown over my throbbing stiffie as I followed her inside where, to my surprise, there was no sign of Freddie. I asked where he was and she gave me a sexy little smile and murmured: "Oh, he's next door in room twenty-two. Between you and me, we usually sleep in separate rooms because Freddie snores so dreadfully he often wakes me up in the middle of the night. It's a great shame but when we get home he is going to have an operation to clear his sinuses, which hopefully will solve the problem."

'She beckoned me to sit down next to her on the bed and spread out the copy of *Vogue* that she wanted to show me. "There, look at page forty-seven," she said, and as we leaned forward together to look at the photograph of her in a swanky fur coat, she gave me a perfect view down the front of her nightie.

'I thought I was going to come then and there as I peered down at Clare's hard, pointy tits. I was so carried away by the sight of her luscious breasts that I didn't even try to conceal my erection which had popped out through the folds of my dressing gown. However, this didn't appear to bother her for she made no attempt to move away when I put my arm across her shoulders and asked if she were feeling a little cold.

'"Oh no," she answered promptly. "If anything I'm too warm. You don't mind if I make myself more comfortable, do you?" And before I could reply, she stood up and pulled her nightie over her head and shoulders to stand in front of me totally nude.

'Clare looked at me with a whimsical smile playing about her lips and then she said softly; "I think I'll be even more comfortable sitting on your nice strong thighs." And quick as a flash she pulled away my dressing gown and parked herself on my knees, facing me as she made herself comfortable. Then she glanced down at my boner which was waving wildly up in the air and circled her fingers around my shaft and very gently started to toss me off. I slid my arms around her as we exchanged a passionate kiss and Clare's hand slicked up and down my cock faster and faster whilst our tongues slid into each other's mouths.

'"Slow down, or I'll come over your hand," I gasped as she continued this delicious wank. She gave a throaty little chuckle as she slid off my knees to kneel in front of me. "Don't worry, there won't be any evidence," she muttered and bent her head down to close her wet lips around my knob.

'I swear that I felt like pinching myself to see if I were dreaming, but I knew I was awake all right and that fluffy mass of blonde hair was no illusion. Clare moved her head rhythmically back and forth, avidly sucking my cock whilst she lashed my throbbing tool with her tongue until she let my prick slip out of her mouth for a rest, which was just as well because otherwise I would have shot my load in seconds. Then she kissed my knob and tongued my shaft before sliding her head down to lick my balls and then she transferred her attentions back to my chopper. This time she managed to take the whole of my shaft deep into her throat and I just couldn't hold back any longer. I spunked inside her mouth and she gobbled my cock till she had gulped down every drop of jism.

'"M'mm, that was yummy," she giggled happily as she gave my shrinking shaft a final kiss and scrambled up onto the bed. "Take off your dressing gown, Simon. I'm sure a strong young guy like you can come more than once a night."

'"I'll do my best," I promised hoarsely as I looked down at this gorgeous girl who was lying down on her back with her legs wide apart. Now I don't know about you but even when I was in my teens, I needed a rest after shooting my load. So although I was desperate to fuck Clare, my cock was hopelessly limp, but I didn't have to worry because she went on: "Good, but would you first like to eat my pussy?"'

'I bet she didn't have to ask twice,' remarked Adrian wryly and Simon chuckled: 'I should say not – after all, I didn't get a distinction in oral French for nothing! In a trice I was kneeling between her legs and I dived down to kiss her fluffy little pussy bush. I could see that her love lips were already slightly open as I rubbed my lips up and down her moist crack before slipping my tongue inside her quim. Almost at once I found her clitty and twirled my tongue around the fleshy nub. The faster I vibrated it, the more excited Clare became, letting out tiny gasps of excitement and arching her body in ecstacy as I pressed the tip of my tongue against her erect love button. By now, my cock had stiffened up again and I was just about to heave myself up over her and slide my pulsing prick inside her juicy wet cunt when I fancied I heard the sound of the bathroom door opening behind me.

'"Did you hear that noise?" I panted as she grabbed hold of my cock and guided it into her sticky honeypot. "What noise? I didn't hear anything," Clare whispered as she put her arms around my neck and pulled me against her. She opened her legs wide and then, hoisting her hips up, she wrapped her thighs around my waist whilst I sucked on one rosy nipple and flicked the other between my fingers.

'"Fuck me, Simon," she cried out, though I scarcely needed any further encourgement and pistoned my prick in and out of her clinging sheath. What a wild fuck that was! I slammed my shaft in and out of her love funnel like a man possesed and on every stroke she rose up to meet me, rubbing her clitty against my cock as I drove in and out of her.

'Her cunny muscles tightened themselves so sweetly around my cock that all too soon I felt myself rushing up to the finishing line. "I'm coming, Clare, I'm coming, I can't stop," I groaned and she shrieked out: "Yes, yes, let it go, spunk into my cunt, you lovely big-cocked boy!"

'We managed to climax together for when I deluged Clare's cunt with a fountain of creamy jism, my spunk mingled with her own love juices and she held on to me tightly as she shuddered her way to a tremendous orgasm. After Clare had milked my cock of the last drains of seed, I collapsed down upon her soft curves, panting with exhaustion. But then I nearly fell out of the bed with fright when to my horror I heard Freddie's fruity voice call out: "Well done, Simon! You were very good, really first class."

'I turned my head and my mouth fell open and I looked at him in horror. He was naked and from the blob of come on his cock I guessed he had been tossing himself off whilst he was watching me fuck the arse off his pretty wife. But there was no anger in Freddie's voice and he came across the room to sit on the bed and patted me on the shoulder. "Clare does enjoy fucking with a randy young stud, don't you, my dear?" he said fondly. She shrugged her shoulders and said in a matter-of-fact way: "So what? You must enjoy watching me being poked or you wouldn't have encouraged me to take lovers in the first place."

'"Quite so, sugarpuss, I don't deny it," he admitted. "And you warned me before we got married that you would want some freedom if I didn't satisfy you between the sheets. Of course I should have realised that it would be difficult for any man my age to keep up with a sexy wife eighteen years younger than himself."

'"Look, I think I had better be off," I began but Freddie went on: "Please don't go, Simon. Clare was quite right, I find it fascinating to see her on her back being shagged by an athletic young stud like you and she really doesn't mind my looking on."

'"Is this true?" I asked Clare and she gave an embarrassed little grin and confessed that it made her even more horny knowing Freddie was watching her being fucked by another man. "But please don't think you've just been used for his pleasure," she added hastily. "Honestly, Freddie will tell you that I fancied you from the minute we saw you and your girl friend come into the hotel."

'"That's exactly what she said to me," confirmed Freddie. Clare lay back on the bed, her pert nipples standing up like little red soldiers as she thrust her blonde pussy mound forward as if begging for my cock. "So how about one more fuck for the road before you go to sleep? I would love to join in this time so, if you prefer, Clare will suck you off whilst I ream out her juicy little quim."

'I was tempted to take up the offer but we all had to make an early start in the morning and I was concerned that Sharon might wake up and wonder where the blazes I had got to, so I thanked Freddie and said that perhaps I could take a raincheck till the next time, saying that Clare had told me that we could meet up again in St Tropez.'

'Did you fuck the fair Clare again?' enquired Adrian and Simon chortled: 'Is the Pope Catholic? I gave her the name of our hotel and I screwed her silly when she and Freddie arrived in St Trop a few days later. We tried to get away on our own but on one occasion I'm pretty certain from the panting noises I could hear from behind the door that Freddie was peeping through the keyhole and giving himself a hand job when I was giving Clare one up the bum.

'Oh well, what do they say? Different strokes for different folks,' he concluded, glancing at his watch. 'Listen mate, I've got to get back home and change. The film won't start till about eight thirty but there's bound to be a queue so we'd better get a move on.'

'Okay,' agreed Adrian. 'It's my turn to drive so I'll pick you up at quarter to eight, sharp. If we're going on to *La Miraggio* I might as well leave the Jag in the office car park and we can jump on a bus to Piccadilly Circus.'

However, little did Adrian Klein know that one of the three spaces in the Rose and Griffin car park was already occupied by a large black Humber which belonged to Carola Watforde, the agency's financial director. A good-looking woman in her late twenties, Carola had attracted the attentions of her male colleagues from the day she joined Rose and Griffin some nine years before, but the word soon spread that Carola was not interested in men. Though she rose to head her department, her affairs with several well-known female artistes as well as with a succession of pretty secretaries were often the subject of shocked gossip in showbiz circles.

Nevertheless, she was very much respected (and slightly feared) by Teddy Dixon, the agency's managing director. So long as her predilection for nubile young girls was kept out of the Sunday papers, Carola knew she was free to pursue her own particular pleasures. Her latest conquest was a lithe seventeen-year-old dancer named Trish who was booked to appear in the chorus line of a new revue opening in three days time at the Prince of Wales theatre. Carola had no compunction about bringing Trish back to the newly decorated bedroom suite on the third floor of Rose and Griffin's plush offices, after spending the afternoon with her in Carnaby Street buying the pretty redhead a new Autumn outfit.

After two large gin and tonics, Trish was in no mood to complain when Carola suggested they lie down for a rest before dinner, although the previous evening a group of her friends had warned her of Carola Watforde's lesbian fancies. 'I'm not that bothered, I can look after myself,' Trish had said lightly, who in any case had rather enjoyed her previous lesbian liaison with one of the teachers at the small private dancing school from which she had graduated only three months before.

So the pretty teenager offered no resistance as she sat on the edge of the bed. She was happy enough to close her eyes and drift along with the sensation when Carola began to stroke her cheeks with her fingers as she breathed: 'Raise your arms, love, it would be a shame to crease this lovely new dress.'

'Yes, of course,' Trish murmured and Carola expertly peeled off the dress and moved away to hang the garment on a hanger in the wardrobe. Then she returned and tenderly lowered the girl down onto the bed, sliding out one of the pillows under her head and slipping it under her tight little backside. Waves of lust swept through Carola's body as she sat down on the edge of the bed and imagined how gorgeous it would feel to burrow between Trish's lissome thighs and tongue her juicy pussy whilst she played with her erect pointy nipples.

'Let's make you really comfortable,' she said softly and reaching down behind Trish's back, she deftly unhooked the lacy half-cup bra. 'Ooh, you shouldn't do that,' whispered Trish but she just closed her eyes and smiled blissfully whilst Carola slid her fingers inside the cups and eased out her luscious breasts into her trembling hands.

Now kneeling on the bed next to the nubile young dancer, Carola leaned down and traced the outline of Trish's ear with the tip of her tongue. Unable to contain herself any longer, Carola forced open Trish's lips and plunged her tongue into her mouth. Trish responded by opening her mouth and enthusiastically returning an urgent wet kiss which thrilled Carola to the core, for now she knew for certain that she could remove the last remaining barrier to Trish's lush body. She rolled down Trish's tights and then tugged down her frilly white panties, whimpering with desire when she saw the tawny moist thatch of pubic hair.

Rising from the bed, Carola swiftly pulled off her dress and underwear to stand naked for a moment in front of Trish before sliding back next to her and in an instant the two girls were locked in a passionate embrace.

Carola moved her mouth down to Trish's uptilted breasts and licked each of her long, inviting nipples in turn. Then with an audible sigh she sucked one into her mouth. Now it was Trish's turn to mew with pleasure as Carola's tongue swirled around her rubbery tittie, nipping and teasing it up to erection. She brushed a stray strand of auburn hair from her face whilst Carola repeated the exercise on her other nipple before moving her head further down to Trish's pussy and buried her face in her glistening bush of pubic curls.

'Do you like me naked?' she asked coyly and Carola replied huskily: 'You have a wonderful body, my darling, and I'm simply dying to make love to you.'

Trish smiled with satisfaction and spread her legs wide as Carola angled her head to press her lips between her pouting love lips and flick the tip of her tongue up and down the ridges of her cunt, her lust fired even further by the soft downy curls brushing against her cheeks. With practised expertise, she worked Trish's thick outer cunny lips with her tongue and thrilled to the girl's ecstatic shivers as she lightly lapped on the stiffening nub of her clitty.

'Oooooh!' wailed Trish when Carola slid her tongue inside her slit and twirled it over the sensitive skin inside her quim whilst she licked up the pungent love juice which was now cascading out of Trish's juicy honeypot. She stroked her gently and Trish cried out in exquisite agony when Carola pushed two fingers deep inside her cunt and began sliding them in and out of her tingling crack.

'Oh God, I'm so wet! Please put more fingers inside me,' pleaded Trish and Carola immediately obliged, inserting a third and then a fourth digit inside her squelchy snatch, working her fingers to and fro as Trish drummed her heels against the mattress in a fresh frenzy of passion.

Carola slid her left hand down towards her crotch to play with her own pussy whilst she continued to finger-fuck the nubile teenager in earnest, faster and faster as Trish's cunny became wetter and wetter. She smiled wickedly when she found the stiff little button of her clitty and frigged it mercilessly with her thumb and forefinger, making Trish shriek with joy as she spent profusely over Carola's fingers.

'Now darling, how would you like me to suck your lovely little quim and bring you off again?' panted Carola passionately and Trish giggled: 'Yes, please,' as she closed her legs to trap Carola's head between her soft, warm thighs. She dipped her head and licked all along the edges of her puffy love lips whilst she clasped Trish's jouncy bum cheeks in her hands.

Trish squirmed her pussy even more firmly against the lapping tongue as Carola's lips closed over her dripping cunt and, with deliberate slowness, she pushed her tongue deep into the moist love hole, fondling the soft flaps of skin with her fingers. Licking up and down the length of Trish's slit, Carola was lost to everything but her own growing sensations which were sweeping like wildfire throughout her body.

'A-a-a-h!' she groaned as her own passion exploded. She

sucked up Trish's cuntal syrup and her body convulsed. She nipped sharply on Trish's clitty when the orgasm finally exploded, sending delicious ripples of ecstasy coursing out from her sated quim. Her climax triggered off Trish's spend and she pressed her pussy harder against Carola's mouth, drenching her face with tangy love juice. Shaking her head back and forth along the tender cunny flesh, Carola rubbed her nose against Trish's clitty to heighten the teenager's pleasure.

Carola slithered herself up the bed and lay next to the slender young girl, scooping her up in her arms as she said: 'I've a good idea, sweetie. Why don't we stay here for a while? Teddy Dixon always has a nice bottle or two of wine and something tasty to eat in the fridge and then later on we could go across the road to *La Miraggio*. We do quite a lot of business with the owner and he told me yesterday that he was expecting Diane Daniels to come to the club for a late-night supper after her concert tonight. So there'll probably be quite a few showbiz people there and I might be able to introduce you to one or two important television producers like Phil Massey or Ion Trewin.'

As it happened, neither of those august gentleman was in the audience when Carola and Trish arrived at the club a little after quarter past eleven. Nor indeed was the famous Miss Daniels who, as Angelo Calabro explained apologetically, had been whisked off to a surprise party thrown by her record company at the Caprice.

'But do stay for a drink, Miss Watforde,' he went on hurriedly when he saw Carola's face cloud over with disappointment. 'You and your guest are just in time for the cabaret. This month we booked this new comedian called Allan Godfrey from Rose and Griffin and he's had the audience eating out of his hand. In fact, one of Nipper Segal's boys was in the club the other night and said he was going to see if he could book Allan into *Babes in the Wood* at the Croydon Empire this Christmas.'

'I remember Teddy Dixon saying to me how impressed

he was with this young man,' remarked Carola. She looked enquiringly at Trish who said eagerly: 'Oh yes, do let's stay. After all, there still might be some people here who you want to introduce me to and if there aren't, at least we'll have a had a good laugh.'

'All right then, Angelo, find us a nice table for two, please,' smiled Carola. The club owner personally escorted them through the crowded restaurant to a small vacant table almost at the back of the room.

'Angelo, haven't you anything better than this?' asked Carola rather petulantly as she gestured towards a second empty table far nearer the stage.

'I'm very sorry, Miss Watforde,' he answered with genuine regret, for like everyone else who had dealings with Rose and Griffin, Angelo Calabro had no desire to offend the woman who signed the agency's cheques. 'But you're pointing at the only other unoccupied table for two and that was booked earlier this evening by your colleague, Mr Klein.'

'Well, you can unbook it right now and sit Adrian and his companion here instead. If he complains, you just tell him to come over and see me,' Carola commanded the hapless Angelo, who spread his hands in resignation as, along with Trish, he followed Carola to the better placed table.

'Would you like a Buck's Fizz, dear?' Carola asked Trish as they sat down and the pretty redhead giggled: 'I don't really know, it sounds a little bit rude. What exactly is a what-did-you-say?'

Carola smiled at her indulgently and explained that a Buck's Fizz was a cocktail made up of equal parts of champagne and orange juice. 'Try one, it's the best way to drink inferior sparkling white wine like the champagne which they serve up here at five pounds a bottle.'

'Miss Watforde, how can you say such a thing?' protested Angelo, but he was not over-concerned at her comment because Carola always grumbled about the quality of the food and drink at *La Miraggio* whenever she frequented the popular night club.

'Very easily,' she responded with a shrug. 'Still, as I'm sure you won't put the extra Saturday night cover charge on our bill, we'll have a bottle of house champagne and a jug of orange juice, please.'

'*Si, signorina*,' Angelo sighed as he gave her order to a passing waiter. He walked back to the entrance where Adrian Klein was standing with the young man who had been driving the red MGB when he had seen them a few hours ago. At the time, he was driving home from a hectic tea-time romp with two of the leggy showgirls who were currently appearing in the club's cabaret.

He bustled over to them and pumped Adrian's hand. 'Gentlemen, I'm so glad you could come at such short notice but, alas, I have some bad news. I'm afraid Diane Daniels is being treated to a slap-up dinner at the Caprice. However, the cabaret will be beginning in five minutes and you'll really enjoy seeing that new comedian Allan Godfrey, who your agency made me book in for this month. He's a very funny man and as sharp as mustard with any hecklers.'

'Damn, Simon and I were really looking forward to having a few words with Diane. Oh well, I dare say it's not that important,' grunted Adrian, but when the club owner led them to the table for two at the back of the room, he protested: 'Hey Angelo, what's the idea? I always have the table where that red-haired girl is sitting by herself.'

Angelo rolled his eyes upwards and took hold of Adrian's arm as he muttered quietly: 'She's not sitting by herself, and you know her companion who must have just gone to the powder room for a moment.'

Simon looked appreciatively at Trish and asked: 'Hold on, Ade, if you know her companion and she's anything like the redhead, why don't we try and make up a friendly little foursome?'

'I don't think that would be a good idea,' answered Angelo with a wan smile and he turned to Adrian and said: 'The girl's with Carola Watforde. What a waste, eh?'

'You can say that again,' agreed Adrian as he sat down and

Simon frowned: 'Carola Watforde, I know that name. Hold on, isn't she Rose and Griffin's financial director? Bloody hell, what a great Saturday! Fulham lose four-one at home, we see a very average film, Diane Daniels doesn't show and the only single girl here is chummed up with a raving lezzie. Otherwise, everything in the garden's lovely!'

'You're right, it's been a very disappointing day but you can't win them all,' sighed Adrian. Simon was about to give a salty riposte when his attention was caught by the sound of a man's voice coming from a table on their right. His jaw dropped open as he clutched his friend's arm and gasped: 'Christ Almighty, look over there, Adrian. Do you see that thick-set guy in a blue suit who's sitting next to a blonde whose tits are almost falling out of her dress?'

'M'mm, she's quite a stunner,' Adrian answered mildly. 'But they seem to be very close and I can see from here that she's wearing a wedding ring, so why the great interest?'

'I'll tell you why, old son,' hissed Simon in his ear. 'Because those two love-birds are none other than Freddie and Clare Norrice, the husband-and-wife swingers I was telling you about this afternoon! Listen, with any luck we might still be able to dip our wicks tonight. That's if you don't mind sharing, of course.'

Adrian gave a nervous laugh. 'Thanks, though to be honest I don't fancy dipping my wick after you and Freddie,' he muttered. A wolfish smile spread across Simon's face as he retorted: 'Don't worry, Ade, you'll be first after me. If Freddie doesn't like it he can go and play with himself, which wouldn't worry him too much because I have a funny fancy that's what he likes doing best.'

'Wasn't it Groucho Marx who said there's something to be said for wanking,' chuckled Adrian. 'At least you meet a better class of person!'

'Freddie and Groucho can have a Barclays Bank if they want to, but I prefer a damn good fuck any day,' retorted Simon. 'And you can take my word for it that the lovely Clare's not just a good fuck but a really great one! When they sit down I'll go over and ask if we can join them. I'll bet you a pound to a penny that they welcome us with open arms.'

The band finished their rendition of *Yesterday* with a flourish and Simon pulled back his chair to stroll over to the Norriccs, but as he stood up the lights dimmed and after a short roll on the drums a spotlight picked out Angelo Calabro in the centre of the stage. He put a hand microphone to his mouth and announced: 'Ladies and gentlemen, good evening, it's cabaret time at *La Miraggio*. So please put your hands together and give a big welcome to our very own Angelo's Angels!'

The band struck up *There's No Business Like Show Business* and six long-legged chorus girls strutted out onto the stage dressed in scanty tight-fitting silver bras and tiny bikini bottoms which were little more than *cache-sexes*, for they were little more than slender thongs passing between the gleaming cheeks of their naked bottoms. The dancers giggled and pouted sexily as they went through their routine and at the end of the number, as they skipped past the two men to a generous round of applause, a luscious auburn-haired girl ruffled Adrian's hair with her hand as she glided past them.

'Hey, what after-shave are you wearing?' quipped Simon and Adrian grinned: 'Aramis, which I happen to know she likes, but that's not why I was given a come-on. Her name's Tanya Gordon and she and I had a little scene a few months ago which was fine whilst it lasted* but Gigi, the girl I was living with at the time, found out about it and cut up two of my best suits before she packed up and left me!'

'Oh yes, of course, I remember Gigi,' said Simon sympathetically. 'Frankly, I can't blame her though, the poor lass was nuts about you. Still, Tanya must have offered some wonderful consolation, you lucky sod!'

'Unfortunately, things didn't turn out that way. She took up a job dancing at the *Moulin Rouge* in Paris and this is the first time I've seen her since she came back to London,' explained

---

* see *Sweet Vibrations* by Jeff Charles [Headline Delta]

Adrian as Angelo came back to give a build-up to the star of that night's show.

'He's an up-and-coming comedian, a marvellous new talent and we'll all be able to say that we saw him first at *La Miraggio* so, ladies and gentlemen, a warm welcome please for Mister Allan Godfrey!'

A tall, good-looking young man bounded out on to the stage and his quick-fire patter kept the audience's attention from the first few seconds. He began: 'Good evening, ladies and gentlemen, there that proves I'm not rude even though I've had a terrible time this week, a terrible time. I got a puncture on the Old Kent Road and as I was changing the wheel a car drove up and a big geezer jumped out and opened my bonnet. I shouted, "What the hell you are you doing?" and he says, "If you're having the tyres, I'll have the battery."

'Mind, it would take more than a puncture to stop me working at an elegant club like *La Miraggio*. Did you know it's so posh that the mice have a choice of cheese in the traps and the waiters bring your bill on a silver tray so you can't see your change.

'My wife would love it here, she could do with a break. She's so out of condition that she gets winded after a game of Monopoly. It's not surprising she's run down though, we've had her mother staying with us the last couple of weeks. Now I'm not saying my mother-in-law's a frightening lady but when we took her to the circus the lion picked up a chair and a whip.'

Then correctly judging that his sophisticated audience would appreciate some *risqué* material, he changed tack and went on: 'Enough of her though, do you know how Snow White and Pinocchio make love? She sits on his face and makes him tell her lies.'

Fifteen minutes later he walked off to a storm of applause and Adrian remarked: 'That guy could make it, especially if he writes any of his own material. I'm glad we've signed him up and I'll make sure that we squeeze a good screw for him from Lou Baum if he wants Allan for a panto at Christmas.'

'What's that about Lou Baum?' said a husky feminine voice behind him and Adrian swung round to see Tanya Gordon standing behind him. She had taken off her showgirl costume and was dressed in a tight-fitting black mini dress which barely covered her pert little bum. 'Hi there, Tanya,' smiled Adrian. 'What's this, you on strike or have they sacked you?'

'Neither,' she replied promptly. 'But I twisted my ankle coming off stage and Angelo kindly told me that I could pull out of our second number. Good to see you again, Adrian. Now are you going to ask me to sit down or am I interrupting an important business conversation?'

'No, you're not interrupting anything and, even if you were, I would be only too happy if a gorgeous girl like you joined us for a drink,' said Simon smoothly and Tanya rewarded him with a sweet smile as she signalled to a waiter to bring her a chair.

'Who's your friend?' she asked and Adrian grunted: 'Tanya, meet Simon Byrne, we were at college together. Simon, this is Tanya Gordon. Perhaps you'll be able to have a chat with him later but unfortunately he was just leaving to have a word with some other close chums.'

Adrian jerked his head towards the Norrice's table and Simon grinned: 'Oh yes, so I was. However, I hope we'll have a chance to become better acquainted, Tanya. In the meantime, you two must promise not to leave the club without me.'

'Don't worry, we won't,' said Adrian in a slightly grumpy tone of voice. Simon kissed Tanya's hand in Continental style before he moved off to renew his association with Clare and Freddie Norrice.

Tanya looked at him and giggled teasingly: 'Why, Adrian Klein, if I didn't know you better, I would say that you were worried that I might be attracted by your friend. Would I leave one of the hottest agents in town just because his pal happens to be extremely good-looking and has an agreeable way about him?'

'You left me once before,' replied Adrian defensively and Tanya opened her large brown eyes wide as she rebuked him. 'Adrian, that's not fair. We were only good mates and you were still involved with that girl Gigi – and anyhow, I didn't leave you, I left London and that was because of work and not for any other reason.'

'Friends?' she enquired as she held out her hand and Adrian pursed his lips for a moment before smiling broadly and copying Simon, he took her fingers and pressed them to his mouth.

'Friends,' he repeated and recalling that the ravishing girl rarely drank anything more alcoholic than a lemonade shandy, he released her hand and called over a waiter to bring a tomato juice. 'Easy on the Worcester sauce, if memory serves me,' he added and Tanya beamed: 'How clever of you darling! Now let's not beat about the bush, who have you been seeing while I've been away?'

'No-one special,' Adrian promptly replied and when she let out an amused cackle of disbelief, he took hold of her hand again and repeated with genuine emphasis: 'Honestly, that's the God's honest truth, Tanya. I won't deny I've had a few one-night stands but there hasn't been one girl who I've dated more than a couple of times since we split up. Listen, if there were any, would I be spending Saturday night with Simon?'

'No, not unless you were on the turn and I can't very well imagine you as a woofter!' she laughed and before Adrian could ask her a similar question, Tanya pulled her chair next to him and snuggled up against his side. 'I suppose you would like to know what I've been up to in Paris,' she commented but Adrian shrugged his shoulders and said: 'You don't owe me any explanations, love. You're free, white and over twenty-one.'

'Only just,' she corrected him as the waiter set down a tomato juice in front of her. 'Actually, I celebrated my twenty-first with Jennie, another English girl in the troupe, down in the South of France.'

'H'm, it's all right for some,' declared Adrian, filling his glass from the bottle of Remy Martin which Angelo had placed on the table. 'How did you wangle that?'

Tanya shook her head. 'I didn't have to wangle anything,

Jennie and I had a few days holiday and we caught a train from Paris to St Tropez for a break in the sun,' she explained as they clinked their glasses together. 'We shared a room in a small hotel and on the first morning, which happened to be my birthday, we had planned to enjoy a lazy day sunbathing and follow that with a quiet birthday dinner together at a bistro on the sea-front.'

'And did things go according to plan?' enquired Adrian as Tanya moved her chair next to his so that she was able to snuggle up against him as she shook her head and giggled: 'Not exactly, though to be honest I wasn't unhappy with the way things turned out. You see, our boss had told us that although girls *can* sunbathe topless in St Tropez these days, you still get hassled by gawpers and recommended that we went to a quiet little beach away from the crowds just outside the town. So we took his advice and arrived there at about eleven o'clock in the morning and sure enough, even though it was a lovely hot day, there were only a few people around and we laid out our towels and li-los in a secluded spot behind some rocks where no-one could see us.

'Jennie switched on our transistor radio and we undressed down to our bikini bottoms and plastered each other over with suntan oil before lying down on the warm white sand for a nice snooze. It was all so peaceful that I dozed off almost immediately and – well, I know I don't have to hide any secrets from you – to be truthful, I had quite a sexy little dream about making love to one of the good-looking boys in our show.'

She paused and lightly dug Adrian in the ribs with her elbow as she continued: 'Don't look shocked, Ade, it could never have happened because all the male dancers I worked with were as queer as coots – and believe it or not, I hadn't had a single fuck since I left London.

'Anyhow, I must have been asleep for about half an hour or so and then through my drowsiness, I heard a familiar male voice say in English: "That's it, Jennie, super. Now open your legs a little wider and put your hand on your thigh as if you're stroking it." There was a click and whirr of a camera and I opened my eyes to see Jennie lying down on her rubber beach mattress and a hunky broad-shouldered young guy wearing only a tight-fitting blue swimming costume looking through the viewfinder of his Leica and muttering: "Great, that's nice, very nice," as Jennie arched up her back and thrust up her beautiful bare breasts at the camera.

'"Oh, that's perfect, darling," cried out the photographer when Jennie lifted her bum and scrunched up the material of her bikini bottom to accentuate the swelling of her mound and I racked my brains trying to recall where I had seen him before as he snapped away.

'"Damn, that's the end of the roll," he said crossly and while he squatted down and took out the film from his camera, I remembered where I had met him before and this is where you come into the story, darling.'

'Me? How come?' said a bewildered Adrian and Tanya chuckled: 'Well, I'll explain – I sat up and locked my hands across my knees as I said brightly: "We've met before, I think – aren't you Nick Clee of the *Daily Sketch*? You probably won't remember me, but we met at the party to launch Alan Brooke's last LP back in April."

'He looked at me hard for a moment and then grinned: "Of course, I remember you, Tanya. Do you think I would forget how I tried to chat you up and how disappointed I was to find out you were the girl-friend of Alan's agent, what's his name now, Adrian Klein. Come to think of it, Alan's left Rose and Griffin, hasn't he?"

'"Yes, and Tanya's split up with Adrian Klein and she's also on a three-month contract to dance at the *Moulin Rouge*," chipped in Jennie and she turned to me and went on: "This could be our lucky day, Tanya. Nick's doing a freelance job for a new men's magazine and they're paying twenty-five pounds to each model he uses, even if they don't use the photographs."

'"Yup, and it's going to be a high-class mag, a bit like *Playboy* but more pix and less waffle," said Nick as he finished loading the new film and looked across at me with a smile. "Are you interested?"

'"I don't know, Nick," I shrugged. "Thanks for the offer but it's my birthday today and I don't particularly feel like working."

'"But there's not much work involved," he observed and then rubbed his fingers against his bronzed cheek as he mused: "I'd need a different background as I've already taken quite a few pix of Jennie round here, but we'd only have to trundle across to the next beach. There's a smashing little cove there where we wouldn't be disturbed."

'"I'm not that keen—" I began but he cut in: "Hey, I've a great idea. It's your birthday, right? Now don't argue, I'm going to treat you and Jennie to lunch. Take my camera bag along with your stuff and meet me at the cove in ten minutes – look, you can see it just over there on the right – whilst I bring over something tasty from the beach café. All right?"

'"Thanks, Nick, that would be fab," said Jennie excitedly and, though I won't deny I was vaguely attracted to Nick, I genuinely wouldn't have minded staying there and letting Jennie have lunch with him by herself because I could tell that she really fancied him.'

'But you let Jennie persuade you otherwise,' said Adrian drily and Tanya nodded: 'To be honest with you, Ade, I didn't need much persuading and I can't say I'm sorry I went along with her because Nick brought back a tray of crusty French bread and cheeses with two bottles of Veuve du Verney and we had a smashing lunch.'

'And I can imagine what Nick Clee had for dessert, the jammy bugger,' commented Adrian thickly and Tanya giggled: 'Well, we all enjoyed it far more than rice pudding and custard! And as I just said, it was clear that Jennie had the hots for him so I suggested that as she was on the books of a model agency, Nick should take some more photographs for her portfolio whilst I went for a little walk.

'Now before I go on, it's only fair to say that Nick kept topping up our glasses till we had finished both bottles of wine and Jennie and I were feeling a bit light-headed. Anyhow, to cut a long story short, I had quite a shock when I came back from my walk! I had guessed that Jennie would be in some outrageous pose because she was a bit of an exhibitionist who loved to wear outrageous clothes. At our first rehearsal she turned up in a pair of ultra-tight jeans and from the way she had pulled the seam right up into her pussy, it was obvious that she wasn't wearing any knickers. So I wouldn't have been totally surprised if I had returned to discover Jennie in her favourite bikini panties which were so short that you would see the top of her muff at the front and all but the crack of her peachy bottom at the back.

'But in fact I was dumbfounded to find the radio blaring out rock n'roll and Jennie lying stark naked on a towel, brushing her cunny lips with her fingertips whilst she looked up at Nick who was squatting down in front of her as she said archly: "How about a close-up shot of my cunt? Do you think that would turn on the readers?"

'"I should bloody well say so," Nick croaked as he mopped his brow and when Jennie moved her finger up and down her slit, easing open her pussy to play with her clitty, I could see a huge bulge forming in the front of his swimming costume.

'"Let me see what effect I've had on your cock," she said huskily and Nick didn't have to be asked twice – he put down his camera and I have to confess that my own quim began to tingle when he pulled off his costume and his erect prick bobbed up, curving slightly to one side in front of Jennie's face.

'"Would you like me to kiss it?" she asked coyly and my hand slid down between my legs to rub myself whilst I watched Jennie curl her fingers around his long thick shaft with its big pink knob.

'"Is the Chief Rabbi Jewish?" he panted and Jennie smiled as she began licking his cock as if it were an ice-cream cornet, flicking her tongue up and down the underside.

'Nick let out a low moan when Jennie took his ballsack into her mouth whilst she fondled his chopper. However, she quickly freed his balls and hissed: "Fuck me, you randy sod, plug my pussy with your fat prick!"

'And before you could say Jack Robinson, she pulled him over on top of her. I watched Nick take hold of his todger and push his helmet between her squishy love lips. His tight little bum cheeks bounced up and down as he fucked her but then she whispered something to him and they changed positions so that he could fuck her doggie-style. Jennie knelt on her hands and knees and pushed out her bum as she reached between her legs and spread open her pussy lips. With a throaty growl, Nick scrambled up behind her holding his cock in his hand and Jennie gave a tiny yelp when he slid it into the cleft of her bum and into her juicy honeypot. He held onto her shoulders whilst he pumped in and out to the rhythm of a Rolling Stones record which was blaring out of the radio, smacking his belly against her backside as he reached forward to squeeze her breasts and then he cried out when his spunk flooded out to cream Jennie's crack. Seconds later she also reached Nirvana and squealed with delight, her body quivering all over whilst Nick successfully managed to stay inside her and waited until she had finished before taking out his meaty wet shaft. I felt very embarrassed when I noticed that it was still semi-stiff.'

Tanya paused to sip her tomato juice and Adrian tugged at his own erection which was pushing against his trousers as he mumbled: 'Well, so what? I don't see why you should have felt self-conscious about watching Nick Clee fuck your friend. If anyone should have felt embarrassed, it's Jennie and not you.'

'Maybe so,' agreed the luscious girl whose cheeks coloured a deep shade of pink as she lowered her voice and continued: 'But the truth is that I was embarrassed because my pussy was aching so much for cock that when Jennie saw me standing there with my hand inside my bikini rubbing my pussy, she called out: "Don't be shy, come and join the party."'

'This sounds interesting,' observed Adrian and then added chivalrously: 'Of course, you don't have to tell me any more if you don't want to.'

However, Tanya shook her head and said: 'No, Ade, I've started so I'll finish. When I heard this I rushed forward and unhooked my top myself as Nick took me into his arms. He kissed my nipples, making them stand up like little red stalks, and then he whispered: "Lie down next to Jennie and let me eat you."

'I lay back and spread my legs as Nick positioned himself between my thighs and I lifted up my bum so he could slide my bikini bottoms off. He made a sheath of the white towelling material round his forefinger which he inserted to the hilt into my cunt, wriggling it about, driving me into a wild frenzy and saturating my bikini with pussy juice. Then he gradually eased off the soaking material and frigged me with his bare fingers till Jennie hauled herself up and commanded him to lie down on his back.

'"Don't worry, he'll fuck you as soon as I've sucked his cock back up again," she said to me as she swung herself over Nick, facing his feet with her pussy directly over his mouth. She sat herself down carefully on his face and leaned forward to take his cock between her lips as I wondered where I was supposed to fit in. But she soon motioned me to get down and start licking his knob which I did and soon Nick was going out of his mind as both our wet tongues slid up and down his trembling thick tool. Neither of us had shared a prick before but there was something about Nick's cock and balls which sent the pair of us wild with desire and we gobbled him with great relish.

'"For God's sake, stop or I'll come too quickly," he panted and so Jennie pulled her head back and wiggled her bum whilst Nick tongued her pussy and I straddled him and eased myself down on his rock-hard shaft which slid into me with no trouble at all.

'Jennie was facing me as I rode his cock and I came again and again as we French-kissed and played with each other's titties whilst I pumped up and down on Nick faster and faster. He must have responded with his tongue on Jennie's clitty because she suddenly grabbed my shoulders and shrieked out: "Aaaaah! Aaaaah" as she achieved a frenzied climax and filled his mouth with cunt juice. With that, Nick jerked his hips upwards and spunked into my cunt and I shuddered with joy as a huge orgasm swept through me as his warm jism filled my love funnel.

'I bounced up and down on his lovely cock till I felt it shrink and then I rolled off him and we lay together in an untidy heap till we recovered our senses. Then we dressed ourselves and Nick rightly made us sit for the rest of the afternoon under an umbrella because we would get burned staying out in the sun for too long on our first day.'

Tanya paused and smiled as she looked down at the protrusion in the front of Adrian's trousers, reaching out to squeeze his stiff shaft as she murmured: 'My word, you certainly enjoyed listening to my naughty confessions.'

'Yes indeed,' gulped Adrian as Tanya nibbled his ear and breathed: 'You will be taking me home soon, won't you?'

'I should say so,' he answered instantly. 'I suppose you moved out of that super garden apartment you shared with your friend Lesley in Kilburn when you went to Paris?'

'Yes, of course,' said Tanya. 'But Jennie came back to London with me and she found us a nice two-bedroom flat in Hampstead Garden Suburb.'

Adrian gave a throaty chuckle: 'Anywhere near Willifield Way? That's where Teddy Dixon, my boss, has lived for the last fifteen years.'

Tanya shook her head. 'Gosh, he must be worth a few bob to live in such a posh road! No, Jennie and I have rented a flat above the shops in Market Place.'

'And very nice too,' commented Adrian, who was well pleased that her new pad was conveniently near his own luxurious flat in St John's Wood High Street. 'Look, I promised to tell my friend Simon when we were leaving the club as we came into town in my car and he might want a lift back. It wouldn't take us out of our way because Simon shares a house with two other guys on the Finchley Road near Swiss Cottage.'

'Sure,' she agreed and jerking her head towards the table where Simon was deep in conversation with Clare and Freddie. 'Though I don't think Simon is planning to go home by himself. Look at the way he's smooching with that pretty blonde.'

'You're right – and what baffles me is that the older fellow with the blonde happens to be her husband who encourages her to take young lovers like Simon,' said Adrian. He pulled back his chair and stood up. 'Beats me why he does it, if I had a gorgeous wife like that I certainly wouldn't share her favours even with my best friend!'

'One man's meat,' shrugged Tanya as Adrian slipped across to where Simon was sitting with his arm wrapped around Clare's waist.

'Good evening, young man,' said Freddie Norrice as he approached them. 'You must be Adrian Klein. Do sit down and have a drink, Simon's been telling us all about you.'

'Oh dear, has he really? Well, I shall take the Fifth Amendment,' grinned Adrian. 'And I'm sorry I can't stay for a drink, I'm about to take my girl friend home. Simon, I presume you don't need a lift back with me?'

'No thanks, Ade, but the night is young. Why don't you bring Tanya over for a night-cap before you leave?' asked Simon, beckoning over the dancer as he spoke. 'All right, so long as Tanya doesn't mind,' concurred Adrian as she joined them.

In fact Tanya readily accepted Simon's invitation and Angelo Calabro himself brought them two extra chairs as they squeezed themselves in between Freddie and Clare. 'Angelo, a bottle of the '64 Moet and Chandon, if you please,' said Freddie who didn't seem to mind in the slightest when the others left the table to dance.

However, after a minute or so rubbing her lissome body against Adrian with her arms around his neck to the drowsy slow rhythm of *A Foggy Day in London Town*, Tanya murmured: 'Poor old Freddie, he looks so lonely sitting by himself. Let's go back and talk to him. In any case, Angelo'll be very cross if he sees me dancing with you with my twisted ankle.'

'Okay,' agreed Adrian and he escorted her back to the table

where he said cheerfully: 'Hi there, Freddie, we've come to keep you company.'

'That's very kind of you, but please don't feel obliged to sit here if you'd rather dance,' he beamed. He turned his head to watch Clare and Simon glide by them, rocking gently to and fro with their arms wrapped around each other as their lips met in a passionate kiss.

Adrian could not keep quiet any longer and burst out: 'Freddie, I hope you won't take offence, but don't you mind just a teeny bit seeing your beautiful wife being groped by another man?'

'Not in the slightest,' he replied promptly. 'You might think I need a psychiatrist but when envious friends and business colleagues tell me how lucky I am to have such a stunning young wife as Clare, I always say to them: "Well, if you think she's that gorgeous, why don't you come round to our house and fuck her?"

'Of course, nineteen times out of twenty they think I'm joking, but it's one of my greatest pleasures to see Clare being shagged by another man. As you say, she's so beautiful that I think it would be very selfish of me not to let other chaps enjoy her. Besides, she's only twenty-eight and in her prime whilst I'm in my late forties and quite candidly, I doubt if I could have satisfied her by myself even ten years ago. Clare loves a good night's fucking but these days I shoot my load pretty quickly and need at least an hour to recover. She needs virile young fellows like Simon who can fuck like rabbits for hours and hours non-stop if required and, take my word for it, that's exactly what keeps Clare happy. I'm not an idiot and I've never expected a girl twenty years younger than me not to want to have lovers so, from the beginning, I said to Clare she can have as many chaps as she wants providing I have the right of veto over any man I consider unsuitable and that I'm allowed to see her perform with her gentlemen callers. Luckily, Clare's a natural extrovert and she enjoys knowing that I'm tossing myself off while I watch her being fucked!'

'And this arrangement has worked out all right for you

both?' asked Adrian. Freddie nodded cheerily: 'Very much so. You might think me weird but I find the sight of my pretty young wife sucking her lover's cock incredibly exciting. The sound of his moans when he shoots his spunk down her throat makes my balls ache and my prick swell up bigger and harder than it ever was before I met Clare.'

Tanya looked at him thoughtfully and said: 'I can appreciate that, Freddie, but doesn't this make it difficult for you to ever fuck Clare yourself?'

'Not in the slightest,' he answered. 'When we're alone together we share some wonderful moments. For instance, I love to lie on my back and have Clare slide up and down on my cock whilst I tickle her bum with a feather duster which she thoroughly enjoys.

'We also take great pleasure in thumbing through the album of photographs I've taken over the last year or two of Clare with big hard cocks in her mouth, having her pussy eaten or being fucked doggie-style. It makes me so proud to think that, despite being constantly propositioned by handsome young men to run off with them, Clare always stays with me.'

He shrugged his shoulders and ended by saying to Tanya: 'You may think our relationship rather bizarre, my dear, but it suits us well enough and as far as I'm concerned, that's good enough.'

'My goodness, yes,' remarked Tanya warmly. 'Listen, I've always been of the opinion that what consenting adults do in the privacy of their own homes is nothing to do with anyone else – so long as they aren't involving kids or anything like that. Don't you agree, Adrian?'

'Absolutely,' he grunted, looking at his watch. 'Freddie, would you mind very much if Tanya and I took our leave? It's well past midnight and, ridiculous though it is, I can't have a lie-in tomorrow morning. Simon and I are both pencilled in for a football match starting at eleven o'clock and there'll be all hell to pay if we don't turn up.'

Freddie clapped him on the back and said heartily: 'Off you go, my boy, you're quite right to worry about letting your friends down. Of course, you are both most welcome to join Clare, Simon and me at our place round the corner in Park Lane.'

'Thanks, but another time perhaps,' rejoined Adrian politely and after he and Tanya shook hands with Freddie, they made their way to the exit, waving their goodbyes to Clare and Simon who were still entwined in a fervent hug on the dance floor.

Angelo was waiting with his bill on which Adrian scribbled his signature and instructed him to put it on the agency's account. He saw Carola Watforde and Trish standing in the line to retrieve their coats from the cloakroom and he gave the financial director of Rose and Griffin a somewhat evil grin as he greeted her effusively.

'Carola! What a surprise!' he cried out. 'Did you enjoy the cabaret? I wouldn't have thought a vulgar comedian like Allan Godfrey would appeal to you. Still, I hope you had a pleasant evening.' Then he deliberately looked across to Trish and smiled at her and added: 'I don't think I've met your friend.'

'I doubt if you have,' said Carola coldly and as they shuffled forward in the queue, she muttered quietly out of the side of her mouth: 'Keep your hands off, Adrian, she's not into men.'

I'll wager she would be, given half a chance, Adrian thought to himself as he responded: 'Fair enough, but in return I don't want any questions raised about my expenses tonight. I only came along to make contact with Diana Daniels but she never showed.'

Carola quickly decided to accept this proposition. 'All right, Adrian, you have a deal,' she mumbled as she searched for the cloakroom ticket in her handbag. 'Angelo mentioned something about Diane Daniels to Teddy Dixon and me yesterday though I'm beginning to wonder whether it was just a clever ploy to fill the club this evening.'

'I wouldn't put anything past Angelo,' stated Adrian as he gave in his ticket to the grey-haired Italian lady behind the counter. 'Still, I'm glad we understand each other.'

But what neither of them had seen was that Trish and Tanya were already deep in conversation and if he had heard what was being discussed between them, Adrian would have learned that his conjecture about Trish's sexual inclinations was entirely accurate. However, Adrian was unaware of this when he gave a generous tip to the cloakroom attendant in exchange for Tanya's green summer coat and his own expensive raincoat which he had purchased the previous month at Harrods. He said goodbye to Carola as he slipped on his coat and struggled through the crowd to where Tanya was waiting by herself, Trish having wandered off to the toilets.

Adrian drove well within the speed limits back to Hampstead Garden Suburb and parked his Rover outside the entrance of Tanya's flat in Greenhalgh Walk. 'That's a good omen,' remarked Tanya as she scrabbled inside her handbag for her front door key. 'There's not often a space till you go right up to Brim Hill.'

She found the key as Adrian jumped out and walked round the front of the car to open her door. 'Ah, you're a real gentleman, Adrian,' she said, blowing him a kiss. 'Not many guys bother to open doors for girls these days.'

'Call me old-fashioned,' he smiled as he helped her out of the car. After Adrian had locked the door behind him, they linked arms to climb the steps to Tanya's flat.

'We must be very quiet because Jennie didn't go out tonight and she's probably asleep. She's dating an airline pilot and he's spending the weekend in Greece, the lucky devil,' said Tanya. But as she opened the door, the sound of a piano could be heard from inside the flat.

'Christ, she must be a real night bird, it's past one o'clock,' whispered Adrian, trying to keep a note of disappointment out of his voice. Tanya kissed his ear and answered: 'Don't worry, darling, Jennie's a good sport and won't interfere with us.'

'I bloody well hope you're right,' thought Adrian as he followed Tanya through the long passage style hall into the living room where a pretty long-legged girl in a pink silk dressing-gown was lying across a sofa with a paperback book in her hands and her bare legs hoisted over the arm. When she saw Tanya and Adrian enter the room, she swung her legs down to the floor to greet her flat-mate.

'Hello, love – God, is it that late?' she asked. 'I switched off the telly after *The Forsyte Saga* but I couldn't get to sleep and I've been listening to music and reading your copy of *Fanny Hill* since eleven o'clock.'

'You should have borrowed my vibrator as well if you've been poring through that rude book for the last two hours,' responded Tanya with a smile. 'Jennie, this is Adrian Klein – Adrian, meet Jennie Osborne.'

'Pleased to meet you, Adrian,' said Jennie brightly as they shook hands. 'Tanya told me so much about you when we were in Paris together that I've particularly wanted to meet you.'

'How nice, I've felt the same about you since I heard all about your exciting holiday in St Tropez,' grinned Adrian whilst he took off his raincoat. 'Especially since all three of us share similar tastes in classic eighteenth-century literature.'

'You like *Fanny Hill* too?' said Jennie as she put the book down on a side table. 'I thought that men might find it a bit tame because although it's very naughty there isn't a single rude word in it.'

She gave a little yawn and said: 'Oh, I beg your pardon, folks. Tanya, I'm off to bed. Good night, Adrian, it was nice meeting you, I dare say I'll see you in the morning!'

Jennie sashayed out of the room and Adrian tried unsuccessfully not to let his eyes follow her wriggling buttocks as she passed by him.

'I'm also going to leave you,' announced Tanya as the music stopped and she gestured to the record player and went on: 'Put on another L.P. whilst you're waiting, I'll be back in five minutes.'

'Sure,' he said and he shucked off his jacket before squatting down beside the pile of records which, he noted with some surprise, was mostly of classical music. This did not faze Adrian for after an initial unwillingness at the age of nine to attend a weekly lesson and to practise, he had enjoyed learning to play the piano. He had reached a high standard of proficiency until like so many others, he had dropped out in his mid-teens, pleading pressure of schoolwork.

Nevertheless, Adrian had retained a fondness for classical music and it was with true pleasure that he found a recording of Mozart's Piano Concerto in C Major which he slipped onto the gramophone. He moved the arm to the middle of the disc and then settled down on the sofa to listen to the haunting second movement.

'Adrian, who wrote this lovely music? I keep hearing it on the radio,' he heard Tanya ask. He called back: 'Mozart and it's in the American hit parade because it was used as the background music for *Elvira Madigan*. Actually, I haven't yet seen the film myself so, if you fancy, we could go tomorrow night. Sunday is your day off, isn't it?'

'Thanks, darling, I'd love to,' she answered and Adrian let out a satisfied grunt as he heaved himself off the sofa and stretched out his arms. He wondered whether Tanya had gone to the kitchen to make them a coffee. After a few moments he wandered out into the hallway.

'Tanya?' he called out questioningly and then noticing that the door on his left was slightly ajar, he slowly pushed it open. Adrian caught his breath sharply when in the low light from a bedside lamp he saw her standing by the bed. The nubile dancer looked at him sensuously, her eyes dark and moist. Her hair fell loosely over her bare shoulders as she tugged at the zip at the side of her strapless dress. Her tongue slid slowly across her lips as she pulled down the black silk garment and stepped out of it with a graceful ease, her glistening body shining like satin in the soft reflected light. She stood naked except for a cream half-cup bra, over which her breasts spilled so excitingly, and matching panties that were pulled tautly over her mound and exposed the outlines of her pussy lips.

'Don't just stand there, you impatient man. If you had waited a little while longer I would have come out to you.' she murmured huskily. 'Still, I suppose you have saved me the journey. Come in and shut the door behind you.'

Adrian gulped as he stepped forward and closed the door with the back of his heel as Tanya unhooked her bra and yanked it off as she moved forwards towards him. Her small, jutting breasts jiggled enticingly as she approached him and for a moment they stood facing each other without speaking as Adrian passed his hands over the gentle curves of her thrilling body.

'It's been a long time,' breathed Tanya and Adrian looked at her tenderly as she tilted her face upwards to offer him her lips. 'Too long, far too long,' he whispered as they slipped into a tightly held warm embrace. Adrian kissed her with a fiery urgency, his hands roaming over her quivering breasts as they staggered backwards and fell back onto the bed.

'Take off your clothes,' Tanya muttered and, as he kicked off his shoes, she helped him tear off his shirt and trousers. Adrian finally divested himself of his clothes and lay naked beside her. His whole body shuddered when he felt her finger-tips move deftly across his chest, sliding along his belly and arousing every inch of flesh as she twined her fingers inside his pubic hair as they moved around the base of his throbbing erection.

'A-r-g-h!' he gasped and his mouth opened wordlessly in suspense as Tanya's finger traced a sensual passage up and down the sensitive underside of his stiff cock before she closed her fist around his shaft and worked it up and down his pulsing prick. Then, straining to encircle the smooth purple helmet, she sucked some three inches of his hot shaft into her mouth, bobbing her head up and down until she had taken him deep into her throat.

Adrian responded by pulling her over him so that her pert backside was directly over his mouth. He rolled down her panties and, still with her lips clamped firmly around his cock, Tanya raised her feet to allow him to pull the frilly little knickers over her ankles and fling them away. She leaned forward again, lashing her tongue around his trembling tool and, when her bottom rose in the air, Adrian parted her buttocks and feasted his eyes on the petal-pink folds of her cunt which were completely exposed to his gaze. He licked his lips in anticipation as Tanya slowly lowered her curvaceous little bottom onto his face. She purred with pleasure when he licked up the creamy slick of moisture which was already dribbling out of her honeypot.

Their two bodies melded into one as they lapped lustily away in a classic *soixante neuf* but Tanya rightly sensed that Adrian would soon come inside her mouth if she continued sucking his warm, velvet smooth shaft. So she lifted her head and twisted round to lie flat on her back, her legs open wide as she ran her forefinger delicately along her slit and giggled: 'Now you must fuck me, Adrian, my pussy is aching for your beautiful big boner!'

'The feeling's mutual,' he croaked hoarsely as he rolled on top of her, rubbing his bursting cock against her hairy bush as their lips flattened together and their tongues darted into each other's mouths.

Adrian did not delay but pressed his knob between her yielding pussy lips. Tanya squealed with delight as he dived deep into the well of her luscious love channel and, hoisting her thighs up towards his hips, she locked him inside her squelchy notch with her legs.

He began to fuck the delectable girl in a slow, regular rhythm, his cock sliding sweetly in and out of her juicy honeypot, his hands working in unison over her erect strawberry nipples. They moved together with an easy grace, sending thrills through the other's body with every stroke and Adrian went wild with passion as he felt his cock so deliciously enveloped by Tanya's moist quim. He began to fuck her harder and faster, plunging his prick in and out of her squishy slit as his hand moved down to Tanya's swollen clitty. As his knob reamed out her juicy cunt, he played with her erect love-bud, rubbing it until Tanya was close to achieving her climax.

Her cunny muscles tightened around his throbbing shaft, squeezing him so hard that Adrian knew that he had reached the point of no return. 'I'm going to spurt, here it comes, take it now, take it!' he cried out, pressing his cock in to the hilt and holding her hips tightly to make sure that he didn't slip out.

'Oh Adrian darling, I'm coming too,' she panted. 'Ooooh, there I go, it's like fireworks exploding all over me!'

Tanya's cuntal muscles squeezed his shaft again as her spasms shot through her entire body and a fierce spout of sticky jism spurted out of Adrian's cock. Instinctively they ground themselves together as the wild torrent of liquid lust splashed against the walls of her cunny until he was spent and he collapsed down on top of her.

Adrian lay there inert with his face cushioned on her breasts until he had recovered and then he rolled over on his back and slid his arm around Tanya. She snuggled up next to him with her head in the crook of his shoulder. In no time at all they were both fast asleep.

Adrian was woken up at dawn by the feel of a soft fist deliciously sliding up and down his erect shaft.

'Good morning, lover,' said Tanya brightly as he sat himself up. He had time only to blow her a kiss before she dived down to rest her head on his thigh. He saw her pink tongue flash out to swirl across the dome of his circumcised cock. She opened her mouth wide and swallowed his knob and Adrian gave a low groan when Tanya began to suck her fleshy lollipop with gusto.

Then he suddenly realised that they had been joined by Jennie who was awake and lying naked on his other side. She took his hand and guided it to her fluffy chestnut bush whilst Tanya released his cock from her mouth and straddled him, though this time she sat on his thighs facing him. Then she lifted herself up and slowly lowered herself on his twitching tool, working it in to her wet, welcoming snatch. She began to bounce happily up and down on Adrian's rock-hard shaft whilst he raised his hands to cup her firm uptilted breasts and their perky red nipples.

'Wowee, he's filling me with his big fat chopper,' she gasped to Jennie who was gently fingering her pussy with one hand and caressing her breasts with the other. 'I don't think his cock is as big as Jean-Paul's, but that doesn't matter.'

'Size isn't everything – frankly I often felt a bit sore after Jean-Paul fucked me,' replied Jennie as she continued to diddle her pussy. Slightly irritated by this exchange, Adrian asked who this Jean-Paul might be.

'No-one important,' answered Tanya breathlessly as she lifted her body up and speared herself down on his swollen shaft. 'He was a good-looking young scene-shifter at the *Moulin Rouge* who was supposed to have possessed the thickest prick in Paris. Like most of the other girls in the show, we were curious to find out whether there was any truth in this rumour.'

'And was there?' pressed Adrian and Tanya chuckled: 'I'll tell you about Jean-Paul over breakfast. Let's finish this fuck first.'

She upped the pace and Adrian tried desperately to keep Tanya's clinging cunt from milking his excited cock too quickly. He looked to his left to watch Jennie play with herself next to him with her eyes fixed upon his shaft as it slurped in and out of Tanya's juicy crack. Now he slid his hands around her waist and clutched her bum cheeks as she bounced up and down faster and faster until she screamed: 'Yes! Yes! Yes! Empty your balls!'

Adrian gritted his teeth and immediately complied which was easy enough to do for the juices of Tanya's orgasm so lubricated her love channel that he swiftly ejaculated a deluge of cum into her tingling cunt and her sopping slit continued to hold and squeeze his cock until he withdrew his drained shaft and Jennie brought herself off with an excited squeal of triumph.

'I don't suppose there's any chance of a fuck,' said Jennie hopefully as she looked at Adrian's limp tool which was now dangling forlornly over his balls.

'Sorry, I'm completely worn out,' Adrian apologised with a heavy sigh. 'But give me half an hour's kip and I should be ready for action again – so long as Tanya doesn't mind, of course.'

'Oh, I don't mind sharing,' said Tanya as she ruffled her hand through his hair. 'Now lie back and have forty winks, Ade, you deserve it.'

'Ta very much,' mumbled Adrian as he closed his eyes and for a moment or two he idly wondered whether Simon Byrne had also exercised his wedding tackle, but in less than a minute he was in a sound sleep from which he did not wake until half past nine.

In fact, just as Adrian was getting up the next morning, Simon woke up from the deep slumber into which he had fallen after an orgy of fucking and sucking at Freddie and Clare Norrice's luxurious apartment in Park Lane. Much to his delight, on his way to the gentleman's washroom at *La Miraggio*, he had struck up a conversation with Trish Jackson after inadvertently bumping into her whilst she waited for Carola Watforde to retrieve their coats from the cloakroom. After he had made a profuse apology, Trish had smiled: 'That's all right – um, weren't you sitting with the chap who works with Carola before you moved to another table?'

'Yes, Adrian Klein and I are old mates from way back,' he had replied. 'We didn't have a row or anything like that, but one of his old girl friends suddenly appeared so I thought it best to exit stage right and leave them to it.'

This friendly exchange had continued and much to Carola Watforde's annoyance, Trish had accepted an invitation from Simon to join him at Freddie and Clare Norrice's table. In vain Carola pleaded with Trish to leave the club and spend the rest of the night in her bed but the young dancer refused to budge and the financial director of Rose and Griffin finally stomped out of *La Miraggio* seething with anger at what she perceived to be her erstwhile partner's treachery.

Of course Trish did not see things in the same light. She considered she had paid her dues for the favour Carola had done for her in obtaining a place in the chorus line of Dickie

Segal's new musical revue at the Prince of Wales. Whilst the pretty teenager had no objection to a kiss and cuddle with other girls, she preferred bedroom romps with her boy friend – although they had split up a month or so before when Trish discovered he had been fucking her twenty-year-old cousin since the beginning of the year – and she was greatly attracted by Simon Byrne's fresh-faced good looks.

Therefore she needed little persuasion to join Simon and the Norrices who were only too pleased to welcome her to their table. After helping to finish the bottle of champagne that Freddie ordered, she readily accepted Simon's invitation to finish the night at Freddie Norrice's plush apartment on Park Lane. The two of them had retired to bed although Trish was unaware that Freddie and Clare were watching her through a two-way wall mirror whilst Simon fucked her doggie-style as she knelt on her hands and knees on the eiderdown; nor did she or Simon know that after Clare had swept in to join them and lick out her pussy as she sucked Simon's cock, that Freddie was taking a Super-8 home movie of the lascivious scene. Freddie himself had briefly linked up with them to make what he called 'a whoresome foursome' but soon afterwards the Norrices left for their own bed and Simon and Trish had gone to sleep alone in each other's arms.

Simon eased himself slowly into consciousness, turning his head to bury his face into Trish's shock of tousled auburn hair, beathing in its warm scent. Some fine strands tickled his nose, making him smile as he looked fondly across at the nubile curves of her naked body. Then he looked at his watch and muttered to himself: 'Hell's bells, it's an eleven o'clock kick-off this morning and I've got to go home first and pick up my kit.'

With a heavy sigh he slid his arm around Trish and leaned over to kiss her lips. 'Time to rise and shine, I'm afraid,' said Simon regretfully as he heaved himself up into a sitting position. 'I don't know if Freddie and Clare are up yet but, if not, I know they won't mind us making ourselves some breakfast before we go.'

'What's the rush, sugarpuff?' yawned Trish sleepily. She ran her hand down from Simon's chest and slid her fingers around his flaccid cock which began to stir when she pressed her soft lips against his cheek.

'There's no point getting up whilst you still have some lead in your pencil,' she added, slicking her fist up and down Simon's fast-stiffening shaft. 'Because whether you like it or not, you're not moving out of this bed until we've made love.'

'Oh, I'll like that all right.' he said thickly. All thoughts of his forthcoming football match left Simon's brain when Trish released his cock and ran her hand across her reddish-brown pussy bush and murmured: 'Ooooh, I'm so wet, darling, fuck me with that big cock, you naughty boy.'

A wordless groan of desire escaped from Simon's throat as he leaned over and Trish pulled him down on top of her, wrapping her arms around his wiry torso. Their hot bodies glued themselves together and with a deep growl he plunged his prick between her pouting pink cunny lips and thrust his swollen shaft deep inside her wet, welcoming love sheath.

Simon fucked the gorgeous girl with powerful, sweeping strokes and Trish moaned with delight as his sinewy thick cock swished to and fro, entering and re-entering her juicy honeypot. Trish lifted her thighs higher and gripped his waist between her legs as they rocked together, faster and faster, in perfect rhythm and she let out an uninhibited yell of ecstasy when she orgasmed and a stream of cunt juice flowed out of her pussy.

Then it was Simon's turn to tremble all over as with one almighty thrust he slammed in his shaft one last time into her love tunnel. 'Hooarr!' he panted hoarsely, signalling the approach of his own climax: Seconds later Trish squealed happily as a flood of sticky spunk washed the walls of her cunny which set the excited girl off on a second blissful journey to paradise.

For a while they lay panting with exhaustion but then Clare entered the room and exclaimed: 'Oh dear, am I too late?

Freddie's still snoring away and I'm dying for a fuck. How about it, Simon? I hope you're not going to disappoint me.'

She slipped off her dressing gown and ran her hands down her gleaming naked body before climbing onto the bed and knelt on all fours, with her beautiful bottom pushed out provocatively and her legs slightly parted as she waited for Simon to mount her doggie-style.

'I'll do my best to oblige,' answered Simon as he slicked his hand up and down his meaty, semi-erect shaft, but his cock stubbornly refused to harden any further until Trish good-naturedly slithered across his thighs and began to suck his balls. Within a very short time this sensuous tonguing had the desired effect and Simon's prick was soon as stiff as a poker and ready for action. He hauled himself up and Trish now took hold of Clare's wiggling bum cheeks and pulled them apart, leaving him free to slide his thick tool through the narrow crevice between her buttocks and directly into her luscious love channel.

'Yes! Yes! Give it to me, Simon, stuff it right up my cunt!' shrieked Clare, tossing her head from side to side as he pumped his prick in and out of her juicy quim.

Nothing loath, Simon grabbed her hips and began pounding into her at an even faster rate. Clare's body gyrated so wildly that his cock slipped out of her cunny, but when she reached round and grabbed his shaft, which was now well greased with her cuntal juices Clare did not replace it in her sopping slit but instead moved his knob upwards to the wrinkled little entrance of her arsehole.

Simon hesitated for a moment or two before gingerly pushing forward into the tight-fitting orifice, but Clare responded to every shove as he engineered some full five inches of his shaft inside her bottom. His balls bounced against the deliciously soft rounded bum cheeks as he moved back and forth in a slow, regular rhythm. He snaked his hand around her waist and slid his fingers through her luxuriant bush of pussy hair and rubbed them against her cunny lips.

Clare's voluptuous backside wriggled joyously as Simon

drove in even deeper whilst he frigged her cunt. Then Trish ducked her head underneath him and for a second time popped his tightening ballsack into her mouth.

'I'm going to spunk!' bellowed Simon and Clare whooped back: 'Go on then, shoot your load NOW!' and with perfect timing he lubricated her back passage with frothy white jism in a thrilling mutual climax. They slid down together with Simon's cock still enclasped between Clare's rolling bum cheeks and he pulled it out with a *plop* before sinking down between the two girls.

They lay in silence for a minute or two until Simon rolled himself out of the bed and blew the two women a kiss. 'Ladies, that was absolutely fabulous, but *tempus fugit*, and I must be on my way,' he announced and then he wrinkled his brow and added: 'Christ, I'm absolutely drenched with sweat. Clare, may I use your shower before I go?'

'Of course you may,' she smiled. 'But as the games mistress at my old boarding school used to tell us, horses sweat, men perspire and ladies glow!'

As Simon disappeared into the bathroom, Trish turned to Clare and said: 'I bet you went to a posh private school like Roedean or Cheltenham Ladies College.'

'Yes, St Evadne was a private school but certainly not in the big league,' said Clare as she cuddled up next to the curvy young dancer. 'Actually I rather enjoyed my schooldays, even though St Evadne's was single-sex, of course. As we were stuck in deepest Herefordshire, there weren't any young men around to disturb our studies and almost every girl passed at least four 'O' levels. Still, Miss Caughey, the headmistress, was no prude and by the time I was in the sixth form, most of us had chummed up with boys from Osbourne House, a boys' boarding school about five miles away. Their sixth form used to visit us quite regularly for debates and lectures from people like the local MP or some other dignitary and twice a term we used to go over to the boys' school for an evening of country dancing.'

'No chance to be naughty then,' grinned Trish but Clare

shook her head and replied: 'Don't you believe it, my girl. I lost my cherry to one of the lads from Osbourne House.'

Trish looked at her in surprise. 'Gosh! Did you really?' she exclaimed. 'Was it very painful?'

'Not in the least,' Clare answered promptly. 'I say I lost my cherry but, to be honest, I was a virgin in name only because my best friend at St Evadne's had one of these new electric vibrators and like most of the oldest girls, I had already shagged myself silly with it by the time Peter Thornton's prick pistoned into my pussy. Not that I didn't enjoy being fucked by Peter because I did!'

'You lucky thing, my first time was a quick knee-trembler behind the back of the Odeon,' murmured Trish wistfully. Clare looked at her sympathetically and said: 'You poor little bunny, what a shame. I was lucky to enjoy my first time though it nearly ended in disaster. Would you like to hear about it?'

'Yes please,' said Trish and Clare gave a throaty chuckle as she slid her arm around the teenager and went on: 'It happened on one of the evenings when a coach was coming round to take us to the boys' school for the country dancing. However, Miss Caughey wanted to return a book she had borrowed from one of the masters of Osbourne House and she asked me if I would go there half an hour earlier by bus and deliver it back to him before the dancing started as he needed it to prepare his lessons for the next day.

'"Here's a shilling for the fare, the bus leaves at six forty-five and stops just a few yards away from the gates of Osbourne House," she said to me. "I've asked you to run this little errand, Clare, because I know you can be trusted."

'It was just as well that neither of us knew what fate had in store or I might have thought twice about agreeing to deliver the book and Miss Caughey would have had thirty thousand fits! To cut a long story short, I caught the bus and delivered the book as asked but there was still twenty minutes or so to kill before the other girls arrived in the coach. So I wandered through the school and found myself in the corridor leading to the sixth-form boys' studies. I had been there once before when this guy Peter Thornton and I had managed to sneak away from the hall for a little snog. Now I remembered that his study was the third door on the left and for the life of me I still don't really know why I didn't knock first, but I just blithely opened the door to see if Peter was there.

'He was there all right though I don't know who was more embarrassed, him or me, because Peter was lying naked on his bed with a blissful expression on his face, a copy of *Playboy* in one hand, fisting his hand up and down his huge hard-on with the other! I was so flabbergasted that I just stood there speechless but poor Peter almost died. He flung the *Playboy* to the floor and threw a towel over his cock as he stammered out an abject apology.

'"That's all right, Peter, it's not the first time that I've seen a stiff cock," I reassured him and, shutting the door behind me, I went forward and picked up the magazine from the carpet, purposely not bending my knees but bending forward naughtily so that he could see down my blouse. I could see his cock twitching under the towel and this made me feel terribly randy so I said to him roguishly: "Wanking won't do you any harm but it seems wrong for a healthy lad like you to have to play with yourself. Anyhow, from the way your friends were talking at the last dance, I was given the impression that you were all screwing the arses off the local girls from that village on the Collington road."

'"Chance would be a fine thing," he said gloomily. "The other fellows here might tell you differently, but the truth of the matter is that none of us have ever gone further than a bit of heavy petting although I promise you that hasn't been for want of trying!"

'"I see," I replied, trying hard to suppress a smile. "I do admire your honesty which deserves to be rewarded.

'"Now what kind of prize would be suitable?" I continued thoughtfully as I sat down on the bed and stroked his thigh with my hand, my eyes rivetted to the quivering bulge which was twitching like fury under the towel.

'This made my pussy begin to moisten as I snapped my

fingers and said coyly: "Peter, answer me truthfully, have you ever seen a naked girl before?" His face crimsoned as he hung his head and muttered: "No, never."

'"Then it's high time you did," I declared and without further ado began to unbutton my blouse, trying hard not to smile when I saw the look of amazement on Peter's face. Then I kicked off my shoes and unzipped my skirt and let it fall to the floor. I noticed how his cock had shot up to make an enormous tenting bulge under the towel. I sat down on the bed and peeled off my tights and I turned my back to him and said: "Why don't you take off my bra?"

'The poor boy was all fingers and thumbs but he managed to unhook it and I stood up in front of him naked except for my blue school knickers which I drew down slowly watching Peter's eyes widen as he glimpsed his first-ever sight of a pussy bush. Now I hadn't planned to go any further but the devil was in me and, throwing caution to the winds, I said: "You Osbourne House boys aren't the only ones to miss out on rumpy-pumpy. We girls also have to rely on our own devices to pleasure ourselves. Let me show you one of my favourite ways of bringing myself off."

'He didn't reply but his jaw dropped and his mouth flew open as I wrapped my fingers around the elastic of my knickers and yanked the crotch up inside my saturated cunt and across my hardening little clitty. Peter gawped with amazement at the way my fleshy cunny lips were forced apart by the taut wet strip of cotton and his hand dived under the towel to fondle his rock-hard cock.

'This sent me right over the edge and I pulled the towel off his throbbing blue-veined boner. I curled my fingers around the velvet-skinned chopper but to my dismay, his shaft began to soften. I wasn't too worried at first because I knew this often happened when lads became over-anxious and I kept my hand around it while I laid down beside him and we exchanged a slurpy open-mouthed kiss.

'However, it only thickened up slightly so I broke off the kiss to bend my head down and give his cock a nice little lick which, thank goodness, did the trick. Peter gave a tiny sigh as my lips slipped over his knob and his shaft hardened up again when I sucked his prick into my mouth. I swirled my tongue over his helmet and, letting it pop out between my lips, I pulled myself up again and Peter slipped a finger up my cunt, moving it round in a circular motion that made me even more hot to trot.

'"Fuck me, Peter, fuck me!" I panted as I pulled him over me and spread my legs wide, taking hold of his cock to guide it into me. His knob slid smoothly between my yielding love lips and he was so excited that he rammed in the rest of his shaft in one big stroke. I gasped with surprise when I felt his balls slap against my bum and my legs seemed to have a mind of their own as they wrapped themselves around his waist. Then he began to fuck me in earnest. I matched him stroke for stroke so that I could feel his cock ream out every inch of my dripping quim and I squealed: "Oooh, you really are a big boy, Peter Thornton. Go in deeper, aaaah, that's gorgeous.'

'He pistoned into me with gusto, his body rising and falling as he fucked me with such passion that part of the time my bum was raised completely off the bed as he pounded in and out of my juicy honeypot. I was enjoying myself immensely but I was nowhere near a come when I felt Peter's prick shiver inside my sheath and with a loud moan he spunked inside me. There was nothing I could do but relax as gobs of sticky jism splashed against the walls of my love channel. Peter knew he had spunked too soon and he groaned in frustration but I said it didn't matter, I'd still thoroughly enjoyed the fuck which was absolutely true.

'"Perhaps we can try again," he said hopefully but I looked up at the clock on the wall and said: "By all means, but not right now. The coach with all the other girls will have arrived by now and we had better get along to the dance before they decide to send out search parties for us!"'

Trish cleared her throat and remarked: 'That all sounds very nice to me – but I thought you said this affair nearly ended in disaster.'

'I haven't quite finished the story,' chuckled Clare as she slid her hand between Trish's legs and began to play with her moist pussy. 'You see, Peter's clock was ten minutes slow and so our absence had already been noticed at the country dance session. One of the Osbourne House masters volunteered to find us and, not realising the time, we were still lying on the bed together when we heard the sound of footsteps clumping through the corridor. I had time only to slide under the eiderdown when the door was flung open by a tall, dark-haired man in his early thirties dressed in an open-necked white shirt and light grey trousers.

'"Thornton, what the blazes is going on here? You should be taking part in the country dancing," he thundered and Peter's face turned as white as a sheet. Now perhaps because this guy was a total stranger I was angry rather than frightened and hauling myself up and exposing my bare breasts to him, I retorted: "That's a bloody silly question – can't you can see for yourself that he has better things to do? Now please go away and leave us alone. Go on, shooh!"

'He stood there dumbstruck but Peter hissed in my ear: "For heaven's sake, Clare, this is my form-master, Mr Crewe."

'"I don't care who the hell he is," I maintained stoutly and, conveniently forgetting that I had been guilty of the very same act, I continued angrily: "He had no right to come barging in here like that without first knocking on the door."

'Peter was now already out of bed and pulling on his clothes as he stammered out a grovelling apology (I didn't blame him because the poor boy was in danger of being expelled only a fortnight away from his 'A' level exams) whilst Mr Crewe folded his arms and looked down sternly at me. I had already noted the appearance of a slight swell in the front of his trousers, however.

'"Don't worry, Peter, you run down to the hall and tell them I was unavoidably detained but that I'll be along in ten minutes," I commanded him as I looked pointedly at Mr Crewe's crotch. With a worried look on his face, he opened his mouth as if to protest but I repeated my instruction and added: "Just do as I say, all right?"

'He looked helplessly at Mr Crewe who passed his hand across his brow and muttered gruffly: "Just do what she says, Thornton. I'll speak to you later about all this."

'This time Peter didn't argue but silently pulled on the rest of his clothes and hurried on down to the hall. After he closed the door behind him, Mr Crewe looked down at me and grunted: "So, young lady, what have you got to say for yourself?"

'"Not a great deal really, except that my name's Clare," I replied brightly. "What's yours? I can't call you Mr Crewe if I'm going to suck your cock."

'"It's Tom and what was that you said?" he spluttered as I pulled off the eiderdown to reveal the rest of my naked body. Then I flipped over onto my tummy and crooking my finger to beckon him over, I cooed: "You heard me, Tom, come over here and let me see what's bulging out between your legs."

'"This is sheer madness," he mumbled but he shuffled forward until his crotch was only inches from my face. I unzipped his fly and slid my hand inside to pull out his cock through the slit of his boxer shorts and I must admit that it was a very impressive todger. Of course I had only planned to suck the schoolmaster's cock as a bribe for his silence about what Peter and I had been up to, but the sight of Tom Crewe's thick tool thrusting out as stiff as a baseball bat did make my pussy tingle. I took it in both hands, one dipping to fondle his big hairy balls and the other halfway up the shaft. Then I leaned forward and ran my tongue round the ridge of his uncapped helmet and then taking a deep breath, I swallowed his entire shaft in one quick movement. I could feel the tip of his knob at the back of my throat as I slurped on his thick fleshy cock although I did not gag whilst I grabbed his balls with one hand and used the other to try and pull him further inside my mouth. However, I shouldn't have been so greedy because now I did choke on Tom's colossal cock and instinctively I jerked my head away from him.

'"Oh I'm so sorry," he panted as he retracted his throbbing boner until his knob lay motionless on my tongue. This was far more comfortable and I moved my head forward and closed my lips around his swollen shaft and began to suck him off. "Arrrgghh!" he groaned as he bucked his hips and thrust his huge tool deeper down my throat. Then he held my head in his hands and cried out wildly: "Jesus Christ, I'm coming, brace yourself, Clare, I've going to shoot!"

'With a deep growl he pressed his prick between my lips to release the flow and I held his shaft at the base just as Tom started to squirt. I used my tongue to catch and swallow his jism. He shuddered all over from the waves of ecstasy running through his body but he held my head steady until I had gulped down every last drop of his salty seed.'

Clare smiled at the memory of this lascivious scene and rubbed her finger up and down Trish's dripping crack as she said: "We didn't waste any more time and I dressed in double-quick time to join Peter and the rest of the boys and girls for the country dancing. I told Miss Caughey that I had a bout of severe stomach cramps from my monthly which was due to begin the next day and this explanation satisfied her. As for Mr Tom Crewe, I need hardly tell you that he never said a word about finding Peter and me *in flagrante delicto*.'

At this point Simon came back from the bathroom with his face buried in a towel. Catching Clare's last few words, he called out: 'What's all this then? Who was caught *in flagrante*—'

Then he pulled the towel away from his face and stopped short as he saw that Clare and Trish were locked in a passionate embrace, kissing rapturously with Clare frigging the young girl's pussy, her fingers sliding in at speed in and out of Trish's thatch of damp auburn hair.

Trish parted her legs even further and Simon looked on with growing interest. His cock began to thicken when he saw her excited erect clitty which had burst out of its pod and was projecting out like a miniature cock between her cunny lips.

'Ooooh, here I go!' she called out. Simon watched with

fascination as an arched fountain of love juice spurted out from Trish's cunt and her lithe body bucked and heaved as she closed her eyes and luxuriated in the throes of a blissful orgasm.

'Now let me finish you off,' she insisted when the delicious sensations finally ebbed away. Nothing loath, Clare laid back and relaxed with her legs open wide and it was now Trish's turn to lean over and rub her fingertips between her yielding pussy lips. Trish kissed the stalks of her nipples and then rolled on top of her partner, pressing her pretty face between Clare's large breasts whilst she eased two fingers inside her squelchy slit. Her thumb prodded the aroused clitty and Clare shivered with delight as Trish withdrew her fingers and ran them wickedly up and down the full length of her saturated quim.

'See, the parting of the ways,' observed Simon wittily as Trish swivelled herself between Clare's raised thighs. Her beautiful bum cheeks jiggled high in the air when she dived down to lick and lap the moisture oozing from Clare's cunt, forcing her tongue deep inside the juicy love funnel whilst Clare threshed around wildly under this thrilling oral stimulation.

Simon moved towards them and let out an agitated gurgle of excitement as, with his erection bobbing stiffly between his thighs, he joined in the fun by positioning himself behind Trish and sliding his cock into the cranny between her tight bum cheeks and into her sticky wet honeypot. Her cunny muscles tightened around Simon's pulsing prick, squeezing his shaft so hard that he almost shot his load too soon.

'Wowee! Keep going, sweetie, that's the ticket,' puffed Trish and she continued to nibble on Clare's fleshy clitty whilst Simon ploughed his quivering cock in and out of her flooded quim.

And it was Clare who was first to explode, rubbing herself up to a glorious come against Trish's mouth. The teenage girl yelped with glee when Simon ejaculated and creamed her cunny with a coating of warm gooey jism.

They sank down in a sticky tangle of perspiring nude bodies and Simon panted: 'Phew, that was a wonderful screw but I'm going to have to take another shower.'

'Hey, that's not fair, you haven't fucked me yet,' protested Clare but Simon said apologetically: 'I'm sorry, love, if I don't leave now I'll be late for the game, so I'll have to take a raincheck as the Yanks say. Tell you what, I've a manuscript to read this evening, but if you like, I could come round here at about ten o'clock and I'll be more than happy to shag you all night, especially if there's any chance of locking Freddie away for a bit.'

'You're on,' she said promptly. 'In fact, Freddie has to travel up to Manchester next week to see his old auntie so I'll persuade him to go tomorrow. He always stays with her overnight so we'll have the place to ourselves.

'Mind, I'm sure you wouldn't have any objections if I invited this pretty little kitten to join us, would you, darling?' she went on and with a grin, Simon shook his head and turned to Trish as he said: 'Sounds like a splendid idea to me. How about it, love?'

'Sorry, but I've already arranged to go out for a meal with a girl friend,' Trish replied but then she smiled and added coquettishly: 'On the other hand, if you brought along Adrian Klein with you, I'm sure I could persuade Beth to come here afterwards.'

Simon's eyes sparkled as he hauled himself to his feet and said: 'No problem, love. It won't be necessary to put Adrian in an arm-lock to get him here. He hasn't got such a big cock as me, of course, but it'll pass muster in an emergency!'

CHAPTER TWO

Match of the Day

Adrian Klein and Simon Byrne were not the only members of the Hampstead Hotspurs football team to have enjoyed a good night out. Twenty minutes before their game with the Fleet Street Casuals, a team of sportswriters, jobbing actors and TV executives, three of their own players had yet to turn up.

'Where the fuck can they be?' fretted Mike Harper, the goalkeeper and captain of the Hotspurs, a loose gathering of young men who met on Thursday nights at the famous Bull and Bush pub on North End Road and who shared a common love of football.

'Mike, don't worry, Jimmy Ward's picking up Melvyn and Spike and he'll be here any minute,' said Roger Tagholm, the University lecturer and veteran centre-half who at the age of thirty-eight was still one of the fittest men in the Hotspurs team.

'I wish they wouldn't cut it so fine because the Casuals still have three former Pegasus men in their side and we'll get slaughtered if Jimmy and the others don't turn up,' grumbled Mike, a geologist with an oil company who had played a few games as an amateur for Leyton Orient and whose feats between the posts were one of the main reasons why the Hotspurs had lost only once in the last seven games.

'They'll be here, never fear,' Adrian assured his captain and then he turned to the brawny young man pulling up his shorts next to him, a stockbroker named Rodney Hill, and asked him if he had enjoyed his Saturday night.

'Not too bad, thanks,' answered Rodney as he sat down to lace his boots. 'Mind you, I found myself in a right pickle on Friday evening. Do you remember I told you how Ivor Lovell, this rich American client of ours, keeps inviting me to his indoor swimming pool in Hertfordshire? This guy owns a chunk of one of a Hollywood production company and some of the stars from Elstree Studios are always popping in for a swim. Well, I had a meeting with him on Friday afternoon and he insisted that I stayed for supper. Then he said: "Look, Rod, I've a few Transatlantic calls to make. Why don't you go down and take a dip in the pool?"

'I replied: "Thanks, Ivor, I would have liked that but unfortunately I haven't brought a cossie with me." He waved this objection away and declared: "Oh, that doesn't matter. I always swim in he nude myself when I'm alone or with close friends – believe me, it's much more fun in the water without a costume. Off you go, Rod, you'll find plenty of towels at the pool."

'Why not? I thought to myself so I trotted outside and stripped off in one of the two large cabins Ivor had built at the sides of the pool. I was down to my Y-fronts when I heard someone dive in. I assumed that Ivor hadn't been able to get through to the States and had come to join me for a swim, so I pulled off my pants and, slinging a towel across my neck, I strode out only to find that it wasn't Ivor in the water but a pretty dark-haired girl in a tiny blue bikini.'

His team-mates burst out laughing and Simon chuckled: 'Lucky you had a towel to hide your wedding tackle. Although I daresay if she was short-sighted it wouldn't have mattered very much!'

Rodney ignored the jibe and continued: 'I could have coped with this admittedly embarrassing situation and indeed I whipped the towel around my waist as I called out: "Sorry about that, Ivor didn't tell me that anyone else was using the pool."

'Then I almost jumped out of my skin when a girlish voice behind me giggled: "That's all right, you're not showing us anything that we haven't seen before." I turned round and my face turned as red as a beetroot when I saw three other stark naked gorgeous girls, one with long blonde hair down to her shoulders and the other two wearing shower caps, all standing behind me with wide smiles on their faces.

'They had obviously been changing in the other cabin and although I was shocked, my cock sprang to attention as my eyes swivelled up and down their beautiful nude bodies. Even more surprisingly, the girls didn't seem disconcerted in the slightest by my presence and the blonde said to me: "Hi there, I'm Michelle, this is Corinne and Debs and that's Livvie down there in the water. We're working at Elstree Studios as extras on *Here We Go Round the Mulberry Bush.*"

'"I'll look forward to seeing you in the film," I said, trying to recover my composure. "Have any of you read the novel? It could be a bit of a naughty movie."

'"Some nudie shots, you mean?" said the ravishing tall bird. "We haven't been asked to show our tits though that wouldn't worry us, would it, Debs?"

'"No, but I think it might bother him a bit," grinned her friend, looking pointedly down at the outline of my cock which was twitching underneath the towel. "What's your name, sir, are you connected with the film business?"

'I answered: "Not exactly, my name's Rodney, I'm Ivor Lovell's financial advisor and before you ask, I'm not a naturist, I didn't bring a swimming costume with me and Ivor said nothing about anyone else using the pool when he told me to go for a dip."

'Now I didn't know it at the time but, to be fair to the girls, they had just come from a party at the studios thrown by the producer to celebrate Denholm Elliott's birthday and Ivor had genuinely forgotten that he had invited them round for drinks that afternoon. Nevertheless, to say the least I was quite unprepared for what was to follow after Michelle giggled: "Come on, Rodney, don't be shy."

'Her hand shot out and pulled off my towel and her eyes widened as she went on: "My word, you don't need to be bashful with a cock like that!" Anyhow, Ivor arrived about ten minutes later with two bottles of Moet et Chandon and the other girls made Livvie take off her bikini while we cavorted around in the pool.

'After a while we climbed out and we let the warm evening sun dry off the moisture from our bodies. I found myself talking with Livvie, a petite but provocatively curvaceous girl with a pretty face and long dark hair which she had to keep pushing back from her face while we talked. Well, one thing led to another and when we found ourselves alone after the others had gone into the cabin to change, we moved behind a bush and I had my tongue in her ear and she had her hand sliding up and down my cock. Then with her back against the side of the cabin, Livvie grabbed my shoulders and opened her legs as I took hold of my cock and slid my knob inside her juicy cunt. She opened up even wider and, with her hands locked behind my head, her legs clasped around my waist and her heels drumming against my bum, we fucked away like crazy to the cheers of Ivor and the other girls who had quietly gathered round to watch whilst Livvie urged me on to fuck her silly.

'"Don't worry, Rod, I'm on the pill," she panted and then, as if we had rehearsed it beforehand, our bellies slapped together and I jetted spurt after spurt of spunk into her as she writhed away in the throes of her own orgasm.

'The only sad thing is that the girls couldn't stay any longer as they had to get back to work and I don't know how to contact them again. Ivor flew out to New York yesterday and it won't be easy trying to find them at the film studios, especially as I don't even know their surnames!'

There was a momentary silence in the dressing room as Rodney finished his story until the three missing players burst in and Mike Harper waved a weak greeting at them.

'Bloody hell, talk about a breathless hush in the close tonight!' exclaimed Jimmy Ward anxiously. 'Did you kick off early and we're six down at half-time?'

'No, we're all wondering how any chick could fancy Rodney Hill,' grinned Mike Harper, deftly ducking the football thrown at his head by the stockbroker. 'Hurry up, chaps. You should have been here twenty minutes ago.'

'Sorry, Mike,' apologised Jimmy as he put down his kit-bag. 'Melvyn and Spike were ready and waiting but I was half an hour late in picking them up from the tube station. The fact is a mate took me out for a Chinese dinner last night and I think the sweet and sour pork was off. Anyhow, I've been up half the night so be gentle with me, as the actress said to the bishop. Put me down for a left-wing berth, skip, and keep passing the ball to the right-hand side of the field.'

'Okay, Jimmy,' sighed Mike Harper heavily. 'I was going to ask Rodney to play wide on the left but he had better tuck in behind the strikers in an attacking midfield role. Adrian, you'll be at right back and Simon, will you play up front with Fred and Clive?'

'No problem,' assented Simon as the referee came in and asked Mike if he was ready to take the field. 'Yup, we'll be out in a minute,' replied the Hotspurs captain. 'Come on lads, we're going to hammer the Casuals. I'll be disappointed if we don't win by at least three clear goals!'

Alas, after only fifteen minutes play Mike Harper was picking the ball out of the Hampstead Hotspurs net for the third time and so let us draw a curtain of charity over the match which was taking place only a quarter of a mile away from the palatial five-bedroom house of Dickie "Nipper" Segal, managing director of Associated Entertainment Productions. The powerful impresario was himself about to engage in some strenuous indoor exercise.

In the absence of his wife who was spending the day with her parents in North Finchley, Dickie had taken the opportunity of inviting to his house a nineteen-year-old *ingenue* named Cindy Shackleton who he had seen at a recent audition for his new revue at the Prince of Wales. Unlike Trish Jackson, she had been unsuccessful in gaining a place in the chorus line, but Dickie had been struck by her fresh-faced good looks and shapely figure and he had sent a minion round to the dressing room to tell Cindy to call his office as there might be a role for her in *Babes in the Wood*, the Christmas pantomime A.E.P. was putting on at the Croydon Empire.

He had brought Cindy into his sumptuous study and after pouring them both a glass of sherry, Dickie explained what he had in mind. 'It should be a good show, we've lashed out on a good script, some lovely costumes and Pearl Carr and Teddy Johnson have already been booked as the King and Queen of Wessex. There's a clever young club comic named Allan Godfrey who I've pencilled in as the male Babe and I'm looking for a bright girl to play alongside Allan as the female. This is a starring role with lots of singing, dancing and a love scene with the Prince of Wessex who'll be some pop singer to please the older kids. Now I know you worked in panto last year in the chorus of one of Lou Baum's shows in the West Country – but do you honestly think you're ready to take on a major part?'

'Naturally I think so, but of course you're in a better position to judge that than me,' smiled Cindy. She bent down and unzipped the small hold-all she had brought with her and handed Dickie a demo disc she had hurriedly cut at a small recording studio after accepting his invitation to come over to his house and look at the script. He placed the disc on the record player and nodded approvingly as he listened to Cindy's rendition of *House of the Rising Sun*.

'You've a strong voice and know how to put over a song,' said Dickie who himself had started his showbiz career as a crooner with a dance band after being demobbed from the Army in 1945. 'Now if you can dance as well as you can sing, I may well speak to your agent tomorrow morning.'

Cindy picked up her holdall and said eagerly 'Fine, I've brought a costume and my tap shoes – is there somewhere I can change?'

Dickie heaved himself out of his chair and replied affably: 'Sure, you can slip them on here whilst I pop out and make a couple of phone calls.' The impresario threw her a friendly smile and patted her shoulder as he walked out into the hall, increasingly confident that this sexy girl understood how she could ensure that he would indeed contact her agent.

To be fair to Dickie Segal, he had never offered work to girls simply on the basis of their willingness to be laid, but when there was little to choose between those who had agreed and those who had refused a session on the casting couch, he showed his gratitude for past favours.

In fact, he had no phone calls to make but he walked briskly across to the kitchen and instructed the *au pair* (a chubby Greek girl chosen by his wife, who knew nothing of Dickie's peccadillos but was sensible enough not to place temptation in her husband's way) to put of a bottle of white wine in the refrigerator and prepare two cold beef salads for himself and his guest. As he left, Dickie added: 'I'll be in conference, Elena, so don't interrupt us. Just leave everything here and when you've finished, you can have the rest of the day off. It's lovely outside, why don't you go for a walk on the Heath?'

He returned to the study and knocked on the door. 'Come on in,' Cindy sang out and Dickie felt a familiar stirring in his groin when he opened the door and saw the stunning young girl had changed into a scanty low-cut pink jumper and a white miniskirt. She was now bare-legged except for a pair of short white socks and her black tap shoes and his cock began to thicken when she turned to her left and bent down to tie up an errant shoe-lace, exposing her firm little bum cheeks which were covered by only a tiny pair of bikini panties.

Cindy nodded when he asked her if she could work out a routine to the Temperance Seven's version of *The Charleston* and so, after putting the record on the turntable, Dickie slumped into an armchair to watch her perform. By the time the last notes had died away his cock was pushing up uncomfortably out of the slit of his boxer shorts against the confines of his trousers, a fact that did not go unnoticed by Cindy when she stood in front of him to await his judgement.

He gave her a thumbs-up sign as he cleared his throat and chuckled: 'Good enough, love. You might need to work on your time steps but that's nothing a bit of coaching from Sarah Watts can't sort out.'

She clapped her hands together in glee. 'Thank you, Mr Segal!' she squealed happily. 'I can't tell you how grateful I am for a chance to show what I can do.'

'You can show your appreciation by staying for a bite of lunch with me,' suggested Dickie with a smile. 'And perhaps I can think up a few ideas about how you can further your career. You're with Midas Management, aren't you? I'll have a word with Steve Williams about you first thing tomorrow morning.'

'Mr Segal, I hardly know what to say,' she answered excitedly and Dickie gave her a good-natured grin. *Giving me a blow-job would be a good start,* he added silently before he shrugged: 'If I like the look of an artiste there's no reason why she shouldn't get to the very top.'

Cindy flashed a saucy look at him as she replied: 'Then you must see another of my routines. Just go outside again for a minute till I call you back inside.'

'It's all right, I don't need to see anything more right now,' he protested but she held out her hand and hauled the reluctant Dickie out of his chair and she repeated that it would only take her a jiffy to get ready. 'You'll love this, I promise you,' Cindy assured him as she shepherded him towards the door.

Dickie did not have to wait more than a minute to find out what the frisky young filly had in mind. 'I'm ready for you,' he heard her call out, but he stopped stock still in the doorway after he had flung open the door. For Cindy was standing with her feet slightly apart in front of his desk, leaning forward with her face cocked to one side facing him and her cheek resting on the polished maple surface.

'I was told you liked to begin at the bottom and work upwards,' she said with an impudent giggle and Dickie slammed the door shut behind him as he gave a low growl of approval. He strode across the room and lifted her short skirt to reveal her bare backside. As he brushed his hands across the pliant rounded globes, he noticed that Cindy's knickers and bra were perched on top of a sheaf of papers on the side of his desk.

'M'm, I love having someone I like smoothing their hands over my arse, it really turns me on,' she cooed.

'Good show,' muttered Dickie and Cindy heard the impresario fall to his knees and she let out a squawk as he squeezed each of her tight dimpled buttocks in his hands.

The soft flesh of her beautiful bum cheeks so close to his face made him tremble with desire. As he parted the rounded globes, his cock throbbed frantically at the sight of Cindy's diminutive puckered rear dimple and the pink, pouting lips of her quim.

Without further delay he forced his head between her thighs and slid his tongue inside her moist crack and to his gratification, the sensuous girl let out a sigh of delight as the curled point of his tongue found the edges of her clitty. Dickie's hands snaked upwards under her jumper to cup her small jutting breasts. His tongue now slipped in and out of Cindy's cunt with ease, coated with the love juice which had begun to trickle out of her luscious honeypot. His lips closed over her clitty and he sucked hard, causing an immediate explosion of pleasure which racked through Cindy's slender frame as Dickie rolled her hard nipples gently between his fingers.

'Fuck me, Dickie, fuck me,' she moaned and, nothing loath, he scrambled to his feet. Cindy turned her head and, as she watched him tear down his trousers and pants, she smacked her lips when she saw his massive stiff shaft which would soon be sliding its way between her bum cheeks and into her moist snatch. Size might not matter, according to the sex manuals she had read, but no-one could persuade Cindy that a prick like the well-endowed Dickie Segal's which measured over nine and a half inches long wasn't worth its weight in gold.

'Okay, here we go!' he grunted as he nudged her knees slightly further apart. He took his todger in his hand and slowly guided the glistening plum-like helmet between her rolling bum cheeks and into the soft folds of her cunt.

Once Dickie was fully embedded inside her sheath, he slid his hands round her sides to caress her breasts as he started to fuck the quivering girl with sharp, jabbing strokes. Cindy quickly caught his rhythm and jerked her hips to and fro in perfect time with his quick short shoves in and out of her sopping slit.

'Aaah! Aaah Aaah!' panted Dickie as she urged him on. He changed the pace and style of the fuck, driving the full length of his rigid rod inside her, riding his prick in and out of her clingy quim until Cindy felt herself being swept into the ultimate ecstasy. She howled with joy as the force of a powerful orgasm rocketed throughout her body. Dickie grunted heavily as his climax followed almost immediately and he creamed Cindy's cunt with a fierce fountain of sticky warm spunk before withdrawing his deflated shaft from her saturated love channel.

However, Cindy Shackleton was a feisty lass who was not satisfied by one short bout of lovemaking. 'Come on, Dickie, don't stop now,' she demanded when she turned round and saw him mopping his brow with a handkerchief. 'Take those two cushions from that armchair behind you and we can have a nice fuck on the floor.'

Dickie shook his head. 'Sorry, love, but it's been a good few years since my old man could carry on after only a few minutes rest.'

'Never mind,' said Cindy comfortingly whilst she slid her hand up and down his limp shaft to make sure there was no chance of coaxing it back into action. 'I loved the way you brought me off with your tongue.'

'Okay, I'll see what I can do,' he agreed. 'But the au pair will have gone out by now so as we've the house to ourselves, let's go upstairs to bed.'

Taking her hand, he led the way up the staircase to one of

the spare bedrooms. Cindy laid herself down on the eiderdown, pulling out a pillow from behind her head to slide underneath her bottom whilst Dickie climbed up and placed himself between her creamy thighs. He took a deep breath and Cindy giggled as she pulled his head down to her fluffy brown bush where he kissed her soaking cunny lips.

'Woooh! That's brilliant, oooh, I just adore having my pussy eaten,' she gasped, wriggling her hips from side to side in order to press Dickie's face deeper between her thighs. He breathed deeply of the musky scent of their previous come and, licking the pink slit in front of him, he played with the delicate folds by flicking his tongue up and down the long crinkly lips of Cindy's cunt. She let out an anguished cry when he momentarily paused to draw breath and then she purred with pleasure as he swirled the tip of his tongue over the hard nub of her clitty before plunging it deep inside the sticky honeypot of her quim.

At once Cindy began to tremble with passion. She felt the growing strength of an approaching orgasm seeping through her entire body as Dickie lapped inside her cunt with increasing intensity. The warm sensations rapidly built up and then rose to a climax and she screamed out: 'Oh yes, lick me out, you lovely cunt-sucker!' as her erect clitty vibrated under the remorseless frigging of Dickie's tongue. When Cindy climaxed, a shower of tangy pussy juice spurted out of her excited quim into his mouth. Dickie gulped it down and continued to suck even harder, pushing his lips up against her cunt and moving his head back and forth whilst his tongue twirled along the silken grooves of her cunt as he swallowed the jets of come which were pumping out of the wriggling girl's sodden slit.

With each stroke Cindy arched her body in ecstasy, pressing her twitching clitty up against his flickering tongue as her cunny exploded one final time and Dickie's face was spattered with a further outpouring of cuntal juice.

'Y-e-s-s-s!' Cindy screamed so loudly that Dickie was worried in case his next door neighbours heard her cries of passion. He pulled his face away from her dripping muff and whispered a warning to her to keep the noise down.

'Sorry, darling,' she apologised as she took a series of deep breaths whilst she recovered from her exertions and then added with a reproachful chuckle: 'But you're to blame, Dickie Segal. Nobody has ever managed to bring me off so beautifully with his tongue. Good grief, you make me feel so randy, you old sexpot, that my pussy is beginning to tingle again. Come and lie down next to me and we'll see if your cock is now ready for some more fun.'

Dickie obediently hauled himself up and slumped down next to her as Cindy nuzzled against his side. She played with the fuzzy hairs on his chest and slowly let her hand run down over his abdomen which, despite his middle-age, was still lean and firm. Then she encircled the meaty tube of soft flesh lying across his thigh and Dickie leaned his head back against the pillow and closed his eyes when Cindy carefully ran her clenched fingers up and down his stiffening shaft.

'Oooh, I think we have lift off,' she giggled as, constantly changing the pressure and speed of her hand motions, she rubbed his cock until it had swelled up to its full throbbing length. Cindy swung her leg over his hips and, still manipulating his prick, positioned herself directly above him. Dickie steadied her with his hands as she lowered herself until the tip of his knob touched her pouting pussy lips and she began to gently rub her clitty with his cock. Back and forth, with long slow strokes she teased herself with his hardness as Dickie groaned with desire whilst his steel-hard shaft pulsed in her grasp.

'Please,' he begged her. 'Please,' and Cindy gave a wickedly knowing smile as suddenly she speared herself on his cock which slid up into the welcoming clingy wetness of her cunt.

'There, is that better?' she asked and he gasped: 'God Almighty, that's fantastic!' as she drove herself down so quickly that Dickie felt as though his embedded cock now belonged to Cindy as much as it did to him.

Her lithe young body rocked to and fro and he rubbed

his palms against her stalky red nipples as she bounced on his pulsating prick. Then he grabbed hold of her jiggling bum cheeks whilst he jerked his hips upwards to meet her downward thrusts and her sticky love channel slipped up and down his shuddering shaft. However, the sensations of her cuntal muscles nipping his tool were so strong that although Dickie would have liked to have continued the joust a little longer, his jism shot out and drenched Cindy's cunt. She let out a short screech and thrust herself forward, rubbing her elongated rubbery titties against his chest as she erupted into a mind-wrenching orgasm.

She slithered down to lie in his arms but the force of his second come totally exhausted Dickie who lay panting heavily with fatigue as they drifted off into a delicious post-copulatory doze.

Meanwhile, the only consolation for the Hampstead Hotspurs was that fifteen minutes into the second half they had conceeded only two further goals. The score could have been worse but, perhaps taking pity on the clearly outclassed side, the referee had whistled up for a penalty when Simon Byrne's long shot was deflected into the upper arm of a Casuals defender and Jimmy Ward had smashed the ball into the net to make the scoreline look slightly more respectable. This put new heart into the side and another goal looked certain when a long through pass from Adrian found Simon with only the goalkeeper to beat, but his foot caught a divot of turf and he stabbed the ball gently towards the corner flag.

'You stupid turd!' angrily bellowed a thickset young man who had been standing at the touchline for the past ten minutes. Beside him was a tall blonde with huge baby blue eyes and long shoulder-length fair hair parted in the middle and who was dressed, like the man, in a rumpled shirt and tight-fitting blue jeans. She had also done a fair share of cat-calling and Adrian couldn't understand why the pair of them seemed bent on barracking him and Simon so unmercifully.

Simon glared at her boy friend – he assumed it was her boy

friend, for they had been standing there arm in arm whilst he had hurled a continual stream of abuse against the Hotspurs in general and Adrian and Simon in particular whenever they had found themselves in the thick of the action. Goaded beyond endurance, Simon ran across to the stockily built youth and shouted at him angrily to keep his mouth shut.

'If you don't like it, take up tiddlywinks,' he retorted aggressively and Simon spat out: 'I'll give you tiddlywinks, you fucking—' but Adrian had run up to him and clamped his hand over his mouth.

'Forget it, mate! For Christ's sake, it's only a game,' commanded Adrian as he removed his hand from his friend's mouth. To his surprise he heard the girl laugh and say: 'Okay, Garry, you win! You're right, they can dish out the aggro, but it's a different matter altogether when they have to take it themselves.'

There was something familiar about her boy friend's face, thought Adrian vaguely, but he banished all thoughts from his mind as the Casuals outside right raced by him and chipped the ball perfectly past the advancing Mike Harper for their sixth goal.

To complete a miserable match for Adrian, five minutes later he was forced to limp off the field with a painful pulled calf muscle but as he slowly hobbled past the incensed spectator he suddenly recognised who had been jeering at him and his team and he said to him excitedly: 'Hey, aren't you Garry Horne, the Fulham centre forward?'

'In person,' he replied with a complacent grin. 'And if I'm not mistaken, you and your mate were two of the fans who gave me such grief yesterday afternoon. I saw you both up there in the stands shouting your heads off when I missed that sitter near the end like he did just then – and, believe me, I was trying even harder than he was because it's my job.'

'I take your point,' said Adrian and then he held out his hand. 'Simon and I will try and be more helpful in future. No hard feelings, eh?'

'Of course not,' said the footballer as he shook Adrian's

hand. 'Listen, as Belinda here says, you're really entitled to shout what you like because you pay my wages. But we're only human and when the crowd gets on your back, it's hard to psyche yourself up when things don't go your way. It's nice to meet a Fulham fan, there don't seem to be that many left these days.'

'You're absolutely right,' sighed Adrian. 'I remember when you had to pay a spiv to get into a big match. Still, I'm sure the crowds will come back when the team starts winning again.'

The ball came flashing towards them from a rare misdirected pass by the Casuals right back and Garry trapped it expertly under his foot as Rodney Hill came over to take the throw-in. 'Adrian, I'd get yourself into a hot shower if I were you,' he commented as he picked up the ball and the blonde dollybird standing next to Garry snapped her fingers and said: 'Adrian, now I've got it, you're Adrian Klein of Rose and Griffin, right? I couldn't think where I had seen you before but now I remember – it was at the London Theatre Awards dinner at the Hilton back in March.'

Adrian looked at her closely and shook his head: 'Well, I'm guilty as charged but are you sure we met at the Awards dinner? You certainly weren't on my table and – please don't take offence – but I can't believe I would ever forget being introduced to you unless I was smashed out of my mind.'

The girl smiled at him as she brushed away flaxen strands of hair from her face. 'Your crowd did get rather excited when Mike Smiley won the Best TV Actor Award. When I asked your boss Teddy Dixon afterwards whether he was taking Mike somewhere to celebrate, he said he was taking him to *La Miraggio* and invited me to join the party.'

'So why don't I remember seeing you there?' frowned Adrian and she grinned: 'There's a very good reason why not – I didn't accept the invitation because I was on early shift the next morning and had to be in the office at eight o'clock.'

She held out her hand and continued: 'My name's Belinda Headley and I'm on the Diary page at the *Evening News*. I cover showbiz stories so if you want to make up for hurting Garry's feelings, you can let me in on some gossip about Rose and Griffin's artistes. For instance, is it true that Carola Watforde has been having an affair with the pop singer Sharon Saxon?'

'No it isn't and even if it were true, I'm hardly likely to tell anyone, am I?' grinned Adrian and then he grimaced as a twinge of pain shot through his injured leg. 'Ouch! Here's an exclusive for you though – why don't you write a piece about Allan Godfrey, the young comedian who is packing them in at one of London's top night clubs and is in line for his own TV series next year? It's his birthday next week and you could see Allan at work for yourself at *La Miraggio*. He's a genuinely nice bloke and I'll be happy to arrange an interview after the show if you like.'

'Never heard of him,' she replied promptly. 'And his birthday's not exactly the strongest peg to hang a story. Still, I wouldn't say no to dinner at *La Miraggio* although I can't promise that we'll run a piece.'

'Of course not,' nodded Adrian. 'But let's make a date – are you free tomorrow night? I'll be honest, dinner's on the house for Rose and Griffin directors on Monday evenings so you wouldn't have to feel guilty if nothing about Allan ever appeared in the paper afterwards.'

He turned to Garry Horne and added: 'You're also very welcome to come along, Garry. I swear I won't tell Allan you're in the audience so he won't make any cracks about Fulham.'

'That's all right, I've heard them all before – about Fulham planning to sign a Chinaman called We Wun Wunce and how we now take a lap of honour when we win a corner,' sighed the footballer. 'So thanks for the offer, Adrian, but I won't be able to make it. The boss is taking us out of town tomorrow for two days intensive training at the seaside before the game on Wednesday up at Huddersfield.'

A shout of joy from the pitch made them swivel round to see Mike Harper glumly picking the ball out of the Hotspurs net as the Casuals celebrated their seventh goal. 'Oh dear, your team isn't doing very well either,' he continued and Adrian shrugged: 'We've yet to win this season. I don't suppose you've time to come back to the dressing room and give the lads some ideas.'

Garry consulted his watch and looked at Belinda. 'Just for ten minutes. We don't have to be at Auntie Hetty's till about half past one, do we?'

She shook her head and said: 'No, and I wouldn't mind if we don't get there till two because otherwise Mum'll have me in the kitchen peeling the veggies.' Belinda could see that Adrian looked puzzled and explained: 'Garry and I are cousins, his Dad and my Mum are brother and sister.'

Adrian's eyes lit up at hearing this good news. 'I see,' he said cheerfully. 'Well, I'm not going to wait till the end of the match so I'll go for a shower now and see you in about fifteen minutes.'

Adrian limped away and while he trudged back to the dressing rooms he considered whether he might have any chance of making a more intimate acquaintance with Belinda, a pleasant fantasy which was rudely interrupted by the sight of Tanya and Jennie loitering outside the pavilion. They were dressed in open-necked short sleeve tops and shorts and Tanya called out to him: 'Yoo-hoo, Ade, Jennie and I thought we'd come and cheer you on – how's the game going?'

Adrian jerked his thumb back along the path and answered: 'Over there but I wouldn't bother, there's only about a quarter of an hour left and we're seven-one down!'

'Seven-one? Crikey, I'm sorry I asked!' Tanya giggled and then she noticed his limp and she said anxiously: 'Oh, you poor wounded soldier. Did you get a kick on the leg?'

'No, it's just a pulled muscle, I'll be all right after a hot shower and a rub-down,' he said valiantly. Jennie gave Tanya a knowing wink and said, 'Why don't we see if we can make poor Adrian's leg better? After all, I did train as a nurse for two years.'

'Good idea, Jen,' enthused Tanya as she slipped Adrian's arm around her shoulders. 'You take the other side and we'll carry him into the first-aid station.'

'There's no need for that,' Adrian complained but nevertheless he allowed the girls to escort him into the Hotspurs changing room where he sat down on the slatted bench and Tanya knelt down and unlaced his boots whilst Jennie ordered him to raise his arms so that she could pull off his muddy shirt. Then Tanya took off his socks and when he stood up the girls yanked down his shorts and jockstrap leaving him stark naked as they stepped back and looked critically at him.

'A hot shower first, I think,' said Jennie thoughtfully and Tanya agreed: 'Yes, but we had better undress too as we're bound to get wet while we rub him down.'

And to Adrian's astonishment, both girls quickly stripped off and then Tanya skipped out to switch on the shower. Jennie grabbed three towels from the pile on the bench and with his eyes riveted to her peachy bum cheeks, he followed her into the showers.

Tanya was waiting for them inside a cubicle where the water was already streaming out of the nozzle. 'Under you go, love, it isn't too hot,' she said, pulling him in by his prick which immediately started to thicken when it dawned upon Adrian that he was being seduced by two ravishing girls who had pressed themselves against him as the warm water cascaded over his head.

He let out a delighted gasp when Tanya now began to rub his cock whilst Jennie kissed him and sucked his tongue inside her mouth. Adrian caressed Jennie's jutting, uptilted breasts as he felt Tanya slide down to her knees and seconds later his shaft was firmly embedded inside her mouth.

However, Jennie soon broke off the embrace and turned off the shower as she pulled Tanya's lips away from Adrian's twitching todger. 'Let's dry ourselves and then Tanya and I will show you a good yoga position which will help cure the pain in your leg,' she said. He let himself be led out of the cubicle into the first-aid room where they towelled themselves dry.

'So what's this yoga business?' he asked teasingly. 'Have you two girls gone out to see that Maharishi guy the Beatles are going nuts about?'

Jennie shook her head. 'No, but don't knock yoga, Adrian, there's much more to it than just meditation. Yoga also involves creating postures designed to stretch the muscles and release tension. Tanya, why don't we show him the Dog position?'

Adrian watched with growing interest as the two naked girls went down on their hands and knees and stretched their arms forward and stuck their delectable backsides in the air. His throbbing tool now stood up stiffly against his belly as he pondered over the tricky problem over who he should fuck first.

'Eeny, meeny, miny, mo,' he muttered softly but he had already decided to favour Jennie whose legs were slightly parted to reveal her pink love lips which were peeking out so seductively through their light covering of strawberry blonde pussy hair. So, brandishing his thick stiff shaft in his hand, Adrian placed himself behind her and carefully parted her jouncy bum cheeks. A fervent growl burst out of his mouth as he slid his cock into the cleft of Jennie's bottom and directly into her moist crack.

'That feels good,' Jennie panted as she jiggled her rump from side to side, taking care to ensure that Adrian's shaft was kept firmly lodged inside her clingy sheath. She moved round until she was in front of Tanya who twisted herself round to lie on her back with the towels bunched up in a makeshift pillow upon which she rested her head.

Adrian slowly expelled a deep breath as Jennie made the muscles of her love channel nip his shaft. As he pistoned in and out of her exquisitely tight cunt, a perfect frenzy of lust racked through his body. His hands slid round Jennie to squeeze her breasts as the supple girl lowered her head between Tanya's long slender legs and plunged her head between her girl friend's thighs.

This had an instant effect on Tanya who gasped out: 'Oh yes, yes! Eat my pussy, darling!'

Without further ado, Jennie pressed her lips against Tanya's cunt and slurped noisily on her dripping quim. Adrian slid his pulsating prick in to the hilt and he fucked her in a steady, regular rhythm, his thighs slapping against her dimpled buttocks whilst she lapped up Tanya's pungent pussy juice.

This sensual scene of mutual enjoyment was carried out in silence, broken only by gentle moans of delight. Adrian pounded away until he found himself teetering on the brink of his climax and suddenly he remembered that he was riding bareback without asking an all-important question.

'Can I come inside you?' he croaked and Jennie raised her head from Tanya's cunt and gasped: 'Yes, it's okay, we're both on the pill.' She slipped her hand behind her to play with his balls as she went on breathlessly: 'Keep fucking my cunt harder with your big cock for as long as you can though, I also want to come.'

'So do I,' squealed Tanya and Jennie dived back to continue licking out her love funnel as Tanya's hair billowed out. She rocked her head from side to side as a shuddering orgasm pulsed through her cunny. Now Adrian's torso went rigid and he gave one last robust thrust forward, drenching Jennie's cunt with creamy bursts of jism before they collapsed on top of Tanya and the three lay together, bathed in a blissful afterglow of pleasure.

However, this delicious reverie was shattered by a loud knocking on the outside door. Adrian cursed loudly as he hastily scrambled to his feet. 'Fuck! The sodding game must have finished and the boys'll be coming in. Quick, girls, run through and get changed whilst I hold the fort.'

'Aye aye, skipper,' giggled Jennie as they scampered back and, wrapping a towel around his waist, Adrian rushed to the door which Tanya had locked behind her.

'Hold on, lads, I'll just find the key,' bellowed Adrian as he watched the girls throw on their clothes. Luckily for him, when he finally opened the door there were not twenty-two irritated footballers on the other side of the door but only the solitary figure of Garry Horne.

'Everything all right, Adrian?' he asked. 'The game won't be over for another few minutes yet. There's been a couple of injury stoppages, nothing serious although your friend Simon was badly winded when he was in the defensive wall at a free kick. Got the ball right in the nuts, but he'll be all right. Mind, to add insult to injury, the Casuals scored their eighth goal while the poor chap was lying on the ground clutching his wedding tackle.

'Anyhow, I just came to tell you that I can't stop to chat with the lads, after all. Belinda and I had quite forgotten that we were supposed to pop and have a drink before lunch with my Uncle Bernie over in Southgate so we must make a move. Sorry about that, mate, perhaps we'll get together another time.'

Then he brought out a scrap of paper from his jeans and went on: 'Belinda's scribbled down her phone number and she says if tomorrow night's still on, you should give her a ring at about six o'clock.'

'Thanks, Garry, tell Belinda I'll call her without fail,' replied Adrian and he shook hands with the Fulham centre forward. He mopped his brow with relief as he closed the door and turned to face the girls.

'And just who is Belinda?' asked Tanya crossly as she stood facing him with her arms folded over her chest. 'Aren't our pussies enough for you?'

'Of course they are, love,' said Adrian smoothly. 'Belinda happens to be a journalist on the *Evening News* and I want her to write about Allan Godfrey, a new comedian Teddy Dixon found at a working-men's gaff in the Midlands. We've put him into a posh West End club, so I'm taking her to see him tomorrow night.'

Tanya was not entirely satisfied by this explanation but Adrian was saved from further questioning by the arrival of his team-mates. He waved happily at the crestfallen Hotspurs players as they filed wearily into the dressing room.

'Hi there, guys, well played. Not to worry, we can't win them all!'

'No, but it would have been nice not to have been fucking humiliated,' snarled Simon Byrne as he flopped down onto the bench and buried his face in his hands. 'Nine bloody one, that's how it finished.'

'Tsk, tsk,' Adrian nodded sympathetically as he patted his chum on the shoulder. 'But don't forget we were playing with ten men for the last twenty minutes or so. I don't want to blow my own trumpet, but we would probably have kept the score down if I hadn't pulled this flaming muscle.'

Simon looked up and looked curiously at Tanya and Jennie who were standing a few feet away. He grunted: 'Never mind the game, Ade, isn't that the girl you copped off with at *La Miraggio* last night?'

'Yes, that's Tanya,' conceeded Adrian quietly. 'And the blonde bird with her is her mate Jennie, another dancer who she worked with at the *Moulin Rouge* in Paris.' Then he went on to explain how the two girls came to be in the Hotspurs' dressing room.

'So introduce me,' muttered Simon as Jennie sauntered over and said: 'Tanya and I had better be on our way, Adrian. We don't want to embarrass your friends by staying here while they change. By the way, are you coming back to see us this evening?'

'Sure, I've promised Tanya I'd take her to that new Chinese restaurant in West Hampstead.' he answered. 'And of course you're very welcome to join us.'

'No thanks, Ade, I wouldn't want to play gooseberry,' she answered demurely. Adrian let out a sharp yelp of pain when Simon dug him in the ribs with his elbow.

'Ouch! That hurt,' he complained ruefully. 'Jennie, this hooligan is my friend Simon Byrne, lunatic of this parish.'

'Hi there, Jennie, nice to meet you,' said Simon warmly. 'Must you and Tanya rush off? What about going for a drink at the Old Bull and Bush.'

Jennie consulted her watch. 'Thanks, but it'll have to be a

quick one because Tanya and I must get back home by half past one. Her brother is picking us up and taking us to the jazz concert in Hyde Park this afternoon.'

'Just give me ten minutes to shower and change and I'll be with you,' he grinned. 'I'll be as quick as I can but to be honest, I'm usually the last one out because I've got so much more to wash!'

'And if you believe that, you'll believe anything,' grunted Adrian as Tanya came up and he escorted the two girls towards the door.

'Believe what?' asked Tanya as she looked back with interest at the naked figures making their way through to the showers.

Outside the dressing room, Jennie told her about the arrangement she had made with the boys to go to the pub with them and Tanya sighed: 'God, why are fellas so obssessed with the size of their cocks! Even those with the biggest pricks would give their right arm for another couple of inches. I'm fed up with telling them that it isn't the size of the ship that counts, it's the motion of the ocean.'

'I know,' agreed Jennie. 'On the other hand we're the same about our tits – almost every girl I know wishes she had a bigger pair of boobs, – I know I do!'

'You're as daft as the lads then,' retorted Tanya promptly. 'It's quality not quantity that counts and that goes for cocks too. Do you remember that American chap, Norris Barcroft, I went out with last year? He had one of the biggest cocks I'd ever seen but he wasn't such a wonderful fuck.'

'Norris Barcroft, oh yes, he was quite a good-looking guy but a bit on the short side, right?' remarked Jennie as the girls walked across to sit down on a park bench.

'Yes, that's the one,' agreed Tanya. 'I liked Norris, he was a nice man and we had some great fun together. He was very keen on opera, you know, and took me to Covent Garden a couple of times which I really enjoyed. Funnily enough, we'd only fooled around a bit till he took me to see *Carmen* which made me feel so sexy that I decided to let him fuck me when we arrived back in his flat for a night-cap.

'So this time I didn't push his fingers away when he slid his hand between my legs as we kissed and cuddled on the sofa but I whispered in his ear: "Take me into the bedroom, that's the best place to make love."

'His eyes gleamed as he scooped me up in his arms and when we got there he gently laid me down on his bed where we quickly undressed each other whilst we nibbled on each other's lips. When we were down to our pants, he rolled down my knickers and ran his palm over my pussy which made me feel so randy I could hardly wait to be fucked. I ripped down his Y-fronts and I tell you, Jennie, it must true what they say about little jockeys having the biggest whips. Norris's cock was enormous, at least ten inches long with a huge purple helmet. When I took hold of this monster in both my hands and jerked the hot shaft up and down, I wondered what it would feel like to have that thick girth inside my palpitating cunt.

'I didn't have long to wait because Norris could hardly wait to climb on top of me and thrust his cock inside my cunny. His todger was so thick, though, that I could hardly take him all in, even though my pussy lips were stretched wide open and my quim was already soaking with anticipation.

'"I don't think I can take you all in," I gasped as he pulled back a little. I managed to take another inch when he pushed in again and I felt his shaft pulsing inside me. He did this several times and to be fair to Norris, he waited patiently till my cunt muscles relaxed and he was able to fill my funnel with his colossal cock.

'Then he began driving his dick into me and as he liked to see my breasts sway with each thrust, he varied the tempo to see the difference in each movement. Then he cupped them in his hands as he pounded deeper and deeper into me but frankly I'd had enough and I reached down to squeeze his balls which thankfully made him come almost at once.

'Norris rolled off me and lay there wheezing with exhaustion and we both fell asleep for a while. I was the first to wake up about half an hour later and when I saw his tremendous tool lying over his thigh, I flipped it over his balls with my hand. God, even when soft it must have been at least eight inches long!

'He stirred when I gave his shaft a little squeeze and immediately his enormous chopper swelled up again from his curly dark bush. He gurgled with delight as I bent down and kissed his helmet, letting my tongue run all the way round the ridge of his knob which made him shiver with delight. Then I washed the underside of his quaking cock in a series of long, slow licks before nibbling on his hot, heavy balls. I slicked my hand up and down his palpitating pole and lapped up a sticky blob of precum which had leaked out of his knob. Norris was so excited when I opened my lips and took his bell-end inside my mouth that he attempted to cram more of his big boner down my throat and I was forced to pull my head away in case I gagged on his colossal cock. So I composed myself and curling my lips over my teeth so I wouldn't hurt him, I took Norris's chopper back into my mouth and as I sucked his cock I felt my pussy began to tingle.

'He gripped my head tightly in his hands whilst he jerked his hips up and down, pumping his prick hard and fast until his spunk shot into my mouth. His salty spunk flowed down my throat and I shivered all over as I was caught by surprise by the tremors of a lovely orgasm.

'Anyhow, the point of the story is that my pussy was so sore the next day that I never let Norris fuck me again,' concluded Tanya as she waved to Adrian who had just come out of the dressing-room. 'And perhaps it was just as well that shortly afterwards the company he worked for sent him to work in Rome for a year.'

'Did you leave on good terms though?' enquired Jennie and Tanya nodded: 'Oh crikey, yes. We still correspond occasionally and send each other spicy letters. Actually I've got the latest one in my bag and I'll show it to you when we get home.'

'That sounds quite interesting,' remarked Adrian as he

came up to them and slid his arm around Tanya's waist. 'Whatever it is, will you show it to me too?'

Recounting her erotic story about Norris Barcroft's big cock had made Tanya's knickers damp with pussy juice and she declared: 'I might do, but only if you're a good boy and fuck the arse off me tonight. Now will Simon be very long? If he doesn't hurry up we'll have to miss that drink.'

There was no need for Dickie Segal or Cindy Shackleton to race against the clock at the wealthy impressario's palatial mansion in Wildwood Road. Their frenzied fucking had made them both hungry and now after finishing off their lunch with a fresh fruit salad, Dickie and Cindy had wandered back upstairs and were lying naked on the bed whilst the impressario was lazily stroking Cindy's sculpted thigh until their reverie was broken by the shrill ring of the telephone on the bedside table.

'Sod it, who the hell can that be?' said Dickie irritably as he heaved himself up and lifted the receiver. Ronnie, how are you? All right till five minutes ago – why, what did you say? West End Central? Oh my God, that's all we need! No, no, of course you had to tell me. Is he still there? Right then, call Jeffrey Green and tell him to get himself over to the station right now and get the silly bugger out on bail. If he's not at home phone Lempert and Lempert's office, there's always a duty solicitor on call over the weekend.'

Dickie punched the air in frustration as he shouted down the phone: 'I'll kill the fucking little queer! Sod it, we're probably too late to stop the duty sergeant tipping off the papers about him and if the story leaks out we'll have to pull him out of the show. Ronnie, call me back when you've got some news.'

He slammed the receiver back on its hook and slumped back next to Cindy. She sat up and smoothed her hand over his chest as she murmured: 'Oh dear, obviously something's gone very wrong, Dickie. Is it all very secret or do you want to tell me about what's happened?'

'You might as well be the first to know,' he groaned loudly. 'It won't be a secret for much longer. Mark my words, I'll lay a pound to a penny that the next call I'll have will be from Mike Boggs of the *Mirror*.'

He fell silent for a moment and then he said heavily: 'Quentin Ludgate's been caught by the police doing something he shouldn't with a sixteen-year-old boy in the gents' at Piccadilly Circus.'

'You're joking!' Cindy cried, for Quentin Ludgate was an actor who played a girl-crazy Casanova in one of the most popular soap operas on TV. Dickie shrugged: 'I wish I were, but it's not the first time he's been picked up for cottaging. We managed to hush everything up last time – luckily one of the inspectors at the nick was a member of my masonic lodge so they let him off with a caution after I gave a hefty donation to the station's Benefit Fund. He's been transferred though even if he were still there, I doubt if he would stick his neck out again for Quentin – and frankly, nor would I. But the stupid bastard's the second lead in my new revue which opens on Wednesday at the Prince of Wales! It's a family show so I'll have to kick him out, though Christ knows who we can get in his place at three days notice.'

'Couldn't Quentin sue you for dropping him?'

'He could try but there's a clause in his contract which states that the performer must do nothing to compromise himself in such a way that would adversely affect the production,' he answered gruffly. 'I'd better have a word with his agent, Teddy Dixon of Rose and Griffin. He might be able to suggest somebody who can fill the gap. Now what's his number?'

'Can't that wait till tomorrow?' Cindy enquired as she snuggled up to him, sliding her fingers around his limp prick and giving it a gentle squeeze. 'Why don't we relax for a bit and then you can work out a plan of action.'

However, the public reason for Dickie Segal's nickname of 'Nipper' was very different from the accidental damage to his cock caused by an over-enthusiastic exotic dancer. It related to his stated formula for success which was to nip trouble in the bud before it became too hot to handle. Accordingly, although his cock started to swell as Cindy fisted her hand up and down his shaft, the impresario ignored her and picked up the telephone to dial Teddy Dixon's number.

He caught the managing director of Rose and Griffin just as he was leaving home for his usual Sunday afternoon round of golf. 'That's terrible news, Dickie,' he said sympathetically. 'But I can't be of much help, I'm afraid, except to say that we won't be seeking any compensation for cancelling the contract. Look, I'm off to Australia next week and young Adrian Klein's looking after Quentin's affairs. I'll get him to ring you first thing in the morning.'

'Can't we contact Adrian this afternoon?' asked Dickie urgently. 'I want to sort things out as quickly as possible so we'll have something to tell the papers tonight.'

'I'll give you his home number, but I know he was playing football on the Heath this morning. Mind, the match should be over by now and you're more likely to catch him at the Old Bull and Bush. He always goes there for a drink after a game.'

'Thanks, Teddy, I'm on my way,' said Dickie after scribbling down Adrian's telephone number on a scrap of paper. But as Teddy had warned him, there was no reply when he dialled it and Dickie let out a grunt of annoyance as he slammed down the receiver.

He turned to Cindy and said: 'Sorry, love, I have to be off. I have to meet Quentin's agent. I shouldn't be more than an hour though – would you do me a great favour by staying here and answering the phone. Write down the name of anyone who rings and tell them I'll be back at four o'clock. Oh, and if my wife calls, for God's sake tell her you're a new secretary from my office or we'll both be for the high jump.'

With those instructions, Dickie flung on his clothes and scuttled downstairs where he picked up the keys of his Bentley from the hall table and ran out towards the garage. Fortunately, the Old Bull and Bush was less than five minutes away and he even found a place to park opposite the pub in North

End Road. His good fortune continued for he immediately saw Adrian standing outside the pub with Simon, Jennie and Tanya as he dashed across the road and grabbed hold of Adrian's arm.

'Hello, *boychik*, good to see you,' he puffed and Adrian looked at him in some surprise.

'Hi, Dickie, don't tell me you've decided to agree that Paul Cooper's worth five hundred a week after all. I said I'd give you till Tuesday to think it over.'

'Never mind all that,' said the impresario grimly. 'We need to talk about something much more important which I heard about half an hour ago.'

From the agitated look on his face, Adrian could see that Dickie Segal had something serious to tell him, so he excused himself from his friends and walked back with him to the Bentley where Dickie informed him of the news of Quentin Ludgate's arrest.

'Oh shit, I thought he'd given up cottaging since that Spanish waiter moved in with him,' groaned Adrian as he drummed his fingers against the rosewood dashboard. 'Dickie, you're a mason, is there any chance of dropping a few quid to the coppers in your lodge to let him off with a caution?'

'No way, it's not the first time you know,' answered Dickie heavily. 'You realise I'll have to boot him out of *West End Extra*, I've spoken to Teddy Dixon and he understands my position. The point is, we must have some big name like Quentin, preferably with his own material, to step into the show or we'll lose the coach parties. So I'm giving you first crack before ringing round the other agencies tomorrow morning.'

Adrian frowned as he mentally ran through a list of all the artistes on Rose and Griffin's books. 'You won't get anyone worthwhile at such short notice,' he declared roundly. 'Why not pitch in an unknown? It would make some great copy for the press especially if he turns up trumps.'

'All right, who have you got in mind?' sighed the impresario and Adrian grinned: 'Well, there is a young comic called Allan

Godfrey who I know won't let you down. We snapped him up from the club circuit and he's been wowing the audience at *La Miraggio* for the last two weeks.'

'Never heard of him,' said Dickie instantly but Adrian went on: 'You must have heard of Allan, Dickie, your office sent a scout to watch his act only a few days ago.'

'Oh yes, I remember now, Steve Williams went to see him and said he was very good but his material was bit blue.'

Adrian pressed home his advantage. 'He writes his own stuff, Dickie, and he's got plenty of clean gags because he's done quite a bit of radio and TV in the Midlands. I know he's done panto though I'll be honest with you, you'll have to get Jill Zabeida to give him a crash course of dancing lessons.'

Dickie stroked his cheek whilst he muttered: 'Well, he wouldn't have to be a bloody Nureyev for the routines, they're simple enough. I'd want to see the boy for myself before making any commitment.'

'Of course you would,' said Adrian smoothly. 'Look, come down to *La Miraggio* tomorrow night, I'll guarantee you won't be disappointed – if you like what you see, he can start rehearsals on Tuesday morning.'

'All right, though don't get him too excited because I'll still be trying to find someone well-known to slot in for Quentin,' warned Dickie. 'Meanwhile, I've sent a solicitor round to get him out of the nick so I suggest you call me again in about an hour and I'll let you know the score. Incidentally, I don't mind stumping up for expenses so far – it's about time those bloody solicitors earned their retainer – but it'll be down to Quentin if he wants Jeffrey Green to take on his case.

'Oh, and I dare say the press will have found out what's happening by now. If he's been charged I'm going to tell them that Quentin's out of the show. I'll say he's suffering from nervous exhaustion.'

'Good enough, if anyone contacts me, I'll say the same,' said Adrian briskly. 'I'm sorry for the silly bugger but it's all self-inflicted.

'Thanks for tracking me down, Dickie, I really appreciate

it,' he added and they shook hands before the agent hurried back to rejoin his friends.

'Who was that?' demanded Tanya as she gave him back his pint of shandy. 'Watch out, darling, you'll get a funny name for yourself if you go around running off with strange men and sitting with them in their cars.'

'He's not a strange man, love, I'm surprised you didn't recognise him,' said Adrian mildly. 'That was the one and only Dickie Segal of Amalgamated Entertainments and usually I'm the one chasing him. Only we have a problem which needs sorting out *tout suite*. I can't give you chapter and verse until later on but one of our artistes is in a spot of bother. Listen folks, I have to be on my way – so just to recap, ladies, Simon and I will meet up with you again at seven-thirty. See you then, okay.'

He gulped down the rest of his shandy and gave Simon his empty glass. 'Cheers, old boy, get rid of this for me, I have to get back home and telephone a few people.'

Simon stared at his retreating back and shrugged his shoulders. 'I suppose that's what friends are for – that spot of bother must be really serious.' He wasn't too bothered by this sudden departure though because, to his delight, Jennie had agreed to make up a foursome with Adrian and Tanya for a Chinese meal that night.

As soon as he reached home Adrian telephoned Allan Godfrey at his rented flat in Notting Hill Gate and his foot tapped a staccato beat on the carpet as he waited impatiently for a reply.

'Come on, come on,' he murmured, but he was not to know that the comedian was in two minds as to whether to pick up the receiver. For Allan Godfrey had no wish to break off from his embrace with the nubile young waitress from *La Miraggio* for whom he had cooked a spendid Sunday luncheon and who was now perched precariously on his lap.

However he finally succumbed and mumbled: 'Hold on a mo', Diana, I'll answer the bloody phone, but if it isn't anyone important put your hands over your ears in case you hear some language which might offend.'

Allan carefully adjusted Diana's supple body whilst the girl busied herself by unbuckling the belt of his trousers and unzipping his fly as he picked up the receiver and said lightly: 'Bayswater Home for Unmarried Fathers, may I help you? Oh, Adrian. Hello mate, what can I do for you?'

His forehead creased into a frown as he listened to what Adrian had to say and then he exhaled a deep breath. 'Poor old Quentin, but there you go. I didn't even know he was a shirtlifter. So where do I fit in, if you'll pardon the expression?'

As Adrian explained the situation, Diana slid her hand into Allan's trousers and brought out his erect shaft. She clenched it tightly in her hand as she jerked her fist up and down his throbbing tool. He wagged a reproving finger at her and, putting his hand over the receiver, he hissed: 'Stop wanking my cock, Di! It's my agent and I can't concentrate on what he's telling me whilst you're tossing me off.'

The pretty girl pouted at the rebuke but released Allan's twitching todger from her grasp as she slid off his thigh. 'So you're saying I should cut out the blue gags if Dickie Segal's in the audience. No problem, I'll do forty minutes during which even Mrs Whitehouse wouldn't bat an eyelid.

'How do you rate my chances?' he asked and then he let out a strangled gurgle as, now on her knees, Diana grabbed hold of his cock and swirled the tip of her tongue over his wide-mushroomed knob.

'Are you all right, Allan? asked Adrian with some concern. 'Indigestion, was it? You're probably out of condition, working at night and sleeping all day. It would do you the world of good to get out of that chair and go for a walk in Hyde Park when we've finished talking.'

Allan was holding the telephone slightly away from his ear and, hearing Adrian's stricture, Diana gave the comedian a wicked smile as she stood up and began to unbutton her blouse. He gave a tiny chuckle and replied: 'You're dead right, I'm going to get some exercise as soon as I put the phone down.'

'You do that,' said Adrian, blissfully unaware that Diana had now pulled down her skirt and was displaying a pair of white lace-fronted panties with a pink heart-shaped panel which cutely covered the bulge of her mound.

'Adrian, I'll see you tomorrow night then. Must go now, bye,' said Allan hastily. As he replaced the receiver, his prick pulsated even more violently when Diana unhooked her bra to display her creamy bare breasts which were crowned with upstanding tawny nipples which jiggled sexily as she skipped across to him and sat herself back on his knee.

Allan's arms slid round her waist as Diana turned her face up to his and their lips crushed together in a fierce open-mouthed kiss. With their tongues still in each other's mouths, they stumbled out towards the bedroom where Diana pulled him down on top of her on the soft mattress. With dextrous hands, she helped the comedian undress. Then he wriggled down the bed to kneel between her thighs where, with a salacious gleam in his eyes, he rolled Diana's knickers down her elegant long legs.

He licked his lips as he gazed down at the thatch of curly light brown hair which covered her cunt and she looked up at him quizzically and said: 'What's the matter, Mr Godfrey? If you're not interested in the merchandise, I'll wrap it up and put it back under the counter.'

'Oh, I'll buy everything on offer. I'm a real big spender and I'm not just talking about money,' he answered throatily. He toyed with her impudent erect nipples, massaging them between his fingers until they felt like two hard rubbery bullets under his touch. I'll tell you what my Uncle Louis told me on my twenty-first birthday – he was in the RAF during the war – Allan, he said, you should treat a woman like an airplane and take her to heaven at least twice a day.

'It's time for your first flight, petal, so wrap your legs around my waist and let's go!' he exclaimed. He took hold of his palpitating prick but Diana put her hand on his arm and said almost inaudibly: 'Ooh, yes I want to feel your lovely thick prick inside me but if you want to make sure that I'll come, you'll have to lick me out before you fuck me. You don't mind, do you?'

Although he was aching to fuck the delicious girl, Allan chuckled and, ducking his head between her thighs, he kissed her moist crack and then he parted her puffy love lips with his thumbs and slipped his tongue inside her honeypot to lap up her cuntal juices. He pulled out for a moment and looked up at her and grinned: 'No, of course not, Diana. Obviously you've heard that I've been elected captain of the British muffdiving team for the Rome Olympics.'

'Wow! You'll win a gold medal there if you carry on like that,' Diana purred with pleasure. Allan mumbled indistinctly 'M'mm, you're very wet,' as his tongue dipped back into the crevice of her folds. He sucked with relish on her swollen clitty and when her fever of excitement was climbing to its highest pitch, Allan replaced his tongue with his fingers, manipulating her fleshy love bud as he moved his tongue down over the folds of her cunt to the tiny puckered opening of her arsehole. He lapped rapidly around the tight orifice and, after turning his tongue into a probing pink dart, he slipped it into her bottom, his mouth pressed up against the soft skin whilst his fingers continued to flick the quivering clitty button.

With a choking cry, Diana achieved an exquisite orgasm. She seized his head in her hands as her cunny was flushed with thrilling waves of ecstasy. Allan's head came up from between her thighs with a huge smile on his face. He pulled the willing girl forward and hoisted her legs over his shoulders until her buttocks slapped against his knees. Diana mewed with delight as he slid his cock between her yielding love lips.

'Yes, yes, fuck me with that big fat cock,' she moaned as Allan's shaft glided inside her dripping crack and paused for a moment to let Diana's cuntal muscles accommodate his width. He balanced himself by placing his hands flat on the sheet on each side of her head and then pushed his cock deeper into her sopping snatch, stopping only when his balls nestled against her spread bum cheeks.

Tightening his buttocks as he moved his hips, Allan pumped fiercely into her honeypot while Diana wrapped her ankles around his neck and inhaled the musky scent of male sexuality which clung to his skin. She urged him on, thrusting up her pelvis to meet his downward plunges. Now it was Allan's turn to groan as he pistoned his sinewy shaft in and out of the delicious clinging wetness of Diana's cunt. He was lost in her now, his cock gripped by the clinging walls of her juicy honeypot. Diana sighed in sheer ecstasy as wave after wave of sheer bliss flowed out from her tingling love funnel and great, climbing waves of sensation crashed through every fibre of her body.

'Go to it, you dirty fucker!' she screamed out as her orgasm escalated to a fever pitch of excitement and Allan's shaft was washed by a deluge of juice that splashed out of her inner depths. He pumped in and out of Diana's squishy quim at an ever-increasing speed until, with a choking cry, he bathed the walls of her cunt with a coating of warm jism. Allan crashed down upon her heaving curves as the contractions of her trembling sheath quickly milked his cock of its sticky spunk and they held each other close, their sated bodies pressed contentedly together.

Allan would have gladly dozed off but Diana's appetite was not yet sated and within a few minutes the comedian felt a familiar stir in his groin. He opened his eyes to see the lusty girl slicking her clenched fist up and down his fast-stiffening shaft.

'Naughty boy, it's not nice to fall asleep on a lady,' twinkled Diana as she scrambled to her knees and took hold of his quivering cock in both hands, one dipping to fondle his tightening scrotum at the base and the other halfway up his shaft.

Bending the stem to her mouth, she ran her tongue up to the rim and over the glistening knob. Allan let out a low growl of delight as he watched her lips close over the dome of his twitching tool, which throbbed like fury as Diana worked her tongue slowly up and down the length of his pulsing erection. She sucked with relish on the sensitive underside of Allan's cock, slurping her way down the velvet-skinned shaft, skilfully manoeuvring her deliciously moist mouth until she had taken almost his entire shaft between her lips.

He clamped his hands on Diana's shoulders as she circled the base of his boner with her hand and began to bob her head up and down, gobbling his cock with evident gusto. Allan let out a fervid whimper when she released his cock from its delectable prison but she slid her hand up and down his shivering shaft whilst he ducked down to nibble on the wrinkled pink skin of his ballsack. This sent him into fresh paroxyms of sheer, undulterated joy.

'I'm coming, I'm coming,' he gasped and Diana filled her mouth with saliva and sucked his knob until a hot gush of jism cascaded out of his cock which she gulped down, smacking her lips as she milked his member dry.

'That was a tasty little snack,' she murmured as she snuggled into the crook of Allan's shoulder. This time they both sank down into an exhausted slumber from which they were wakened by the strident sound of the telephone bell. Again, Allan was tempted not to answer but he realised that it might be his agent on the line with more news about his possible West End debut, so he heaved himself out of bed and padded out to pick up the receiver.

It was indeed Adrian Klein calling him and Allan's heart began to thump with exvcitement when Adrian confirmed that, as expected, the newspapers had been tipped off about Quentin Ludgate's arrest. 'Dickie Segal has already made a statement about how Quentin is suffering from nervous exhaustion and has checked into a private rest home in Berkshire.'

'Poor old Quentin, he won't get much rest once the newshounds find out where he's staying,' said Allan sympathetically but Adrian chuckled: 'No, he wouldn't but that story's just a cover. Actually, I've arranged for our publicity people to pack Quentin's bags, give him a hundred quid pocket money and then whisk him off to Heathrow where they'll put him on the evening flight to Malaga. He's got a friend in Torremolinos who'll look after him till all the fuss has died down.'

Allan whistled in surprise. 'Crikey, that'll cost a few bob. I didn't realise I'd joined such a generous agency. Will you send me on a holiday to Spain when I need to relax?'

'Don't hold your breath,' grunted Adrian. 'And I'm sorry to disillusion you, mate, but even if he doesn't realise it, Quentin's picking up the tab as we'll deduct our expenses from his next cheque from the *Ask Doctor Jonathan* show. Christ, I hadn't even thought about what the TV boys will do with Quentin. He'd been written out of the series for a couple of months to do *West End Extra* but I bet they'll kill off his character in the series so the poor sod will have fuck all left.'

He let out a weary sigh and went on: 'Allan, you're not that way inclined, are you? Dickie Segal would have my guts for garters if after he took you on you were found fiddling with a boy in a public loo.'

'No chance of that, Adrian,' he retorted quickly as Diana sauntered up to him. 'I've been called many things on and off the stage but never a brown-hatter – and there's someone standing next to me who can prove it.'

'What's that, Allan?' she asked and he put his hand over the receiver and grinned: 'My agent wants to make certain that I'm a normal red-blooded male. Would you like to confirm that for him, love?'

'Only on condition that you fuck me again after I've made us a cup of tea,' Diana cautioned him as he passed the phone over to her and she said: 'Hello there, I understand you would like corroboration that Allan Godfrey isn't a poof. Well he's just fucked the arse off me, if that's any help.'

'Good enough for you, comrade Klein?' smirked Allan and Adrian gave a dainty little cough. 'Yes, quite good enough, thank you,' he commented wryly. 'Not that I was over-worried about whether you liked girls, especially after hearing about how Angelo found the star of his cabaret and Claudia, the hat-check girl, in a compromising position behind the stage last week. Watch yourself there, Allan, her Dad works in security at George Raft's Casino in Berkeley Square and he's got some rather tasty friends who wouldn't take it kindly if anyone took advantage of Claudia.'

'Um, thanks for the tip, Ade, I'll call you in the morning,' said Allan hastily as he saw a dark frown forming on Diana's face. He put down the phone and giving her his most charming smile, he began: 'Look, Diana, I can explain.'

Back in his bedroom lying next to the luscious Cindy, Dickie Segal took a sip of his Johnnie Walker Black Label scotch and ran the fingers of his free hand through the curly bush of nut brown hair between her thighs.

'M'mm, I like that,' said Cindy lazily, stretching herself out languidly as Dickie's fingertips slid up and down her pussy lips. 'And that reminds me of something I wanted to tell you – last week my agent forwarded to me a peculiar letter from a fellow who had seen me in my last job in the chorus of a variety revue down in Plymouth. It was quite a good show and at the top of the bill we had Lewis Wilson, that magician who's been on TV quite a lot recently. Anyhow, I got this strange fan letter and frankly I'm not too sure what I should do about it.'

'You should never ignore the paying public,' declared Dickie, putting down his drink. 'Do you want me to take a look at the letter and suggest a suitable reply?'

'Would you, Dickie?' said Cindy gratefully as she wiggled away from him and dipped her hand down the side of the bed to find her handbag. 'Here it is, and I must say that I'd appreciate any advice about how I should reply.'

Dickie took the sheet and raised his eyebrows when he saw the embossed crest on the notepaper. He burst into laughter and commented: 'My God! You didn't say it was from the Earl of Dartmoor!'

'The letter isn't from the Earl,' Cindy smiled back. 'It's

from his son, the Honourable Beresford Synge-Latimer. You won't believe what he wrote to me – go on, read it out loud and you'll see what I mean.'

Dickie cleared his throat and began:

Dearest Cindy, you don't know me but I've been madly in love with you since I first saw you on the stage of the Theatre Royal. You remind me so much of a former girl friend of mine who was almost as pretty as you. She came from a dreadfully strict family though and we never made love. Three years later I've still never got over losing her and every night I used to fantasise about her whilst I tossed myself off.

But let me tell you what now goes through my mind whilst I rub my rock-hard rammer. I think about you wearing a sheer white blouse with no bra because your firm breasts stand up proudly by themselves and round your waist you're wearing a tight black leather skirt with matching high-heeled boots.

I take you back home and savour each moment as I undress you. As you stand there I kneel before you to unzip your skirt and pull down your panties. Then I bury my face in your pungent pussy as I reach up to fondle your breasts, but I never get any further because I always come before I can lay you down on the bed and make mad, passionate love to you.

Oh Cindy, the very thought of fucking you is giving me a hard-on! I will always have a stiff cock for you and a mind intent on making you happy. I realise there's probably a man in your life who must be very special to have a gorgeous creature like you in his bed, though if he ever lets you down, remember I'm here for you always.

I know it's only a foolish dream, but you turn me on so much that I simply had to let you know my feelings and let you know how much happiness you've given me by just being there.

With all my love for ever, Beresford.

Dickie paused to give Cindy back her letter and then swigged down the rest of his Scotch. 'I don't really know what to say, my dear. To be quite candid, I've never read any fan letter like that before. It's very flattering and I can understand why he's gone overboard for a lovely girl like you, but I think this is something best nipped in the bud.'

He shot a puzzled look at Cindy, who had smiled broadly when Dickie used the phrase which, like other people who had heard the story about the over-enthusiastic oral exploits of an exotic dancer, she understood had led to the impresario's showbiz nickname.

'Cindy, it's not funny,' he protested. 'Not to put too fine a point to it, this chap is potty. Give him the slightest word of encouragement and you'll never shake him off.'

'That could happen, I suppose, but between ourselves, I guessed he was the man who was sending me bouquets of red roses every night during the last week of the show. And when I found out that Beresford was the heir to a twenty million pounds fortune, I haven't been able to make myself chuck his letter in the bin.'

Dickie shook his head. 'Forget him, Cindy, any involvement will end in tears, the man lives in a dream world and deep down couldn't cope with the existence of a real-lfe girl friend,' he advised and she groaned: 'Yes, I know I should, but twenty million pounds, Dickie. What a waste!'

Cindy let out a heartfelt sigh but when she looked down at Dickie's thickening cock, she pressed her soft curves against his side and giggled: 'At least no-one could accuse you of not being able to turn fantasy into reality, Mr Segal.'

He stared at the nubile young girl's succulent breasts and cupped the soft, high-tipped globes in his hands. His arms trembled when he felt the hardening nipples push against his fingertips and Cindy whispered throatily: 'Oh yes, Dickie, squeeze my tits, squeeze them hard! God, I love it!'

Their mouths met and she swallowed his tongue like a hungry animal while her own tongue shot between Dickie's lips to slide wetly against his teeth. Cindy pulled her face away and murmured admiringly: 'My word, you are a big boy,' as she held his swollen shaft tightly in her hand, making his rigid rod throb as she slowly worked her fist up and down the fleshy truncheon.

'Let's see if this cock tastes as nice as it looks,' she remarked. She slithered across his belly and, opening her mouth, swirled her tongue along the smooth underside of his shaft before sliding her lips over the juicy ripe plum of his helmet. Dickie let out a low cry of delight when Cindy sucked in almost his entire palpitating prick down her throat. She wrapped her right hand around the root of his cock and started to frig him gently. Her left hand cradled his hairy scrotum, gently caressing his balls as they tightened inside their wrinkled pink sack.

She could hear the impresario groan in ecstasy when she sucked underneath the rim of his knob, pressing her soft lips against his throbbing fleshy column. Cindy began to swallow in anticipation when Dickie's chopper commenced to jerk wildly inside her mouth. When the creamy jism gushed out of his cock, she gulped down his sticky emission with great enjoyment. He bucked his hips as the uninhibited girl sucked his shuddering shaft until she had coaxed out the final dribble of seed.

Then she released his deflated shaft and looked up at him cheekily. 'Your turn now, Dickie. I don't expect you to be able to fuck me but I adored the way you brought me off with your tongue before lunch. You will do it again, won't you?'

Dickie had time only to gurgle an indistinct reply before she pulled her legs across his thighs and straddled him, moving her lissome body upwards to sit upon his chest so that her damp muff of pussy hair was pressed tightly against his nostrils.

'Atishoo!' he sneezed and Cindy reached back and pulled his limp shaft in mock reproof. 'Mr Segal, I'm surprised at you! It really isn't the done thing to sneeze into a lady's cunt!'

'I'm terribly sorry, love, here, let me kiss it better,' he muttered shame-facedly. When he raked the tip of his tongue along the length of her damp crack, Cindy gasped, in a voice husky with lust: 'Ooooh, I'll definitely accept your apology if you keep licking my quim like that!'

With a tigerish snarl, she adjusted her position to open her quim further for his questing tongue. Dickie slurped lustily on her pussy lips, lapping up the pungent love juice which was now trickling out from her cunt. Cindy clutched at his neck and threw back her head. She squealed with pleasure when he found her erect clitty and attacked the fleshy nub with a series of quick little nips with his teeth.

She felt her climax looming up quickly upon her. She held Dickie's head still while she rubbed her hairy pussy over his face, feeling his nose against her clitty as she pushed herself against him, smearing his cheeks with cunt juice. Cindy came in a series of huge, thrusting spasms before she rolled adroitly off her perch on Dickie's chest and sank down next to him. They lay there in silence until he looked anxiously at his watch. Realising that his wife might return early from her parents', he said with some embarrassment: 'Cindy, it's been wonderful meeting you, but I think we had better call it a day before we're interrupted. Let's get dressed and I'll give you a lift down to the tube station.'

Cindy had thoroughly enjoyed herself, and she was further buoyed by a final repeated promise by Dickie Segal to call her agent in the morning about her starring in panto with Allan Godfrey.

Jennie and Tanya had experienced a frustrating afternoon. Five minutes after being dropped back at their flat by one of the Hotspurs football team, Tanya's young brother telephoned her to say he was suffering from a dreadful headache and so wouldn't be able to take them to Hyde Park for the jazz concert.

'Sorry, sis,' he apologised. Tanya heaved an exasperated sigh: 'That's okay, Ben, go back to bed and try and sleep it off. Bye.' She went back to the living room and reported the news to Jennie who tutted: 'The silly chap, was it a touch of the morning after the night before?'

'No, to be fair to him, Ben's not a great boozer,' said Tanya. 'He suffers from tension headaches and the poor sod always seems to get them on weekends. The doctor's given him all kinds of pain relief pills but they don't really help – all he can do to get some relief is to lie down in a darkened room and wait till the attack wears off.'

'What a shame, still, I suppose we could go in town by bus,' Jennie said doubtfully. 'On the other hand, it's hardly worth the hassle, especially on a Sunday. You know what, we could give this place a good clean-up instead. I'll hoover out all the rooms if you'll tidy up in the kitchen and wash up those saucepans in the sink. After all, we might as well make a good impression on the boys when they come round tonight. We don't want them to think we live in a pig-sty.'

'True, though if Simon's anything like Adrian, I don't think he'll be bothered by a bit of dust,' Tanya commented drily as she picked up a pile of magazines from the floor. 'There's only one thing he'll be looking out for and that's your sweet pussy,'

Nevertheless, an hour later as they were sipping a well-earned coffee, Tanya was ready to concede how much better the flat looked after their hard work. 'There, do you think Simon will be suitably impressed?' she asked anxiously.

'I'm sure he will be,' grinned Jennie as she stretched herself out on the sofa. Then the smile faded from her face as she added: 'I just hope that he doesn't try the same trick with Adrian as Jason did with his friend Mark.'

'Jason? Are you talking about Jason Chalfont, the boy you were going out with till we went to Paris?' enquired Tanya.

Jennie nodded: 'I certainly do and the stunt he pulled with his mate led to us breaking up. Didn't I ever tell you what happened?'

Tanya shook her head and Jennie gave a wry laugh and went on: 'You'll remember that I was between flats before we went and I was living at home with my parents. Anyhow, one night they had gone out to the pictures and Jason came over to keep me company. We were having a cuddle on the couch while we listened to the new Beatles' *Sergeant Pepper* LP he had just bought when the phone rang. I clambered up and knelt on the sofa to answer it and who should be on the line but my friend Mary who wanted to tell me some gossip about a mutual friend. I knew it would take a few minutes because she loves a good chat.

'I hadn't been listening to her for very long when there was a chime on the blinking doorbell so I called out to Jason to answer it. I heard the front door open and close and was surprised when he came back with his best friend, Mark, who we'd seen quite a few times at parties and what-have-you. I wasn't too surprised because Jason had said that Mark might pop round if he could get us two tickets for the Rolling Stones concert at the weekend.

'So there I was kneeling on the sofa resting my elbows on the side table and chatting away to Mary when all of a sudden I felt Jason's hand lifting up my skirt from behind. "Hold on a minute, Mary," I said and covered the mouthpiece with my hand and hissed: "Stop it, Jason! Bugger off!"

'He took no notice though. A few seconds later he threw up my skirt again and pinched my arse. So I reached round and slapped his hand but this didn't have any effect – in fact he began kissing my bum cheeks through my knickers. He just wouldn't stop fooling around. With one ear I was listening to Mary prattling away about some nonsense or other and with the other I could hear Jason whispering to Mark how he would now pull down my panties to show him my beautiful bare bottom.'

She paused and bit her lip. 'I'm going to shock you now, but please don't tell anybody about this,' she said as a pink blush coloured her cheeks.

'Of course I won't,' Tanya assured her flatmate with an easy smile. 'Let's face it, Jen, you know how many skeletons are rattling around in my wardrobe!'

Jennie nodded and moistening her lips with her tongue, she carried on: 'Not to beat about the bush, Jason kept going on and on about my lovely bum and my wonderful pussy. I tried not to take any notice of him but then instead of his fingers I suddenly felt his hard cock brushing over my knickers.

'This made me feel very randy and my pussy began to get wet. This time, instead of smacking his hand, I reached back and, squeezing his shaft, I began to wank his cock. I had trouble keeping my voice steady when Jason pulled my knickers over my bum and slid his knob between my cheeks. Instinctively I pushed back my bottom and he slipped my knickers down to my knees as his shaft slithered into my sticky wet cunt.

'"Wow!" I panted as he fucked me doggie-style in a lovely slow rhythm, pumping his prick in and out of my tingling snatch. Thank goodness Mary kept rabbiting on by herself because I was in no state to carry on a two-way conversation! Finally though, she said: "Jennie, I must go. There's something I want to see just starting on the telly. Bye, love, I'll speak to you tomorrow night."

'"Bye," I gasped and now I could concentrate fully on the lovely tingling in my quim caused by Jason's long, steady strokes. However, when I put down the phone I almost keeled over because Mark shuffled forward. Ripping open his trousers, he pulled out his erect prick which he held in his hand just inches from my face.

'What came over me I'll never know, but instead of pushing him away, I leaned forward and started to gobble him, laying my cheek along his hot, stiff shaft and licking up and down the barrel of Mark's thick tool before taking his knob deep inside my mouth. He whimpered with pleasure as I sucked his cock, bobbing my head up and down his rigid rod, slurping loudly on his boner as the top of his knob slid along the roof of my mouth to the back of my throat.

'Watching me suck off his friend drove Jason wild and he started slamming his cock in and out of my juicy cunt whilst I matched his pounding thrusts with my mouth, pressing my lips tightly against Mark's cock, wanting him to come in my mouth while Jason filled my snatch from behind.

'Mark climaxed first, spurting his salty spunk down my throat and almost immediately Jason jetted a stream of jism into my love funnel. As I exploded into a tremendous orgasm, I heard Jason gasp: "There you are, mate, I told you that Jennie's such a horny girl that she'd love to take on two cocks at once."'

'So Jason had set up the whole episode,' breathed Tanya and Jennie nodded: 'Yes, he later admitted that he had even called Mary earlier and asked her to telephone me at around half past eight. Anyhow, it was crystal clear that the boys were in cahoots – Mark hadn't just brought round our concert tickets but had come prepared with a bottle of wine and half a dozen cans of lager.'

'The rotten so-and-sos,' Tanya murmured and Jennie swept her hand through her hair as she said: 'Exactly how I felt! Honestly, I wouldn't have minded if Jason had only asked me how I fancied the idea of a threesome. It so happens that I liked Mark and as I knew they were both nice lads who wouldn't have attempted to force me into anything I didn't want to do, I would probably have given it a try.'

'You're quite right to feel aggrieved,' declared Tanya roundly. 'Jason was utterly wrong to assume that you probably liked the idea of sucking his friend's cock whilst he fucked you. As our old Latin mistress used to tell us at school "*Quae dant, quaeque negant, gaudent tamen esse rogatae*".'

Jennie looked at her blankly and, with a chuckle, Tanya translated: 'Whether they give or refuse, women always want to be asked.'

'Well, I hope Simon asks me the right questions tonight,' said Jennie forcefully. 'It's all right for you, my darling, you had Adrian Klein all night whilst I've only had a quickie with him in that tatty old changing room this morning.'

'Don't worry,' advised Tanya. 'I'm sure you'll have your fair share of rumpy-pumpy with Simon when we bring the boys back after dinner this evening.'

Coincidentally, as Tanya spoke, a similar thought was spinning around Simon Byrne's head. He lay on his bed reading the manuscript of Ryan Clarke's autobiography which had been commissioned by his firm last year and which the rock star had insisted on writing himself, refusing the offer of a ghost writer. 'I'm going to tell it as it is, man,' he had insisted, which had slightly worried Simon although the early chapters had been just what he had wanted, lots of revelations about debauched nights after gigs all over Britain. It was the kind of material which would help the subsidiary rights director extract a substantial sum from whichever newspaper won the auction to serialise extracts from Ryan's lurid confessions.

However, alarm bells began to ring in his mind when he cast his eyes over the draft of the next chapter which involved Ryan's seduction of Tessa Radlett, a bubbly blonde actress and the live-in partner of Vernon Taggart, a man who hosted one of the most popular chat shows on TV.

'The lawyers'll have a field day with this,' Simon muttered to himself as he scanned through the rock star's randy reminiscences. They began with a phone call from Tessa asking him to go round to the house in Chelsea she shared with Vernon. Ryan had been playing a high-stakes poker game in the luxurious hotel suite of Dave Zwaig, an American record company executive who was making a brief trip to London. "I never go to bed till one o'clock so you won't disturb me if you come round after your game," she told Ryan and curious to know what was to follow, Simon read on:

> After about an hour I was down by more than twelve hundred quid. I wasn't the only loser – the rag-trade magnate Ronnie Bloom had dropped near enough a grand whilst even Lord Burbeck, the Tory peer and the craftiest card player I had ever encountered, had lost almost as much as me. If I hadn't broken the seal on the pack of cards myself, I would have sworn that Zwaig had marked the deck, but in the end the

three of us grudgingly realised that the Yank was just a bloody good poker player. None of us grumbled when he wanted to pack up at half past eleven as he had to take an early flight to Frankfurt in the morning.

Tessa had sounded insistent though, after saying goodbye to eighteen hundred pounds, I was in no mood for anything except going home and kicking the cat. Still, she only lived a couple of hundreds of yards away from my own pad in Redcliffe Gardens. After parking the car, I decided to walk over to Tessa's and find out what was on her mind.

She came to the door herself and her face brightened up when she saw me. 'Oh, Ryan, you are a darling to come over so late, I'm really grateful,' she said, kissing me on the cheek. She took me by the hand and led me through to the living room and offered me a brandy. I accepted and could see from the slightly unsteady way she lifted up the crystal decanter and from her own half-filled glass that Tessa was at least two drinks ahead of me.

So I came straight to the point and taking the glass from her I said: 'All right, Tess, what's the problem? It must be serious for you to ask me over at this time. By the way, where's Vernon?'

'He's recording his show in Manchester tonight,' she replied. 'And that's why I wanted to speak to you because it's Vernon who's giving me grief. He's having an affair with Flick, the dollybird who escorts his guests onto the sofa where they sit while he interviews them.

'Ah,' I said, unsure of how to continue because it was an open secret at the BBC that Vernon would fuck anything under thirty in a skirt, so I went on: 'Are you certain, love? I know myself how I've only got to be seen talking to a bird at a party and next day, in the gossip columns, she's moved in with me.'

'No, there's no doubt, read this. I found it in a raincoat which he asked me to take to the dry cleaners for him.' She pulled a sheet of paper out of the pocket of her silk dressing-gown. I looked down at the hand-written letter which read:

'*Darling Vee,*
I can hardly wait till Wednesday – you must find more excuses to spend the night with me, it's so much nicer spending the night together than snatching half an hour here and there for a quick fuck. We'll have a grand time after the show in Manchester next week. You'll come to my room and I'll give you one of my special blow-jobs that you like so much. This time there'll be no need to hurry and you won't have to come till you're good and ready to shoot your scrumptious sticky spunk down my throat.

Oooh, just thinking about it is turning me on! I'm sitting naked on my bed and feeling so sexy that as you're not here I'm going to have to finish myself off. Shall I tell you how I do it? First, I'll run my hands over my breasts and press them together so that I can lick my big titties. Next, I'll slide my hand down between my legs and run my finger all along my wet crack and then I'll get hold of that wonderful electric vibrator you bought me last month – I adore the way it slides into my pussy! The stiff hard tube fills me up, reaching and probing all the way up my cunt and I pump it in and out of my eager snatch, faster and faster as I get nearer to my come – and then afterwards I'll lick off all the tangy juice whilst thinking how I would rather it was your cock I was licking and not some piece of plastic!

If you get up to Manchester in time, perhaps you would like me to demonstrate this before the show. By the way, my room number is three hundred and twenty four.
All my love,
Flick

'I see what you mean,' I murmured as I passed the letter back to Tessa. She put it back in her pocket and said fiercely: 'Vernon really is a shit, he swore blind to me that there was nothing between him and Flick when some gossip columnist told me that he had been seen holding hands with her at some posh restaurant out of town. "Between you and me, she's a lesbian, so you've no worries, darling," he said. The liar.'

'So what are you going to do?' I asked gently. Tessa looked me straight in the eye and replied: 'What can I do, Ryan? The house is in his name and I've been so busy being the girl in Vernon's life that I haven't worked much this year. Still, I've told my agent that I'm now open to offers and hopefully I'll make myself enough to move out and give Vernon the chuck. In the meantime, I'm staying put and I'm going to have a fling myself – after all, what's sauce for the goose is sauce for the gander.'

'Sure, go out and enjoy yourself, Tess,' I said, but I honestly hadn't cottoned on what she had in mind until she stood up and looked at me with a mischievous smile.

'I'm glad to hear you say so,' Tessa said softly as she stood up and sensuously slid her dressing gown off her shoulders to show that she was wearing only a revealing short nightie underneath, through which I could see the swell of her beautiful breasts thrusting against the semi-transparent material and the fuzzy mound of her bush between her thighs as she walked steadily towards me and sat down on my lap.

'I've always fancied you, Ryan,' she whispered before she wound her arm around my neck and pulled my face towards her – not that I needed any encouragement because by now the penny had dropped and I enthusiastically returned her kiss. Tessa slipped off her nightie before she unzipped my trousers and rubbed my cock whilst I caressed her gorgeous bare breasts, rolling her pointy titties on the palms of my hands.

In no time at all she had helped me whip off my clothes and we were rolling around naked on the carpet.

We were both too excited for any foreplay and Tessa just lay on her back and spread her legs wide apart. I nearly creamed myself just looking down at the thatch of fluffy blonde hair through which her pink pussy lips were peeking. Tessa must have sensed this because she said throatily: 'What are you waiting for, Ryan? Go ahead and fuck me, I've wanted to be screwed by you ever since we first met but I never let on because I felt I had to be faithful to Vernon.'

I could hardly believe my ears but without further ado, she took hold of my throbbing tool and guided my knob inside her squelchy cunt. She hiked her legs over my shoulders to draw me in to the hilt and our bodies were now joined from mouth to groin, glued together so tightly that I felt that my shaft had been welded inside her juicy tight quim.

Then I began to fuck the gorgeous girl, pistoning my prick to the root inside her cunt. Tessa raised her bum to meet me on every stroke, forcing every inch of my hot, twitching tool inside her as she panted: 'Aaah! Aaah! What a lovely big cock you've got, it's much thicker than Vernon's and I know it's brimming with jism. Go on, Ryan, let me have it, I can take all you've got – fill my cunt with your creamy come!'

I speeded up the pace, plunging my prick in her sopping slit and her cunny muscles clutched at my sliding shaft so excitingly that I couldn't hold back any longer. Pressing my shaft inside her cunt I shot tremendous spurts of creamy jism inside her.

'Sorry, I guess I came off too quickly,' I apologised but Tessa simply gave me a salacious smile and lay me down flat on my back. Then, sitting on her knees, the stunning girl bent down. She pullined back my foreskin, swirled her tongue over my knob and in no time at all my shaft was as stiff as a poker again.

'Christ Almighty, who taught you to suck cock?' I panted as she gobbled away, sucking and slurping till she took me to the very brink of another spend. I tried to pull my cock away because I thought she might want to be fucked again but she held tightly on to my cock and wanked my shaft until I ejaculated into her mouth. She smacked her lips as she swallowed my spunk, but I groaned: 'That's torn it, I won't be able to fuck you for at least another hour.'

'Who cares?' said Tessa jauntily. 'That'll give you plenty of time to eat my pussy.'

Simon's hands trembled as he put down the manuscript. Unconsciously his right hand strayed to his groin where he pulled out his erect cock from his shorts. He pumped his shaft up and down till his seed flooded over his fingers and he slumped back onto the pillow.

He reflected that tossing off might not be as good as a fuck, but it certainly gave much-needed relief. Simon wondered whether Jennie would fist his cock as well as the teenage Trish who the previous night had wanked his cock even better than he could have done himself. In his experience, most women were far too unsubtle and pulled his shaft as is they were milking a cow, but Trish knew exactly when to tease and cajole and when to be more forceful.

His mind came back to the question of Ryan Clarke's manuscript. Simon slowly let out a regretful sigh for, even after the Lady Chatterley case and the recent publication of John Cleland's eighteenth-century classic erotic novel *Fanny Hill*, he judged that Ryan's manuscript was too hot to handle. Even if he could persuade the rock singer to tone down the sexual element in his writing, Herald Books would be showered with writs for libel from here to kingdom come if they dared to publish the book. For example, Tessa Radlett had split up with Vernon Taggart and was now sharing a penthouse apartment in Mayfair with a wealthy property tycoon.

He would be forced to abandon the project unless Ryan could be persuaded to allow a full rewrite but the hot-headed musician would probably tell them to get stuffed and that he would publish his book himself. Not that he would get very far on that score because no printer worth his salt would touch it and nor would any bookshop. It was all a great shame because Ryan's story would sell like hot cakes and Simon, who had commissioned the book, would have been set for a handsome bonus at the end of the year.

There's no use crying over spilt milk, reasoned Simon as he picked up the latest offering by one of his firm's bestselling crime writers. He enjoyed a good murder mystery and settled down to read until it was time to change and meet up with Adrian, Jennie and Tanya at the girls' flat.

Simon would have been amused to know that he was not alone in pulling his pud that afternoon. After Adrian finished talking to Allan Godfrey, he sat down to read a Sunday newsaper when the phone rang.

'I'm nothing but a slave to this sodding thing,' he complained to the empty room as he picked up the receiver, expecting to hear a further urgent message from Dickie Segal or the first of several calls he presumed would be coming from the team of Fleet Street showbiz reporters hot on the trail of the Quentin Ludgate story.

To his delight, however, his caller was Wendy Shand, a temporary secretary who had spent a fortnight in Adrian's office whilst working for Rose and Griffin during the summer months. He had been smitten by Wendy's pretty face and lush body, her perfectly proportioned breasts and the thick fluffy patch of dark pussy hair that spread over her prominent mound. Fortunately, she had been equally enamoured by Adrian's good looks and genuine charm. Within seventy-two hours of meeting they could have been found writhing under the sheets in Wendy's bed.

Nonetheless the passionate affair had lasted less than a month because, on her twenty-first birthday, Wendy had accepted a permanent post with Pan-Am which was not only well-paid but offered the opportunity of frequent cheap travel to the USA. However, she had remained good friends with Adrian and two or three times since taking up her new job, Adrian had taken her out for dinner and they had finished the evening with a fervent fuck, once in a threesome with June, Wendy's willowy but uninhibited flatmate.

'Oh, it's you, what a relief!' said Adrian when he heard Wendy's mellifluous voice on the line. She gave a surprised little laugh and continued: 'I'm glad there are other people than me who you'd rather not talk to, but it would be nice to hear a hi-there-Wendy-lovely-to-hear-from-you.'

'Sorry, darling, it's been a stressful Sunday, that's all,' apologised Adrian. He proceeded to explain his worries about the Quentin Ludgate affair. 'No excuses, Wendy, but I'm sure you'll see why I'm in a bit of a state.'

'Well, you're best off trying to take your mind off the problem,' commented Wendy. 'Listen, do you remember what we got up to when you took me to the Old Vic to see *Hamlet*?'

Despite himself, Adrian chuckled: 'Could I ever forget it! Dear God, Wendy, there can't be many couples feeling each other up in the back row of the stalls during the third act of one of the greatest plays in the English language.'

'Well, that's their loss,' giggled Wendy. 'Anyhow, let me ask you a question, Ade. Do you remember those black silk knickers I was wearing at the time? You loved those knickers, didn't you? I've got them on now and I wish you were here to roll them down and lick my pussy like you did in the theatre. Then you could bend me over a chair and shove that big thick cock of yours up my quim. That would make you forget your troubles, all right.'

'I dare say it would, you naughty girl,' Adrian agreed with a smile as he tugged at his burgeoning erection. 'Unfortunately, that won't be possible unless you're ringing me from a call-box round the corner.'

'No, I'm still sharing with June down here in Clapham,' she replied. 'Never mind though, we can still have some fun over the phone – take your prick out of your pants.'

Adrian could not believe his ears. 'What did you say?' he spluttered and Wendy calmly repeated: 'Take your prick out of your pants and keep hold of it. Go on, do as I say.'

Obediently, he unzipped his flies and on Wendy's instruction he grabbed his pulsing shaft in his fist. 'There, doesn't that feel nice?' she enquired sweetly. 'Now, I'm sitting here naked, Adrian. I'm playing with my pussy, slipping my fingers into my juicy honeypot and squeezing my clitty. My cunt is all wet and open, really hungry for your lovely big cock. M'mm, let's both imagine that you're moving that thick hard chopper in and out of my tight little crack.'

Adrian entered into the spirit of the game, his voice rising and falling as he muttered: 'God, my cock's as hard as a rock and I wish you could turn round and see it sliding in and out of your snatch from behind, in and out, in and out.'

'Yes, yes, that's the ticket! Now smack my bum whilst you fuck me, you know how much I like it. But don't stop, make sure you keep your cock inside my cunt.'

The flood of words acted like a whiff of aphrodisiac. Adrian's fist slid rapidly up and down his shaft as he panted: 'I'm slapping your bum, Wendy, I'm slapping it whilst I fuck you but now I'm going up your bum, ooh, it's so narrow and you're wriggling like crazy but, uh, I'm in . . .'

For a while neither spoke. All that could be heard on the line was the sound of the rasping breaths of their mounting frenzy. Then Wendy wailed: 'I'm coming, Adrian, I'm coming! Give me all that creamy come, give it to me!'

She screamed out at the top of her lungs when she exploded into an orgasm. Her cries were matched by Adrian's deep grunts as he pulled a tissue from a box which was standing conveniently by the phone and shot his load into the soft folds of paper.

There was silence again for a few moments and then Wendy crooned: 'There, do you feel better now, Ade? I know I do!'

He gave a low chuckle. 'That was damned good but the real thing would be even better. Is there any chance of meeting up?'

'Only if you can take me out this evening,' she answered promptly. 'I flew in last night from New York and from tomorrow afternoon I'm on the Tokyo run for a week.'

For an instant Adrian toyed with the idea of breaking his date with Tanya but though he wobbled towards expediency, he reluctantly settled for principle and said: 'Sorry, love, no can do. But how about when you come back? I have to go up north later in the week but I should be back by the weekend.'

He settled for a date the following Sunday and then, looking at his watch, he rummaged around in his pocket for the piece of paper with Belinda Headley's telephone number which Garry Horne had given him. Talk about either all or nothing, he said to himself as he dialled the number. For the past three weeks he had lived like a monk and now he had to juggle with as many as three girls – Tanya, Wendy and hopefully Belinda – who were eager to be bedded by him. Still, it was a nice problem to have, he thought, as Belinda answered the phone. 'Hello, Belinda? It's me, Adrian Klein,' he said. 'Did you have a nice lunch at your Auntie Hetty's? Good, I hope it made up for having to stand around this morning watching my team go down to their seventh consecutive defeat. No, I tell a lie, we drew the match before the last.'

'Oh, I enjoy watching football, though I don't often go to see Garry play. Not that he minds, as he says it puts him off when knows I'm in the crowd. Perhaps I had the same effect on you,' she said kindly.

Adrian gave a wry smile. 'I can't even blame your cousin Garry for shouting at us, now we know what it's like being abused from the touchline. Anyhow, I do hope that we're on for tomorrow night. To be honest, I must go to *La Miraggio* as the impresario Dickie Segal will be coming down to cast his eye over Allan Godfrey.'

This information surprised Belinda. 'What, old Nipper himself? This guy must be really good. Okay, Adrian, what time and where shall we meet?'

'I'll pick you up at your flat at half past eight,' he answered. I'm really looking forward to seeing you, Belinda, bye for now.'

Adrian put down the phone and went back to the bathroom to run his electric razor over his face before changing into his new chinos and the blue Italian button-down shirt he had recently bought from Cecil Gee's store in Shaftesbury Avenue. Then he remembered he had yet to book a table at the Chinatown Café. Fortunately there was no problem in making a reservation and Adrian resolved to get to Tanya's flat at seven thirty sharp.

Happily for Adrian, Simon Byrne also arrived punctually at Greenhalgh Walk and he and the girls were equally keen to get to the restaurant in West Hampstead which had become a haunt for many of the showbiz people who lived in that fashionable area. They ordered a feast of crispy Peking duck, chicken with almonds, shredded beef with chili and sweet and sour pork with egg fried rice and noodles washed down with two bottles of light white wine.

'Phew, I'm full up,' said Simon as the waiter cleared the table. 'As they say, Chinese food's like sex, you feel completely satisfied after indulging but a couple of hours later you want some more.

'Well, it's not that silly,' he added defensively when a smile crept across Jennie's face and she winked roguishly at Tanya who chuckled: 'We're not laughing at you, Simon, but I'm pretty sure Jennie's thinking about the Chinese meal we had just before we left Paris.'

'Why? Was there anything special about the food?' enquired Simon and Jennie shrugged: 'Not really, it wasn't as good as the meal we've just had, but it was what took place afterwards that Tanya and I will always remember.' She paused and then looked across at her friend and asked: 'Would the boys be offended if I told them what happened at Madame Suzette's club?'

'Darling, you must be joking,' Tanya answered wryly. 'These two would only be offended if we don't give them

Madame Suzette's address so they can go there themselves on their next trip to Paris!'

Jennie grinned: 'All right, but you must promise not to hold it against me, as the actress said to the bishop! While we were working at the *Moulin Rouge*, Tanya and I gave English lessons to Jules and Pierre, two guys who handled the publicity for the show. They were both learning the language at a proper school but we helped them with their homework and taught them some everyday words and expressions they probably wouldn't pick up at their college – and before you ask, not just rude ones either! Phrases like *the tickets are selling like hot cakes* or *it's raining cats and dogs*, that sort of thing. Anyway, we didn't charge them anything for this but the boys were very grateful and insisted on taking us out for dinner in return for our trouble. Well, we went to this Chinese restaurant which was very nice enough but nothing as spectacular as compared to the rest of the evening!

'As we left the restaurant Jules asked us if we fancied going to see a sex show at one of the famous Parisian *club privé*. He said: "The hottest place in town is Madame Suzette's on the Rue Kowalski. It's very select but I know the doorman and he'll let us in if I give him a few francs."

'"Sure, why not?" I said so we crowded into a taxi and sure enough after Jules had bribed the doorman, we were ushered inside by a ravishingly beautiful black girl who was wearing only a white see-through slip under which you could see her bra, garter belt, stockings and tiny g-string. The bra hardly covered her titties as it was one of those uplift ones which just fit under your boobs and push them upwards. I could see the boys' eyes were rivetted to her gorgeous bum cheeks which jiggled so invitingly as she walked ahead of us and showed us to a table in the dimly lit club.

'Jules ordered drinks from the topless waitress in a microscopic skirt who deliberately let her titties swing in front of us whilst she took our order for four beers. I looked around and saw that most of the customers were male although there were a number of couples and foursomes who were obviously there for a randy night out.'

Jennie paused to pour out the tea and Tanya took up the story. 'I'd never seen anything like it in my life. By the side of the bar there were some low tables where a bunch of naked girls were sitting with their knees up and legs wide apart, offering themselves to any man who passed by.

'A tall Arab dressed in long white robes took up the invitation and, kneeling down between the thighs of a curvy young redhead, he kissed her hairy pussy and began licking her cunt. She must have enjoyed it because I watched her roll her nipples between her fingertips and then pull the lips of her cunny apart so that he could get his tongue deeper inside her.

'Next to them another girl was on all fours with three guys around her. She was sucking one and tossing off another as the third fucked her from behind doggie style. Every so often they changed places so each had a turn at everything she offered and eventually they all came, one inside her cunt, another inside her mouth and the third over her titties.'

Now Jennie took up the story again and carried on: 'I don't mind admitting that I was getting turned on by this red-hot entertainment. My knickers were already getting damp when Pierre slid his arm around my waist and murmured: "I wonder if they have any shows like this in Swinging London?"

'But before I could answer, the black girl walked onto the miniature dance floor in the centre of the room holding a silk top hat. Speaking first in French and then in English, she announced that it was time to find out who had that night's lucky cloakroom number. She drew a ticket out of the hat and called out: "*Numero quatre-vingt-trois!*"

'"*Merde! Ça c'est mon billet*!" cried out Jules, waving his ticket in the air. Two of the naked chicks who had been sitting next to the bar came up to our table and escorted him onto the stage whilst the black girl pulled her slip over her head, unhooked her bra to let her big breasts bounce free and then ripped off her tiny g-string to reveal a shaven cunt.

'I asked Pierre if he knew any of the girls and he told me that the black girl's name was Michele whilst her assistants were called Lulu and Verna. Anyhow, the three girls quickly helped Jules out of his clothes and he was given the lucky winner's treatment. They laid him down on a mattress and Michele started to suck him off, bobbing her head up and down his shaft until his whole length had disappeared into her mouth. At the same time, Lulu was licking his balls whilst Verna was rubbing her soft breasts against his body.

'Then Michele pulled Jules's cock out of her mouth and walked off stage whilst Lulu, the girl who had been lapping on his balls, mounted his rigid chopper facing away from him. Verna straddled over his head and lowered herself down so that he could lick her quim. Then Michele came back holding a really thick dildo and gave it to the girl who was having her pussy pleasured by Jules's tongue.

'"Phew, that's a big one," I breathed to Pierre who whispered back: "It's a very famous dildo which belongs to Madame Suzette, the woman who owns this club and who used to fuck all the famous visitors to Paris – from film stars to heads of state. That dildo is supposedly modelled on a cast taken of the prick of General Eisenhower with whom she had a passionate affair after the Liberation in 1944."

'"My word, I bet it's done sterling service ever since," I murmured as Michele parted her legs and proceeded to diddle herself with it whilst Lulu rode Jules's cock, up and down, backwards and forwards until his hips bucked upwards and he jetted his jism into Lulu's cunt. When she was sure Jules had shot his load, she raised herself up and, with her hands on his knees, raised her tight little bum cheeks into the air. Michele shoved the dildo between them and glided it straight up her snatch.'

Jennie paused to sip her tea and Tanya went on: 'It didn't take long for her to bring Lulu off with it and then the real orgy began. There were some youngsters at a table celebrating their friend's twenty-first birthday and Verna pulled two of them out from the audience to join the action. They didn't need any encouragement to strip off and as they stood in front of her she squatted in front of them and set about sucking their stiff cocks one at a time, her head moving methodically back and forth from one to the other in a sensuous rhythm.

'Michele was now giving Jules another hard-on by sucking his cock and she was joined by a black guy – Pierre informed me later that he was her boy friend – who ripped down his pants and smeared some butter on his cock before parting her cheeks and slipping his knob inside her bottom.

'Michele wriggled her bum from side to side as he gradually pushed his way into her arsehole. I know what's going through your mind! Well, they say black men have big dicks but this guy wasn't particularly well endowed. Just as well, perhaps, because I don't think Michele could have taken a big cock like Rex Harrison's up the tradesmen's cntrance.'

'Sorry to interrupt, but how do you know Rex Harrison's got a big cock?' Adrian demanded and Tanya chuckled: 'Because a friend of mine was an extra in *My Fair Lady* and she saw it for herself.

'Anyhow, across the room there were naked girls getting shafted left, right and centre and one came over to Pierre, ripped open his trousers and bent over to give his cock a good sucking whilst a thickset young man pressed his cock into my hand. I was so worked up by now that I grabbed hold of it and began to gobble his knob.'

'We were both carried away by the erotic situation,' confessed Jennie and she blushed as she continued: 'I felt myself getting wet between the legs and so I let a good-looking fair-haired guy pull off my clothes. Pressing me up against the wall, he pushed his prick up my cunt. He had a big cock but he used it gently and somehow managed to move it from side to side as well as up and down as if he was zig-zagging his way inside my quim.

'I'd never been fucked by a complete stranger before and I probably won't ever let it happen again but I have to admit it was fantastic. When he came, I came with him too, clinging on to his shoulders and pushing myself as hard as I could against him, my whole body trembling as the tension snapped and waves of my orgasm swept through me while I drained his cock dry.

'Well, after a while things settled down and we gathered up our clothes and left,' she concluded. Tanya sighed: 'And believe it or not, all four of us were so tired from all the fucking that the boys dropped us home and we slept through till nine o'clock the next morning.'

There was a short silence and then Simon gave a hoarse laugh. 'Sorry, girls, it might sound selfish but I hope telling us this story hasn't made you sleepy because listening to you both has almost made me cream my pants.'

'Just the opposite in fact,' said Jennie quickly. As Adrian signalled the waiter to bring the bill, she whispered in Simon's ear. 'I can't wait to get back to the flat and let you take off my knickers.'

A wide smile spread across Simon's face. As the foursome walked down Fortune Green Road, he quietly asked Adrian not to waste any time getting back to the girls' flat. 'Otherwise Jennie and I will drench the back seat of your flash car with love juice,' he hissed and Adrian nodded: 'Don't worry, I also can't wait to do something about my stiffie.'

Although Adrian resisted the temptation to cross a red traffic light at an empty crossroads, he drove at speed through the leafy streets of Hampstead Garden Suburb and inside ten minutes Simon was closing Jennie's bedroom door behind him. He pulled off his jacket before taking Jennie in his arms and crushing the nineteen-year-old blonde beauty in a passionate bear hug, smothering kisses all over her pretty face.

'Last one on the bed without any clothes on a cissy,' she teased and giggled when Simon tripped over his own feet in his eagerness to tug down his trousers. Nevertheless, he was lying naked on her bedspread as Jennie rolled down her tights. When she stood nude except for her frilly pink panties, he sat up and with trembling hands yanked down the tiny garment, feasting his eyes for the first time on the fluffy corn-coloured bush which surrounded the pounting lips of her pussy.

Jennie let her tongue pass slowly over her top lip and allowed herself to be pulled down on top of him. Simon turned on to his side and pressed her compliant soft curves into the crescent of his own warmth. Their mouths met and the aroused girl experienced a glorious wave of sensual energy hurtle through her as Simon's hands roamed freely across her breasts. He kissed her pointed nipples which had swelled up to two little red peaks and Jennie cooed with delight when his fingertips ran along the edges of her moistening crack.

She reached down to squeeze his cock but to her surprise she found his shaft was still hanging forlornly over his balls. Sensibly, she refrained from comment though she was surprised that Simon's beefy prick was at best only at half-mast and Jennie wondered if there was anything she could do to rectify the situation. She had first held an erect penis in her hand at the age of fifteen when her boy friend had moved her hand down to the tenting bulge in his lap whilst they necked in her parents' living room. Since then she had seen and played with a variety of pricks of different shapes and sizes, but all had risen to a throbbing stiffness by the time she had touched them.

'Am I doing anything wrong?' Jennie blurted out as she rubbed her palm against the soft fleshy tube, but Simon shook his head as beads of perspiration formed on his brow as he said miserably: 'Jennie, I'm dreadfully sorry but I just don't know what's happened. I've had a huge hard-on ever since you were telling us that story about the orgy in Paris, but a minute ago my cock just collapsed like a burst balloon.'

'Forget it, you're just over-anxious, that's all,' said Jennie encouragingly. She nibbled his ear as she deftly shifted her body so that she lay on top of him and kissed his nipples before sliding her mouth down to his flat, hard-muscled belly and into the crinkly, dark hairs which ringed his flaccid todger.

Half upset and half amused at the plight of his soft shaft which twitched feebly in her hand, Jennie lowered her head and licked around the edge of the smooth, mushroom knob. She tickled the sensitive underside with the tip of her tongue and Simon's anxiety now communicated itself to her when even this delicious stimulation failed to work.

Why should this happen? the bewildered girl asked herself silently as she ruffled her hand through his hair. She wondered why, when Simon had been so eager to possess her, the apparently fit and healthy young man was now unable to accept the freely offered gift of her ripe eager body.

Then a shrewd idea on how to excite Simon's crestfallen cock occured to her and she murmured: 'Sweetie, just lie back and relax— I'd like to tell you what happened to me last summer when I went down to Bournemouth for a weekend with my friend, Glenda. We had planned to go cycling on the Saturday afternoon but Glenda cried off after she copped off with a guy who she met at the pub on Friday night. Still, it seemed a shame to waste the money we had paid to hire the bicycles so I went out on my own and though it was hard work at first, I soon began to enjoy the feel of the hard saddle between my legs, pressing right into my pussy. After half an hour or so my quim was really tingling.

'Anyhow, there I was cycling slowly down a winding country lane when who should I happen to see but Timmy, Glenda's young brother, sitting down on a clump of grass by the side of the road, holding a rucksack in his hands.

'I pulled off the road and laid my bike down next to his machine and said: "Hello there, Timmy, what a nice surprise! Your sister never mentioned you were holidaying down here."

'The lad blushed and told me that he was staying with two other pals but they had gone off with two girls leaving him to his own devices. "And you don't have a girl to pair up with?" I said with genuine surprise, tugging down the crotch of my brief white cycling shorts which had ridden up into my bottom. Now I didn't say this merely to flatter him because Timmy might have been only seventeen but he was already six feet tall, strongly built and very handsome. I must admit that I found him very attractive and from the way he looked at my jiggling bosoms – for I wasn't wearing anything underneath my shirt – and from the bulge in his crotch, it seemed that Timmy was equally enthusiastic about my charms!

'Anyhow, he shared his cold drink with me and as we talked, I coaxed him into admitting that he was a virgin. "That's nothing to be ashamed of," I declared but Timmy shook his head and muttered that all of his friends had told him they had already had their first girl. I nodded sympathetically and said: "Are you sure they aren't simply boasting? Lots of boys brag about their conquests when in fact they haven't even reached first base."

'I paused for a moment and then put my hand on his arm and said softly: "Timmy, if you would like to have sex, you can fuck me if you like." He blushed and hung his head but I guessed he was really dying to lose his cherry but my brashness had frightened him. So I chuckled: "Don't worry, I won't bite, at least not if you don't want me to."

'We were silent for a few moments and then realising that I would have to take control, I leaned over and kissed him. I tried to put some tongue-action into the kiss but Timmy was still shy so I took hold of his hands and placed them firmly on my breasts. This worked wonders! I felt his body shiver and I could feel my pussy getting very wet as the emboldened young scamp pulled my shirt out of my shorts and slid his hands underneath it to cup my bare breasts.

'"Hold on, you randy young so-and-so, we'd better find somewhere comfortable behind the hedge," I giggled. "I'll go first and then you can follow me with the bikes."

'I raced through a gap in the hedge to find a hummock of earth and shucked off my shirt so that when he appeared a few moments later trundling the two bikes, he was greeted by the sight of me sprawled out on the ground with my hand plunged down my shorts, stroking my wet pussy. His cock grew before my eyes, creating a tight bulge in the front of his shorts as I said huskily: "Timmy, why don't you pull off your top and sit down next to me."

'He didn't need to be asked twice and in an instant he was at my side. We kissed again and this time all Timmy's shyness had evaporated and his tongue slid straight between my teeth. He squeezed my breasts whilst I unbuttoned his shorts and out popped his thick meaty cock which I gripped in my fist, slowly jacking it up and down as I watched a blob of pre-come form across his knob.

'I broke off our kiss and slithered across him until his huge, hard and throbbing shaft was just inches from my open mouth. Then I slowly circled his helmet with my lips and tongue whilst I fondled his balls. Timmy was so tense, he actually pulled my head away from his cock – for the first few seconds anyway – but soon he was enjoying his first blowjob, pumping his hips up and down and groaning in ecstasies of delight. Naturally, he came very quickly and when I sensed he was about to let go, I pulled his cock out of my mouth till just his knob was resting on my tongue and wanked him with my hand. He shot a tremendous amount of creamy cum over my lips and teeth which I licked into my mouth and swallowed.

'It took him only a minute to get hard again and now I laid him on his back and climbed on top of him. I straddled his thighs and speared myself on his thick young cock, taking it all the way up my cunt. I bounced up and down on it feverishly as his hands slipped round to clasp my bum cheeks. This time I was the first to come and I screamed out as the divine sensations rushed through me.'

At this point Jennie stopped and looked down. She smiled knowingly when she observed that her erotic confession had broken through Simon's mental block. His cock was now fully erect and quivering with desire when she took the hot, throbbing shaft in her hand. With an unhurried calm, she moved her luscious smooth body across him, the tips of her breasts brushing against his own nipples. She slid downwards until her mouth was level with his uncapped knob.

A low, wrenching groan of ecstasy escaped from his lips when Jennie sucked his cock, bobbing her head up and down on his rampant prick. Then she gave one final long lick from his balls to the tip of his tool and pulled him across her as she parted her long legs and invitingly spread open the pink lips of her pussy with her fingers.

Simon mounted her eagerly. A blissful smile spread across his face as he savoured the delicious sensations to the full when she guided his cock into her lush folds. He took a deep breath and in a single deep thrust buried his shaft to the hilt inside her clingy, wet quim. Jennie lifted her legs high into the air as he entered her, their pubic hairs matting together before he pulled back again for a second onslaught. She twisted her feet around his neck and he fucked the gorgeous girl in long smooth strokes, rubbing her creamy titties against the palms of his hand, his balls slapping against her backside as his cock squelched in and out of her juicy love sheath.

Again and again he slewed his shaft back and forth, sending pulses of sheer ecstasy rippling throughout her entire body. Soon she was writhing in hot, exciting spasms as Simon's cock rammed forcefully in and out of her tingling slit.

'I'm coming! Oh yes, I'm coming!' gasped Jennie, arching herself upwards as she felt the rush of an oncoming orgasm building up inside her. 'Spunk into my cunny, Simon, and fill me with hot, sticky jism, you lovely big-cocked boy!'

Simon gritted his teeth and slammed his twitching todger to and fro, faster and faster until a fountain of creamy cum jetted out of his cock and creamed the walls of Jennie's cunt which quivered all round his shaft as she climaxed with him. The muscular contractions of her quim increased his pleasure even more. They shuddered with joy at the explosive force which racked through their bodies and collapsed down into an untidy heap of limbs when the heavenly sensations finally subsided.

Next door Adrian Klein had experienced no difficulty in getting a hard-on after his and Tanya's warm naked bodies had slithered together in a sensuous embrace on her bed. However, he had been unable to resist ejaculating a stream of spunk down Tanya's throat whilst she was sucking his cock and it was as well that Tanya enjoyed oral foreplay before she was ready to be fucked.

She purred with pleasure when his hands smoothed their way up her thighs, higher and higher until his fingertips reached her moist cunny lips. Then she threw back her head on the pillow as Adrian moved nimbly between her legs and bent his head down to rake his tongue over her already erect love button.

'Ahhh, that's so nice,' she breathed as he slipped his tongue inside her wet cunt. She splayed her legs wider when he began to lap up the love juice which had trickled out of her honeypot. Unlike some of his friends, Adrian genuinely enjoyed muffdiving and he did not flinch when his nostrils were assailed by the strong tangy aroma of Tanya's cuntal fluids. Frantically he attacked her fleshy clit, which twitched and trembled when he nipped at it with his teeth. She jerked her hips upwards, pressing her hands against the sides of Adrian's head as, with a scream, she climaxed and he gulped down her salty spend as Tanya sank down, sated by her glorious come.

Nevertheless, it did not take her long to recover. After releasing his head from between her thighs, she said cheekily: 'M'mm, that was a splendid *hors d'oeuvres*, darling – but what are you going to serve for the *entrée*?'

'Whatever *mademoiselle* desires,' replied Adrian in an exaggerated French accent as he clambered up on his knees and fondled his rigid cock. It was sticking upwards out of the thicket of curly dark hair at the base of his belly. Tanya giggled and opened her legs as he moved himself sinuously over her.

Then she took over and guided home his rock-hard rammer inside her aching cunny, directing in every inch of his sizeable shaft. Once it was snugly embedded inside her cunt, she closed her thighs, making Adrian open his own legs and lie astride her with his pulsating prick well and truly trapped inside her clinging quim.

A growl of delight escaped from his lips as he cupped her jiggling breasts in his hands as she asked: 'Are you comfortable? I love fucking in this position because I can feel every bit of your big thick cock.'

'It's fine,' panted Adrian although it took some considerable effort to pump in and out of Tanya's snatch as her cunny muscles were gripping him so tightly. To compensate for this, however, when she started to jerk her hips, his shaft was massaged exquisitely against the walls of her cunt. His prick pulsed inside her juicy love funnel and then it was Tanya's turn to squeal when he sank his forefinger between her soft bum cheeks and inserted the tip into her arsehole. This made her wriggle wildly in fresh paroxyms of passion. She eased the pressure by parting her thighs to release his cock and now Adrian began driving strongly at breakneck speed in and out of her squishy honeypot.

'Y-e-s-s!' screamed Tanya as the fierce momentum brought her off time and again. She brought her legs up against the small of his back, humping the lower half of her body upwards to meet the violent pistoning of his rampant cock. Adrian's body gleamed with perspiration as he fucked her harder and harder, the rippling thrusts exciting the velvety sides of her quim. When he felt himself on the verge of orgasm, Adrian tensed his frame and, with a cry, he ejaculated spurt after spurt of frothy seed which streamed inside every nook of Tanya's cunny. She squeezed her thighs together and milked his trembling tool, not freeing his cock until it began to shrink and he pulled it out of her slippery slit.

Adrian sat back on his haunches and rested his hands on his thighs. He knew from their previous couplings how Tanya was a veritable tigress between the sheets and that in all probability her appetite was not yet sated. So he relaxed for only a moment before he cupped her breasts in his hands, feeling their jouncy firmness. Sure enough, the gorgeous girl sighed with happiness when Adrian licked her horned-up titties. She slipped her fingers around his cock and started to pump her hand up and down the flaccid shaft.

'I'm sure your little soldier is ready to go into battle again,' she murmured, still gripping his cock tightly as she scrambled up on her knees. 'No, I think he needs a little rest first,' replied Adrian regretfully with a shake of his head. But Tanya was in no mood to take no for an answer and his tool twitched when she leaned forward to place a luscious wet kiss on his smooth ruby helmet.

'On the other hand, you may be right,' he murmured as she sucked his shaft into her mouth. Adrian's cock soon began to swell with excitement when she slid her lips up and down his palpitating prick, kissing, licking and lapping until it stood up proudly again with the tip of his knob just below his belly button.

'Now I want you inside me again,' Tanya whispered fiercely as she turned herself over onto her tummy. With her free hand, she slid one of her pillows down the bed to rest under her hips after which she pushed out her bottom towards him.

Adrian drew a deep breath as he parted her tightly rounded globes of her backside and placed his knob inside the smooth crevice between her impudent young bum cheeks. His lascivious gaze travelled down to the tiny wrinkled rosette of her arsehole and as if reading his thoughts, Tanya said huskily: 'Darling, there's something on the floor which you can smear on your cock.'

He dived down and found a plastic bottle of moisturing lotion which he opened and rubbed the viscous liquid all over his shaft. Then, prising apart her buttocks, he lodged the domed helmet of his cock inside Tanya's arse and his hands clamped down on the soft dimpled hemispheres of her glorious bottom.

'Okay, you can push on,' she panted. Adrian eased his shaft slowly forward into her bum and at first he encountered some resistance so he stayed still as Tanya rotated her rump from side to side in an erotic circular motion as she pressed her face and elbows into her pillow.

She gave out a diminutive whimper when he withdrew all but the tip of his cock from the puckered entrance but the whimper changed to a startled yelp when Adrian stabbed forward and plunged his entire eight inches inside her narrow sheath, his balls thudding against her backside.

However, once she was fully impaled, Tanya began to ride

backwards and forwards on his rigid rod and Adrian panted with pleasure as her sphincter slid up and down his quivering cock. He happily followed her rhythm, working his shaft in and out of her luscious bottom at a quickening pace and they rocked together in a lustful frenzy as his thick tool slithered to and fro inside her anus.

Tanya's excitement was further increased when Adrian slid his arms round her and playfully jiggled her breasts up and down whilst he rubbed her erect rubbery nipples and she lifted her head from the pillow and gasped: 'Woooh! What a super bum-fuck! Keep going, Ade, I'm almost there.'

'So am I,' he choked out. Tanya sighed and pushed back against him as he thrust forward yet again. Her buttocks were like soft, yielding cushions and Adrian groaned with delight on every stroke as he drove home, stretching her bum hole as he pounded away, feeling every inch of his throbbing todger scraping along the engorged furrow.

The sensations were so strong that he soon felt the rush of seed shooting through his shaft. He called out a warning that he was about to spunk, but Tanya was ready for him and she yelled out: 'Yes! Yes! Yes! Cream my bum, you randy sod!'

With a hoarse cry he shot a torrent of warm, glutinous jism inside her. The room echoed with their long sustained moans as the raunchy couple finished the course of their mutual cataclysmic climax.

Adrian flopped down on top of the inert girl and kissed the back of her neck. He pulled out his prick with an audible plop from her bottom and they lay cuddled together. The lusty couple had been so engrossed in their frenetic lovemaking that neither of them had heard the door open. Tanya was rudely woken out of her satisfying post-coital doze to see Jennie lounging against the door wrapped in her pink silk dressing gown.

'Well, well, I only arrived thirty seconds ago but you two have obviously just finished shagging yourselves silly,' Jennie observed brightly as she stepped into the room. 'So would you mind very much if I bedded down with you for a while because

I've left Simon snoring away in my bed and I don't want to wake the poor lad up as he's really out for the count.'

'No, do come and snuggle up with us, love,' replied Tanya hospitably. She sat up and brushed back the long strands of silky dark hair from her face. She turned to Adrian and added: 'You've no objections to Jennie joining us for bit, have you?'

'Of course not, the more the merrier,' he grunted, patting the bedspread. 'There's plenty of room for a slim lady like you.'

'Thank you, kind sir,' said Jennie and, closing the door behind her, she walked across the room and, shucking off her dressing gown to reveal her magnificent naked body, plumped herself down next to him. This made Adrian feel like the filling in an extremely delicious sandwich. Then, with a cheeky smile on her face, the luscious blonde took hold of his limp shaft and remarked: 'M'mm, I can see your cock's been well-exercised. Tanya, may I have my way with this pretty prick?'

But before her friend could answer, Adrian protested weakly: 'Jennie, you must be joking, what do you think we've been doing since we came back from the restaurant – playing gin rummy? I'm sorry but I'm all-in – well, at least for half an hour or so.'

'Dear me, and who said men are the stronger sex?' said Jennie with mock severity as she smoothed her hand between her legs. 'Tanya, I need our little rubber friend – is it in the usual place?'

'Stay there, I'll get it for you,' said Tanya. A puzzled frown formed on Adrian's brow as he watched her swing her legs down to the floor and pad over to a chest of drawers. Then he turned back to glance at Jennie who lay back with a smile on her face as she tenderly parted the moist flaxen hairs around her prominent pussy lips. Her hand was pushed aside by Tanya who continued this sensual frigging by running her forefinger up and down Jennie's pouting crack.

Adrian looked on with growing interest as the two girls kissed, like sisters at first, but then with parted lips, their wet tongues curling together as their mouths eased away from each other, leaving Tanya free to lick Jennie's lush swollen titties.

'Oooh, darling, that's divine,' murmured the blonde beauty. Tanya closed her left hand on her fluffy flaxen bush and Adrian's cock began to stir when he saw that in her right hand she was brandishing a thick ribbed dildo of a kind he had never seen before, with both ends fashioned like the knobs of huge stiff penises. Tanya saw his expression of surprise and said: 'Haven't you seen a Black Mamba before? No? Jennie and I will show you how they work.'

She pressed one end gently against Jennie's yielding pussy lips which instantly parted to allow Tanya to insert it into her honeypot. Next she began to vibrate the dildo in and out of Jennie's cunny with one hand whilst with the other she rubbed her fingertips along her own snatch. When her slit had sufficiently moistened up, she raised herself off Jennie's thighs and pushed herself slowly down on the cock-shaped end of the Black Mamba which was protruding out of Jennie's juicy cunt.

Tanya squealed with joy as Jennie wrapped her arms around her. She pulled her down until the girls were pressed tightly together, breasts to breasts and cunt to cunt. Adrian watched with quiet fascination whilst he watched the double-headed dildo squelch in and out of their cunnies as the girls jerked their hips and rocked to and fro along the rubber shaft. Their motions became more and more frenzied as their excitement mounted. Tanya stretched herself across her partner with the heads of the dildo still clamped firmly inside their sticky, suctioning pussies. She grabbed Jennie's jutting breasts and licked and lapped at the inviting berry-sized nipples as they continued to fuck themselves on their imitation double-knobbed cock.

'Ooooh! Ooooh! Ooooh! Suck my tits, darling!' shrieked Jennie, drumming her heels on the mattress. Tanya paused for a moment to catch her breath, not that there was any real need for her to give any such instruction because Tanya had every intention of sliding her lips around the springy red projectiles. The girls were soon again lost in their erotic reverie, spurred on by an uncontrollable intensity which locked their bodies together until, with loud cries of fulfilment, they climaxed within seconds of each other. Rivulets of pungent love juice streamed out of their pussies and onto the bedspread which was already stained with Tanya and Adrian's previous exertions.

Tanya hauled herself off Jennie's thighs and, as she extracted the dildo from her cunt, Jennie said to Adrian: 'Take out the Black Mamba from my pussy, there's a good boy.'

'With pleasure,' he answered and when leaned over to gently pull out the wet imitation cock from between her puffy love lips, Jennie sat up and rewarded him with a kiss on his forehead. She licked her lips as she looked longingly at Adrian's meaty shaft which was almost fully erect and said to him: 'I'm glad to see you enjoyed our little show. It's great fun bringing myself off but of course it's not as good as the real thing.'

Then she said pleadingly to Tanya: 'Sweetie, would you be awfully upset if Adrian fucked me?'

'I wouldn't be upset at all,' replied her friend generously, making a fist with her fingers to rub her hand briskly up and down Adrian's burgeoning cock until it stood bolt upright with the purple helmet pointing up to the ceiling. 'There now, his tool's good and ready for you.'

'H'm, that's a good-looking specimen,' remarked Jennie as she replaced Tanya's hand with her own and cuddled his cock in her fist. 'Now let's find out if it tastes as good as it looks.'

Then almost as an afterthought she said to Adrian with a girlish giggle: 'I presume you don't mind if I suck your lovely cock?'

'Be my guest,' he answered with a smile as Jennie wriggled down the bed until her head was level with Adrian's pulsing prick, bringing her lips level with the wide mushroom-shaped bell-end. Saliva dripped from the corners of her mouth as she used her teeth to nibble playfully on the smooth dome.

Then she let her tongue run down the length of his veiny truncheon and then back up again to catch a sticky drip of pre-come which had formed around the tiny hole at the top of his cock.

Jennie ran her lips over his knob and opened them wide when Adrian instinctively jerked his body upwards and forced some six inches of his succulent chopper into her mouth. Concerned that he might choke the voluptuous girl, he retracted an inch or two out of her mouth and let his straining shaft lie throbbing on her tongue. This allowed Jennie to close her mouth around its girth, moving her tongue excitingly. Adrian let out a strangled cry as she sucked greedily on his bursting tool whilst Tanya began kneading and massaging his hanging balls.

'Oh no, I can't take too much of that,' he gasped when both girls started to lap on the sensitive underside of his shaft. Jennie gently pushed Tanya's head away from his palpitating prick as she rightly judged that Adrian was close to shooting his spunk over their faces.

'Give him a helping hand instead, I'm more than ready to be fucked,' Jennie suggested as she rolled onto her back with a wicked smile playing suggestively across her lips. She slid her hand between her parted thighs and moved her finger up and down between the moist love lips which stood out in her fluffy bush of blonde pussy hair.

This clear signal was not lost upon Adrian. He crawled up on top of her trembling curves and Tanya curled her fingers round his cock and guided it into position. She rubbed the tip of his knob against the entrance to Jennie's juicy quim and cradled his balls in her hand as he pushed forward and embedded his twitching tool inside her wet welcoming love tunnel.

'Oh Adrian, you feel incredible,' breathed Jennie, reaching up to ruffle through his hair with her hand as she wriggled beneath him. 'You're so big, I can feel you right up against my clitty!'

Adrian nodded his appreciation of the compliment and,

revelling in the clinging moistness of her honeypot, he forced himself to control his entry with a steady deliberation, sliding his shaft slowly into her squishy crack as her cunny muscles contracted exquisitely against his palpitating prick.

Tanya removed her hand from his balls and began to diddle her own pussy as she gazed at Adrian's cock as it plunged into Jennie's pussy, now at a faster pace as he speeded up the tempo. He thrust his cock in and out of her tingling love funnel in short, rapid jabs. His hips rose and fell in a regular cadence and each pistoning stab brought forth a cry of pleasure from the gorgeous blonde. She raked his back with her fingernails as shivering ripples of rapture from her sated cunt flooded out throughout her body.

She squealed with surprised delight when Adrian reached under her and slid his index finger directly into her arsehole, gently rubbing around the rim of the tiny puckered orifice. He rammed his shaft harder and faster into her dripping love funnel whilst he pushed his finger deeper inside Jennie's backside. At first he worked it simultaneously with his cock and then alternately so that when his prick was buried in her quim he withdrew his finger from her bum, and then as he pulled his prick out of her juicy crack, he plunged his finger up to the first knuckle inside her bottom.

Jennie encircled his hips with her thighs, her ankles pressed against the small of his back as the first spasm of her orgasm electrified every fibre of her body. This immediately triggered Adrian into his climax and out of his cock spurted a torrent of frothy jism which gushed into her soaking honeypot. Exhausted from this shattering fuck, Adrian heaved himself off the trembling girl and sprawled down on his belly as, still frigging her own pussy, Tanya scrambled across Jennie to take his place and licked up the dribble of spunk and cuntal juice which was trickling down her thighs.

When she had finished, she looked at Adrian and said hopefully 'I'd adore being shagged again. Is there any chance of another poke a little later on, darling?'

'I don't think so,' replied Adrian apologetically. 'I'd really love to but the problem is that I've a full day tomorrow and must be getting back home.'

'Okay, I understand,' she said generously as she riffled her hand through his hair. 'When you work at night like me, it's easy to forget that most people have nine-to-five jobs, so off you go.'

Adrian hauled himself up and kissed her nipples. 'Thanks, sugarpuss, I'll need all my wits about me in the morning. Anyhow, I'll see you tomorrow night at *La Miraggio*, though I'll be there on business. Dickie Segal suddenly needs a good comedian for one of his shows and he's coming with me to see Allan Godfrey in action.'

'Would you like us to wake up Sleeping Beauty next door?' enquired Jennie. Adrian shrugged: 'I'll leave Simon here, if you like – they don't seem to get into their offices much before ten in publishing, lucky sods – but if you want to kick him out of your bed, I'll take him back to his flat right now.'

'Well, if the lucky lad doesn't have to get up too early, let him stay,' she answered with a smile. 'I dare say he won't mind starting the day with a good fuck.'

'I'm sure he won't,' agreed Adrian as he pulled on his pants and when he had finished dressing, he kissed both the girls and drove back home alone.

CHAPTER THREE

Start the Week

Simon Byrne emitted a soft growl of contentment as he slowly eased himself into consciousness, breathing in the warm feminine scent as he buried his head into a shock of fine golden hair. His eyes fluttered open and he looked fondly at the owner of the long blonde tresses who was sleeping beside him. He glanced at his watch and let out a quiet sigh as he leaned forward and gently kissed Jennie on the lips.

'Hello there, darling,' she mumbled sleepily as she turned towards him and snuggled her head inside the crook of his shoulder. Simon was tempted to follow her example and return to the Land of Nod, but instead he heaved himself up into a sitting position and said regretfully: 'Jennie, I'm sorry but I must be on my way. I've a difficult author due in at ten o'clock to discuss her latest masterpiece and I dare not be late. But I promise I'll call you later today and we'll fix up a date.'

Jennie did not reply at first but instead pulled back the bedspread and then swung her arm over him so that her elbow rested on his abdomen whilst she gently stroked Simon's nipples with her fingers. Then she answered with a saucy smile: 'Fair enough, but only on condition that we first check that your equipment is back in full working order – remember how we had a wee problem to solve last night?'

He opened his mouth to protest but her fingers had already slid down from his chest to his cock. 'It looks like there's plenty of lead in this pencil,' she added happily as she tightened her grip around his stirring shaft.

'Don't do that, Jennie, I honestly don't have the time,' he begged the luscious girl. But his voice was already thick and unsteady as she slicked her fist up and down his burgeoning erection. 'It's already eight o'clock and I have to—'

He stopped short and a fervent groan escaped from his lips as Jennie jammed down his foreskin and swooped down to plant a voluptuous wet kiss on his bared helmet. 'That's not fair,' said Simon plaintively as her lips slithered over his smooth knob, though he made no attempt to pull back her tousled blonde hair when she sucked in his rigid rod into her mouth whilst her hands played with his dangling balls. Instead, he slumped back and closed his eyes as he thrilled to the delicious sensations afforded by Jennie's tongue slurping around his pulsating pole. He clutched at her head and shuddered violently as she circled her tongue around the fleshy purple knob so sensuously that any remaining thoughts about work fled from Simon's mind.

When he opened his eyes he saw that Jennie was now fingering herself whilst she sucked lustily away on his sturdy shaft, rubbing her fingertips along the edges of her pouting pink pussy lips and sliding her forefinger directly into her cunt. He began to pant hoarsely and when Jennie looked quizzically up at him, she realised that watching her masturbate had swiftly aroused Simon to boiling point. With a mischievous glint in her bright blue eyes she drew back her head and, releasing his cock from her mouth, she whispered: 'Wait a minute, Simon, let's do this properly.'

She climbed to her knees and then straddled him, facing his feet so that her pussy was only inches from his mouth. She leaned forward and kissed his pulsing prick which stood high in the air at right angles to his flat belly. Her pink tongue flashed out to wash wetly over his knob. Simon arched his back upwards as Jennie opened her mouth as wide as she could. He felt her teeth scrape the sensitive crown of his cock as she sucked his shaft with renewed gusto.

He placed his hands on her rounded bum cheeks as he watched the delicate slit of her pretty quim open and close when she moved her thighs. Drops of cuntal fluid splattered upon his cheeks as he pulled her down until the delectable cleft was resting upon his lips. Simon used his tongue to good effect, gliding it up and down the long crack, savouring the tangy aroma as he thrust it deep inside her juicy honeypot. He immediately found her excited, erect clitty and a low moan escaped from Jennie's throat as she frantically rubbed her cunt against his mouth whilst she continued to gobble uninhibitedly on his throbbing tool.

This sent Simon into fresh paroxyms of sheer ecstasy and he found it impossible to prevent himself racing past the point of no return. He cried out hoarsely and his hips jerked upwards as he stabbed his finger into the tiny wrinkled opening of her anus and spurted a lavish stream of sticky spunk into her mouth. Jennie gulped down his abundant ejaculation of creamy jism, smacking her lips as she milked his cock, only pulling her lips away when his shaft finally lost its stiffness and drooped limply downwards when she released it from her mouth.

'Your cum has a nice refreshing taste,' she commented as she swung off Simon and sat back on her haunches besides him. He shrugged his shoulders and said modestly: 'Thanks, but I think the credit must go to my diet – not too much red meat and plenty of fresh vegetables.'

Jennie smiled as she held out her hands and said: 'I'm going to make myself comfortable and see for myself if the little trouble we had last night really is behind us.'

She helped to pull Simon up and then she laid herself down lengthways across him, with her bottom resting on his belly, her head resting on the side of the bed and her legs splayed out over the other side. He watched goggle-eyed as Jennie slipped her hand between her thighs and lasciviously teased her fingers across her puffy pussy lips.

As Jennie had correctly surmised, watching her masturbate had the desired effect of making Simon's shaft swell up again and it was soon as hard and stiffly erect as it had been before the ravishing young blonde had sucked him off. She slid back alongside him and Simon leaped on top of her and guided his blue-veined todger into Jennie's welcoming wet cunt.

'Oh yes! That's the ticket! Slam every inch of that big cock into me!' she panted when he jammed in his cock inside her. The hairs of their pubic bushes were rubbing together and his balls slapped against her bum cheeks as his throbbing tool deliciously stretched the inner walls of her tingling quim.

Nothing loath, Simon worked his hips in an ever-quickening rhythm and Jennie bucked and squirmed under the surging strokes of his pulsing prick as it squelched to and fro inside her juicy love tunnel. She whimpered with delight as his hands roamed over her breasts, tweaking her aroused nipples up to two red peaks of rubbery hardness whilst his prick ploughed its way in and out of her squishy sheath.

Again and again his quivering cock lunged backwards and forwards, making the folds of her cunny open like a water-lily. She yelped with joy as sweet waves of ecstasy began to course through her.

'Ooooh! Ooooh! I can feel you right up against my clitty! Oh, yes, I'm coming! I'm coming!' Jennie screamed out. She clawed at Simon's bum cheeks to try and push him even deeper inside her.

With a loud cry she toppled over the edge whilst he continued to thrust into her sopping slit and she sustained a further wrenching climax when he finally emptied himself and drenched her cunt with a torrent of frothy jism. In seconds her pussy was awash in a sticky flood of their mutual jism and another ecstatic squeal escaped from her lips as the force of a third orgasm shuddered through her.

They lay panting with exhaustion for a minute or so and then Simon looked at his watch and murmured: 'Sweetie, I must be off because there'll be all hell to pay if I miss my meeting with Estelle Hendon this morning.'

Jennie slowly rubbed her hand across his shoulders and pouted: 'But you said that's not till ten o'clock. Why not stay here just for some tea and toast and then a nice little quickie to send you on your way?'

'Don't tempt me with such goodies,' he begged her with a smile. 'I would love to stay here all day but I'll lose my job if I'm not in the boardroom at nine forty-five on the dot for a briefing with my chairman.'

Nevertheless, as he spoke, his hand slid down to squeeze one of her smooth white bum cheeks, but the nubile girl giggled and wriggled away out of his reach to stand up and look at her flushed naked body in the mirror. Simon turned to watch her but, forgetting he was lying at the edge of the mattress, he rolled off the bed and crashed down onto the carpet.

He let out a pained yowl and Jennie rushed over to comfort him. 'Are you all right, darling?' she enquired anxiously as she sank down on her knees at his side.

'Yes I'm okay, no bones broken,' grunted Simon as he sat up and gingerly rubbed his hip. 'Just a bit shaken up, that's all.' And to prove that he had been unaffected by his fall, he leaned forward and kissed Jennie's breasts.

'M'mm, carry on, sergeant,' she murmured happily when Simon's hand snaked down into the fluffy bush of flaxen hair at the base of her belly. He dipped a fingertip inside her moist cunny whilst he continued to lick her elongated nipples.

Reluctantly, Simon pulled himself away and scrambled to his feet. 'Sorry, love, but I really have to leave. Look, I'll give you a ring this afternoon and perhaps we can take in a film tomorrow night.'

This pledge satisfied Jennie but it was only after he had reached home and was sliding his electric razor over his chin that Simon remembered that he had already made arrangements with Clare Norrice and Trish Jackson for that evening.

'Damnation,' he muttered as he recalled how he had agreed to be at Clare's flat at eight o'clock where they would meet up with the pretty teenage dancer Trish Jackson who might also be bringing a friend in the hope that Adrian Klein might join them.

'I must call Adrian as soon as I get to the office,' he said to himself and gave another anxious look at his watch, for when he had explained to Jennie why he could not stay longer with her, he had not exaggerated the importance of the formidable Estelle Hendon who was Herald Books' most popular author. If she took umbrage about his non-appearance at the meeting, there was little doubt that his job would be on the line.

Adrian Klein had no reason to be concerned about the security of his employment at Rose and Griffin, although he would not be able to relax until he had persuaded Dickie Segal to sign up Allan Godfrey to replace the errant Quentin Ludgate whose photograph had been on the front page of almost every newspaper that morning. So the agency was faced with losing income from one of its star artistes, and Adrian was faced with carrying out a damage limitation exercise. Normally, Teddy Dixon, the agency's urbane managing director, would lend a hand especially when it came to negotiating with Dickie Segal, but as Teddy had told the impresario the previous afternoon when the news about Quentin had leaked out, he was busy preparing for his forthcoming Australian journey.

So Adrian was in a distinctly snappish mood when his pretty young secretary came into his office carrying a mug of tea which she carefully deposited on a coaster on his desk. Unfortunately she had slightly overfilled the mug and a tiny liquid wavelet spilled out near the edge of a nearby sheaf of papers.

'Careful, Debbie,' said Adrian irritably at the leggy girl whose light green miniskirt scarcely covered the tops of her stockings. 'It took long enough for you to type these letters and we've enough to do today without you having to redo any of them.'

'Sorry, Adrian,' she apologised but he sighed: 'No, I'm sorry, Debs, for flying off the handle, there's no damage done. It's not you but this bloody Quentin Ludgate business which is giving me grief.'

Debbie looked at him with a puzzled expression. 'But you

told me that Quentin's been smuggled away secretly so the reporters won't get to him,' she said and Adrian nodded: 'Sure, only Teddy, myself and our solicitor know where he is. We don't want him talking to the press because, hopefully, we'll be able to sell his story to one of the Sunday papers. He'll need the loot, poor sod, because I'm expecting a call from the *Ask Doctor Jonathan* studio confirming that Quentin's been written out for good.

'What's even more worrying, though, is whether Dickie Segal tries to renege on his promise to see Allan Godfrey at *La Miraggio* tonight. Allan's the only guy on our books who could step into Dickie's new show, but I'll bet a pound to a penny that once they've seen the headlines this morning, all the other agents in London are calling him suggesting someone who could take Quentin's place in *West End Extra.*'

'Oh dear, there can't be too much we can do about that,' remarked Debbie as she picked up her notebook and pencil and sat down to take Adrian's dictation which she did every morning after bringing him his tea.

'There isn't,' he agreed with a resigned grin. 'Not unless we can think of a way of keeping Dickie incommunicado till I take him to dinner. I don't see a way of doing that short of cutting off his telephone and whisking him off to some secret hideout.'

Debbie put down her notebook and said thoughtfully: 'Adrian, I don't know how to sabotage his phone but I can think of a way to get Dickie out of his office and keep him occupied for quite a time. But you might not like the idea.'

'Try me, I can only say no,' said Adrian and she said hesitatingly: 'Only yesterday a friend of a friend of mine found out for herself that what you've always told me about Dickie Segal is one hundred per cent true. The girl in question is a dancer and after going round to his house yesterday and getting laid, she came back with a promise of a part in one of his Christmas pantomimes.'

Adrian nodded and said: 'Yes, I can believe that, though Dickie's not a mug, he wouldn't be where he is today if getting between the sheets was the only criteria he used when booking acts for his shows. On the other hand, I'm sure that at worst, this girl will at least get an audition with the famous Mrs Moser who choreographs all his shows.

'But so what?' he asked and Debbie replied with a disarming smile: 'Haven't you kept the telephone number of that hostess from *La Miraggio* who helped you out when you were having problems with that tough American promoter, Dave Zwaig?' Perhaps she could help you out by keeping Mr Segal busy as well as very happy.'

'You naughty girl, fancy suggesting such a thing,' Adrian grinned back. 'It's certainly worth a try, though it might be bit early to call Elaine. I doubt if she stirs much before eleven o'clock. Still, what the heck?'

He opened his telephone book and when he found the number, he muttered: 'Here we are, let's see how the land lies.'

After only a few rings there was a click on the line and Debbie came forward to listen to the conversation. Adrian cleared his throat and began: 'Hello there, Elaine, Adrian Klein here. How are you? Hope I didn't wake you up, but I wonder if you were free at all today.'

'Hi, Adrian. I can't help you I'm afraid. I'm flying to Nice this afternoon for the rock festival. The promoter has invited about a dozen girls to stay at his villa for the week to escort the stars to all the parties. He's bought the air tickets and is giving us a hundred pounds spending money each. What was it you wanted me for?'

'It doesn't matter now, we just needed a classy girl to keep a guy entertained for a couple of hours this afternoon,' explained Adrian dejectedly.

Elaine replied, 'If that's all you're looking for, I've a gorgeous friend named Sandra who is staying with me for a few weeks who I'm sure would be delighted to help you out. It so happens I was going to call you about her because she wants to be a pop singer and I thought you might be able to give her some tips about how to get noticed.'

'Great. The fellow I want entertained this afternoon is a guy named Dickie Segal and he could do much more for your friend than me because he puts on shows all over the country. Um, I take it Sandra would know what she'd be expected to do?'

'I should say so,' replied Elaine with a hoarse chuckle. 'Why don't you come round and have a chat with her and put your mind at rest? Say in about an hour? I'll still be here as my flight doesn't leave till three o'clock.'

'All right, I'll see you soon,' agreed Adrian. He put down the phone and gave Debbie a thumbs-up sign as he grinned: 'Did you hear all that? I'll go round to Elaine's and check out this girl. She might be expensive but you'll be on a bonus once Dickie Segal signs on the dotted line.'

Debbie returned his smile and said: 'I'll hold you to that, boss. Now, have you any letters for me to type?'

'Yes, thanks for reminding me. I need to confirm Eric Major's spot on *Sunday Night at the London Palladium* on October 22nd with ATV,' said Adrian briskly as he shuffled through the papers on his desk. 'Then I want to send a stiff note to Lou Baum about Sheena Walshaw. He must reckon I'm going soft in the head if he thinks I'll accept anything less than five hundred pounds a week and a suite at the Grand for Sheena if he wants her to top the bill at a top Birmingham club in November.'

After he had finished dictating his letters to Debbie, Adrian walked up one floor to Teddy Dixon's sumptuous office suite to check that the agency's managing director approved of his plan to spirit Dickie Segal away from their competitors.

'I'm not sure whether it's a totally ethical scheme,' commented Adrian doubtfully but Teddy brushed aside his qualms and said with some spirit: 'Don't be daft, dear boy. Do you think any of our competitors would think twice about hitting below the belt, especially where Nipper Segal's concerned? No, of course they wouldn't, so you go ahead and see if you can keep him away from everyone till he's seen Allan Godfrey in action. Listen, we're not holding a gun to his head, are we? If the worst comes to the worst, he might not like Allan's act and then he'll be free to sign up who he wants to take poor old Quentin's place.

'That reminds me, I spoke to Quentin this morning and warned him about leaving Felipe's villa for another day or so. He said he was feeling bored so I told him to make a start writing his life story which he's been threatening to do for the last few years. I know you've got a friend who works for Herald Books, why don't you ask him if he'd be interested in publishing Quentin's autobiography?'

'That's a good idea, Teddy. I'll give Simon a bell as soon as I get back from Elaine's,' promised Adrian as he made his way to the door.

He spotted a taxi across the road from Rose and Griffin's offices and he rushed across Dover Street to claim it as the previous occupant walked away. He slid into the back seat and, opening the glass panel, he called out to the driver: 'Hutchinson Mews please, it's just off Sloane Street by—'

'I know where Hutchinson Mews is, thank you, Mr Klein,' said the cabbie as he switched on the meter. Adrian's eyes shot up in surprise as he sat bolt upright in his seat and spluttered: 'How the blazes did you know my—'

The driver guffawed as he took his place in the queue of traffic waiting to descend the short hill into Berkeley Square and then he turned round to Adrian and grunted: 'One of the few good things about this job is that no-one really looks at you when they tell you where they want to go. Still, you might not recognise me even now, mate. It's been what, six or seven years since we played football together for University College down in Malden.'

In fact at first Adrian did not recognise the cabbie when he peered at the youngish balding man but then he snapped his fingers and said: 'Bloody hell, Frank Hayard as I live and breathe! How are you, old boy? I thought you were going into the family hotel business down in Worthing.'

'Quite right, my friend, I can see you've still got a good memory. Unfortunately, it's now the former family business.

When my parents retired a couple of years back, I took over from them, but last year I sold out to one of the big chains.'

'Oh dear, what a shame,' said Adrian sympathetically but Frank Hayard went on: 'Not really, I got a fair price and truth to tell I wasn't that keen on being a hotelier. It's ruddy hard work twenty-four hours a day in the season and even then we were only just keeping our heads above water. Anyhow, I packed it in and married this girl whose Dad runs a taxi garage up in Islington. As Denise is an only child, he was only too happy to make me a partner and look after the business side for him. It took me about eight months to learn the knowledge and I got my badge back in June. Not that I do all that much driving, but I can always get hold of a cab and make myself a few bob extra whenever we need it – which is almost every ruddy week since Denise announced she was expecting our second early next year.

'But what about you, Ade? I still see some of the old gang and one of them told me you were a theatrical agent. Do you look after any of the big stars?'

'The agency I work for handles people like Bernie Harwin, Warren Lipman, Clare Mahoney and Sharon Saxon,' replied Adrian and his old college chum grunted: 'Sharon Saxon, eh? You lucky so-and-so, I bet you handle her yourself! Adrian, is there any chance of a signed photo which I could put up on the notice-board at the garage? All the drivers are nuts about her.'

'Sure, Frank, just scribble down your address. I'll ask Sharon to write a personal message to you and the London taxi trade on one of her sexy pin-up photographs.'

'Thanks, Ade, you're a scholar and a gentleman,' he called back as the traffic inched forward.

'You must pick up a few characters now and then,' said Adrian as the lights turned red.

Frank chuckled: 'Just one or two. Last week at about midnight I picked up a couple outside Broadcasting House and the man asked me to drive them to a posh block of flats off Highgate High Street. I thought I'd seen the girl on the telly though I couldn't remember her name, but I didn't recognise the older chap at all. Anyhow, to cut short the story, I looked in the mirror and saw the girl cuddle up to the geezer and before you can say Jack Robinson they're necking away like crazy.'

'I always thought that cabbies' driving mirrors were specially positioned so you couldn't see what was going on in the back seat,' said Adrian with a worried frown on his face, for only a month or so ago, after a wild press party, he had been partially undressed in a taxi by two groupies who had taken turns to suck his cock.

'Don't you believe it! Anyhow, the panel was open so I could hear every word they were saying. It turned out that this arty-farty looking fellow was a drama producer and he was complimenting this girl on her performance in the play which had just been broadcast on the Home Service.

'"Darling, you sounded so sexy in that final scene with Conrad," he said to her. "Honestly, Gillian, whilst you were speaking your lines I closed my eyes and began to fantasise about how wonderful it would be to make love to you myself."

'When he mentioned her name I suddenly remembered where I had seen the girl before – would you believe it was Gillian Radley? That pretty girl who played the nurse who ran off with an anaesthetist in *Ask Doctor Jonathan*, the TV soap with that Quentin Thingummy who's turned out to be a shirt-lifter. I kept my eyes peeled on them and watched him slide his hands inside her coat and she wriggled even closer to him as she said: "Phil, you are such a flatterer, I wasn't *that* good."

'"Oh yes you were, my poppet," he insisted and I saw his hand caress her knee as he went on: "When you were telling Conrad how much you cared for him, I began to imagine myself lying naked on a bed with my cock standing up to salute you as you knelt between my thighs wearing nothing but a skimpy pair of panties.

'"Gilly, I almost came in the control room as I thought how I would slowly pull down your knickers and kiss your pouting little crack and then play with your mouth-watering pussy as you lowered your head and began working your lips up and down the shaft of my rock-hard cock whilst you cupped my balls in your hands – then I'd lay you out on the bed and fuck you till we soaked the sheets in torrents of come!"

'"That sounds like an exciting fantasy," she giggled and naughty old Phil slid his hand up her skirt as he muttered: "Doesn't it just? But take my word for it, darling, whilst fantasy's fun, reality is even better."

'Then they started to kiss so passionately that I could hardly concentrate on the road. Lucky old Phil soon had her coat off and was unbuttoning her blouse by the time I reached Camden Town. I almost drove over a red light when he whipped off her bra and fondled her breasts whilst she unzipped his flies and pulled out his boner and began giving him a hand job.'

'By the time we reached Archway she was pummelling his cock so hard that I thought she might pull it off! Then as we were going up Highgate Hill he let out a groan and I watched a huge jet shoot out of his cock and I hoped it had all landed on his trousers as I didn't fancy cleaning his spunk off the seat.'

'Blimey, what would have happened if a police car had pulled up next to you at traffic lights?' said Adrian curiously and Frank shuddered as he answered: 'Christ, it doesn't bear thinking about. I suppose they would have been done for indecent behaviour and even though I was only driving the blinking cab, the Public Carriage Office would have found I'd broken some rule or other.

'At best I would have probably been called as a witness and Denise would have given me hell because she's suspicious about drivers who take on night work because she knows that they're often offered payment in kind, if you take my meaning.'

'And if they're anything like my Uncle Sid, I bet they sometimes take it too,' remarked Adrian with a low chuckle as he thought about his mother's brother, a cabbie who had worked nights in the West End for the last fifteen years.

'I'll take the Fifth Amendment on that one,' laughed Frank

as he swapped V-signs with the driver of a bus as he changed lanes at Hyde Park Corner. 'Fortunately though, there wasn't a copper in sight when I dropped Phil and Gillian off and I must say that he gave a me a bloody good tip – and there wasn't a trace of cum on the seat!'

When Frank dropped him off Adrian stood on the pavement for a minute or two and considered the vagaries of fate which had left him footloose and fancy free on ten thousand pounds a year – clearly far in excess of what Frank Hayard, who had gained an upper second-class degree in Politics, Philosophy and Political Science, was pulling in.

'Luck of the draw, I dare say,' he muttered to himself as he pressed the bell of Elaine's flat.

As he walked up the short flight of stairs he found a slim dark-haired girl waiting for him.

'Hello, Adrian, I'm Sandra Davies,' she greeted him, and Adrian's mouth creased into a smile. She was stunningly attractive in tight blue jeans and black ankle boots with a matching black silk shirt.

'Good to meet you' he replied easily as they shook hands. 'So you're Elaine's friend?'

'We've been friends since we were at school together,' she answered as she escorted him into the lounge. 'And before I forget, I have a message from Elaine for you. She's sorry to have missed you but her brother came round and offered her a lift to Heathrow if she could leave straightaway.

'But don't worry, I know what you want me to do and I'm really grateful for the chance to meet someone as important as Mr Segal.'

'Super, I'm sure you'll get on well with old Nipper,' remarked Adrian as Sandra waved him to an armchair. 'Though he's not a chap to stand on ceremony so there's no need for you to mister him.'

'Oh fine, that'll make it easier to start the ball rolling,' she said with relief. 'But what's all this Nipper business – I thought his name was Dickie?'

'Well yes, it is,' admitted Adrian with a grin. 'Nipper's just his nickname. He tells people it comes from his habit of telling people to nip the trouble at the bud but the truth involves an exotic dancer named Peaches.'

He proceeded to tell the anecdote about the ill-starred fellation which had left Dickie Segal with a sore cock. When he finished Sandra burst into a fit of laughter. 'So I had better not offer him a blow-job if I want him to listen to my demo record,' she observed but Adrian shook his head and said: 'I'm not privy to Dickie's sexual preferences – except that he's supposed to have quite an appetite for bonking and I've never come across any man with a heartbeat who doesn't enjoy being sucked off.'

'Come to think of it, neither have I,' she giggled. 'Now, changing the subject, have you had lunch yet? I was just about to make myself a sandwich.'

'Thanks, I wouldn't say no and—' Adrian stopped short and clapped his hand over his mouth. 'Oh God, I must ring Dickie, I haven't even asked him if he's free this afternoon. I hope I haven't raised your hopes and mine for nothing!'

'The phone's over there,' said Sandra, pointing across the hall. Adrian dashed across and found himself in a well-furnished bedroom. He sat on the edge of the large king-sized bed and dialled Dickie Segal's personal number, known only to a handful of business associates and close friends.

'Come on, come on,' Adrian mumbled as the phone rang out. On the sixth ring there was a click and when he heard Dickie's dulcet voice on the line, he said eagerly: 'Hello Dickie, it's Adrian here. Sorry for the short notice but I've come across a gem of a new singer who you must hear for yourself this afternoon. I'm with her now at her flat just off Sloane Street, it would only take Graham fifteen minutes to drive you here. She's even sexier than Sharon Saxon and I want you to have first refusal for one of the provincial pantos. As soon as her first record comes out, she'll put as many bums on seats as Lulu or Cilla and you can book her in at silly money if you sign her up now.'

'Is that so?' grunted the impresario. 'In that case, bring

her photograph with you tonight and you can tell me all about her then. You're picking me up at eight from my office, right? Must dash, Adrian, old Tony Hammond is popping in to see me this afternoon and I've a meeting with Lennie Lieberman at five o'clock.'

Adrian gnawed his lower lip in frustration for he rightly suspected that Tony Hammond, the managing director of one of Rose and Griffin's largest competitors, was as keen as Adrian to push one of his artistes into the role vacated by Quentin Ludgate. 'Dickie, between you and me, Teddy Dixon's been so busy preparing for his big trip to Australia he forgot to mention her to you. I know I'm asking for a lot of your time but Sandra told me that her manager is taking her to see Lou Baum on Friday morning and I owe you a favour for slotting in time to confirm Allan Godfrey for *West End Extra*.'

'Here, hold on a second, Adrian,' Dickie Segal protested. 'I haven't promised you I'll take this lad on. It all depends if he's as good as you say he is. I've yet to meet an agent who's too modest about his clients' capabilities!'

'Point taken but this girl's really special, Dickie, and I'm sure you won't regret coming over here. It'll only take Graham fifteen minutes to drive you over. I'll have sandwiches and fresh coffee waiting for you and if you tell me afterwards it hasn't been worth your while, I'll have to drop Allan Godfrey's price by ten per cent! Now I can't say fairer than that.'

There was silence for a few moments and then Dickie Segal let out a gruff laugh. 'All right, Adrian, give me her address, I'll be over in about forty five minutes if only to satisfy my curiosity. It's been some time since I've been entertained by Rose and Griffin and now I'm being wined and dined by you twice in one day.'

'Believe me, you won't regret it,' promised Adrian. He mopped his brow with relief as he gave Dickie the address of the flat. Then he rushed back to the lounge and told Sandra the good news. She clapped her hands together and said: 'Great! Look, we've two bottles of white wine in the fridge but I think I'll pop down to Giovanni's Café round the corner, his sandwiches are a darned sight better than mine. I shouldn't be more than about ten minutes.'

Adrian extracted a pound note from his wallet. 'There's no rush, and perhaps you can get some orange juice for Dickie, he never drinks anything else at lunch-time. Here, will a quid cover it?'

'Thanks, that's more than enough,' she said gratefully. 'But I fancy a glass of wine, don't you? Try the Chablis, it's really first-class.'

Sandra put the pound note in her bag and when she had left, he sauntered into the kitchen. Knowing how important it would be for him to keep a clear head over the next few hours, he opened the bottle of wine for Sandra but filled the kettle to make himself a cup of tea. Then after he pulled out some plates from the cupboard he noticed a small pile of notepaper on the kitchen table. 'Hello, hello, what's all this?' he murmured as he scanned the first page of a handwritten letter. To be fair to Adrian, he would have simply gathered up the sheets and put them aside unread had he not clapped eyes on the second paragraph, for this made it abundantly clear that the writer (who was obviously Sandra) was writing a very uninhibited letter indeed . . .

> "I suppose you want to hear all the lurid details about my love life in Swinging London. I wish there was a lot to tell you but, except for last Friday afternoon, I've been living almost like a nun! Actually, I'm dying for a good fuck because it's more difficult than you might think meeting fellas in the big city. I've had to take my pleasure where I can find them . . .
>
> As you warned me, Elaine is definitely bi-sexual but though we share a bed together she doesn't force me to do anything that I don't want to – even though she refuses to take any rent from me till I land myself a job. To be honest, I must confess that I rather enjoy

being pampered by her as she's a sensitive lover and only wants to please me.

For instance, Elaine understands how most girls need time to get turned on. Sure, I'll get excited by looking at a handsome well-hung lad standing in the nude especially if he has a hard-on, but so many men think that just twiddling your titties as they shove their cocks inside your quim is enough – and usually it isn't!

But Elaine doesn't rush our love-making. We spend time in some good old-fashioned cuddling and she knows that I like her to undress me whilst we're kissing. My pussy always gets wet when she unhooks my bra and slides it off my shoulders whilst our tongues are in each other's mouths. Then she squeezes my breasts before unzipping my skirt and pulling down my panties.

Of course by now I'm doing the same to her and we hug and rub our bodies together for a while before we actually make it in bed. There she'll lick the insides of my legs all the way up to my bush and when she's brought me to the peak she laps on my cunt and I begin coming all over her tongue.

This all changed on Friday night when I met a guy who can eat pussy as well as Elaine. It happened at this gymnasium where we work out every week. I'd ricked my back when I was climbing over a vaulting horse. Anyway, Elaine could see I was in some discomfort and she introduced me to this hunky young fellow named Gideon who she said was one of the best physiotherapists in the area and would soon get rid of any aches and pains. He was a really good-looking chap and looked very sexy in his white tee-shirt and tight black shorts.

First we had a couple of drinks at the bar and then Gideon and I went upstairs to one of the private rooms where he told me to undress and lie face down on the bed by the far wall whilst he washed his hands. I was a bit worried about this but after he disappeared into the bathroom I whipped off my leotard and lay down stark naked as he had instructed.

When he returned, Gideon spread a little baby oil on my back and, standing at my side, rubbed it into my skin with his fingertips and proceeded to give me a fabulous massage, just smoothing his hands up and down my back. I closed my eyes and felt the pain seeping out of me as it quickly became clear that he wouldn't be starting any funny business though, truthfully, I found that a tiny bit disappointing!

'Oooh, that's amazing,' I said drowsily and now my cunt really began to tingle so I deliberately raised my bum a little and parted my thighs so that he could get a glimpse of my pussy. My face was level with his waist and when I turned my head I could see a huge bulge between his legs. It was quite obvious that I wasn't the only one who was getting excited!

'Gideon, I'd love you to finish me off,' I said throatily. He looked so shocked that I added: 'With an all-over massage, I mean.'

Without waiting for any further instructions, I rolled over and spread my legs. Gideon blushed as he stared at my pussy lips, which were peeking out through my curly bush. Now I decided to move matters along and told him to start massaging my legs and carry on upwards. He hesitated at first but then he did as I asked and, when he started to stroke my thighs, I became so hot that I suddenly sat up and in one quick movement I pulled down his shorts.

'Oh, I say,' gasped Gideon as I took hold of his sturdy prick which stood up to greet me. Then, with a saucy twinkle in his eyes, he slipped his hands up to my breasts and began to rotate my nipples against his palms. I squeezed his pulsating prick, running my fingers along the warm, velvet skin. I pulled it towards me and swirled my tongue over his knob before lying back on the pillow.

'Goodness me, you are a sexy one! It's been some time since I worked on such a good-looking girl as you' he croaked. Then he leaned forward to lick my titties whilst his hand slid down between my thighs.

'M'mm, this is even nicer than the massage,' I breathed softly as his index finger probed around my moist folds until it found the yielding entrance to my honeypot. 'Come on, Gideon, my wet little pussy is ready and waiting for you to fuck me nice and hard with your lovely thick prick!'

I didn't have to repeat myself for he now moved quickly, sliding himself on top of me. I grasped his quivering cock and guided his knob between my puffy pussy lips. 'Wow, aren't you a big boy, I feel really filled up,' I panted as I hoisted my hips upwards to greet his wide-domed helmet.

Gideon smiled as he pressed home. I wrapped my arms around his neck and clamped my legs around his waist as he slowly inserted inch after inch of his throbbing tool into my juicy cunt. He stayed still for a while once he was fully embedded inside me and then he began to fuck me quite divinely, sliding deeper and deeper in and out of my squishy slit again and again in a deceptively lazy rhythm.

Then he raised the tempo as our lips meshed together, pistoning his prick into me with long, powerful strokes. I raised my bum cheeks on every forward thrust and my clingy cunny muscles clutched at his shaft. He pounded away with such force that the bedsprings began to creak underneath us.

'Can I come inside you?' he gasped breathlessly and I just had time to nod before he rasped: 'Here it comes then, Sandra, take it now, take it!'. He held my hips tightly to make sure that his greasy cock didn't slip out of my quim as he shot a tremendous spurt of spunk into my love funnel. Then he collapsed down on top of me as I purred with pleasure at this wonderful shafting.

When we recovered we dressed ourselves and went back downstairs to Elaine who guessed what had happened and suggested to Gideon that he took me out to dinner as she was working that night. He took me to a lovely Greek restaurant in the King's Road and then back at his flat we screwed ourselves silly till the wee small hours as thankfully Gideon is even more oversexed than me!

Incidentally, he told me that he loved to fuck me from behind because that way he had the best view of my bum and pussy and he could also get his prick in deeper into my cunt. This was fine as far as I was concerned because, as you know, I've always enjoyed being fucked doggie style, although to be truthful I preferred climbing over Gideon to sit on his cock and slide myself up and down his thick throbbing chopper.

In the morning he drove me to Kensington Gardens and we jogged around for about ten minutes but we had to stop because Gideon forgot to put on a jockstrap under his running shorts. When he was running behind me, he got such a hard-on looking at my bum cheeks jiggling in my leotard that we had to go into a clump of bushes where I had to rub him off whilst he played with my boobs.

Sadly though, I haven't seen Gideon since that afternoon when he dropped me home – and that's because the very next day he had a call from Paramount Pictures inviting him to name his fee to come out on the next plane to Los Angeles because Diane Daniels was having trouble with her back again. Gideon had looked after her when she was filming in England last year and she swore that he was the only physio whose treatment worked.

Still, he's due back in ten days time and I hope he hasn't been shagging himself to death every night with all those pretty Hollywood starlets because my pussy's fairly aching for his lovely big stiffie.

Must dash now, sweetie, as lucky old Elaine is off to

Nice in a few hours time but she's arranged for a top showbiz agent called Adrian Klein coming round to see me at lunch-time. She says he's a very nice man who'll help me find work if he thinks I have what it takes to be a pop singer. 'Adrian's a very genuine guy, he won't insist upon a session on the casting couch in return for any favours,' she said to me. Anyway, I'll close now and let you know what he says about me in my next letter."

Adrian's cheeks flushed whilst he read through this last paragraph and his hand trembled as he put the sheets of paper back on the table. 'I must tell Sandra the truth about why I want her to keep Dickie Segal happy this afternoon,' he mumbled to himself as the front door opened and Sandra called out: 'Coo-ee, I'm back.'

He met the pretty fresh-faced girl at the top of the stairs and followed her back into the kitchen where she dumped the carrier bag she was holding on the table and said to him brightly: 'Okay, Adrian, I've got some tasty beef and tuna salads as well some chilled fresh orange juice for Dickie Segal. And there's one and sixpence change for you as well.'

'Never mind the bloody change, there's something more important that you should know,' said Adrian irritably and her face crumpled as she looked at him in hurt surprise and asked 'What's the matter, have I done anything wrong?'

'I'm sorry, Sandra,' he said instantly and almost unconsciously stepped forward to give her a reassuring hug. 'It's me who's in the dock, not you. I've behaved like a right toe-rag.'

Rapidly, he explained why he needed to keep Dickie Segal away from his office till the impresario agreed to sign up Allan Godfrey. 'I'm not saying that Dickie couldn't put you in touch with one or two people in the pop business but he's a busy man and I can't guarantee anything will come out of this afternoon, even if you give him a gobble,' he added miserably as he slumped into a chair.

To his relief, Sandra did not show any anger but coolly remarked: 'Of course I understand that you can't give any guarantees about anything and that includes whether I'll even give him a blow job! But it's up to me to see that Dickie doesn't forget all about me afterwards and anyhow, Elaine said that you would be in touch with some record producers who would make a demo disc for me.'

Adrian shook his head. 'Pop isn't my field, though my colleague, Tony Cavendish, who looks after Sharon Saxon, knows quite a few people in the music business. Whatever happens this afternoon, I swear that I'll put him in touch with you.'

She flashed a grateful smile at him. 'I know you will, Elaine said you were a decent bloke. Anyhow, I'm not exactly a vestal virgin. Come to think of it, I'm no kind of virgin at all, I love a good fuck, especially with a nice man like you.'

'That's good to know,' remarked Adrian. He felt far more cheerful now that he had no need to feel guilty about Sandra having false hopes about fucking her way into show business – not that she would have been the first attractive girl to have tickled a fancy or two in order to get their feet on the first rung of the ladder. He said no more about the matter as he helped Sandra set out their lunch and soon afterwards, when a sharp ring on the bell announced the arrival of Dickie Segal, Adrian went downstairs to open the door for him.

'Thanks for coming, Dickie,' he said genially and the impresario grunted: 'You might not thank me so much if I say you've wasted my time. To be frank with you, the only reason I accepted is that it's been bedlam in my office this morning. Every sodding agent in town has been ringing me up to offer me someone to take Quentin's place in *West End Extra*.'

With a twinkle in his eyes he added: 'And if I didn't know you better, Adrian, I might have thought that was the real reason you suddenly *shlap* me out here so that I wouldn't be tempted to think of anyone else but your boy to fill the vacancy.'

Adrian did not attempt to deny the implied charge for even if the shrewd showbiz mogul had correctly guessed what was going on, nevertheless he had still turned up. So Adrian was happy enough simply to laugh: 'Dickie, how could you think such a thing – as if I'd stoop to such a low trick.'

'Very easily,' he answered drily as they climbed the stairs. 'Now, where's this girl you want me to listen to?'

'In here,' said Adrian as he led the way into the kitchen. He could not prevent a satisfied smirk from spreading over his face when he saw Dickie's eyebrows shoot up as he gave Sandra an appreciative stare.

The stunning girl had unfastened the top button of her blouse. Her rounded breasts were almost completely exposed as she bent over the table to put out the plates of salad. She straightened herself up as they entered and brushing the shiny long strands of dark hair from her face, she smiled at their visitor and said: 'Hi there, Mr Segal, it's so sweet of you to find time to listen to me sing.'

'Think nothing of it,' replied Dickie as he wondered whether the afternoon might repeat itself into an action replay of twenty-four hours ago, when he had fucked the gorgeous Cindy. 'So what's first, lunch or the audition?'

'Let's have a bite first,' said Adrian and he pointed to the jug of orange juice. 'That's genuine freshly squeezed stuff, by the way, not ordinary squash. Sandra went out specially to get it once she heard you didn't drink at lunch-time.'

Dickie nodded his thanks. 'Bless you, sweetie, it isn't that I don't enjoy a glass of wine but I have to keep all my wits about me watching out for all the villains I have to deal with in the crazy business. You wouldn't credit some of the stunts they try to pull.'

'I hope that remark isn't aimed at me,' grinned Adrian and the impresario shot him a long look and said meaningfully: 'If the cap fits . . .'

However, the three of them chatted amicably whilst they ate. Though tempted to help Sandra finish the bottle of Chablis, instead Adrian made himself a cup of coffee. However, when they retired to the lounge, both men succumbed to Sandra's offer of a cognac whilst they listened to her tape.

'Here goes,' she said as she pressed the 'on' button and sat back on the sofa between them with her hands on each of their knees. Sadly, the recording which Sandra had made of two of The Beatles' songs with a backing from a local group back in Cardiff was of such a poor quality that it gave little evidence of her talents.

So when she bent forward to switch off the machine and looked enquiringly at the impresario, he smoothed his hand over his cheek and said: 'It's a terrible shame but it's not possible to judge anything from what we've just heard. Adrian, wouldn't you agree with me on that?'

'I'm afraid so,' admitted Adrian reluctantly. 'Mind you, Dickie, it sounded to me that Sandra can sing in tune.'

Dickie nodded his agreement and continued: 'Perhaps, although I reckon she could probably do with some lessons in voice control. Anyhow, these days so much pop stuff is recorded by session singers and musicians, that hardly matters. A few years ago almost anyone with enough chutzpah and a bit of luck could waltz into the studios and churn out a hit record. But record sales have been going down for the last few years and now you need a first-class songwriter to write something for you.

'Still, at least you look the part and there's no doubt you score in that department,' he added comfortingly. Sandra gave him a rueful glance and said: 'Thanks, that's something I suppose, but I don't know where to go from here.'

'I'd recommend a good agent who has the time and know-how to promote beginners,' advised Dickie, putting his arm round her waist and giving her a friendly squeeze. 'I think Adrian will bear me out on this, his company is a bit too high-powered for someone like you. But give me your phone number and I'll pass it to Terry Blacker, he's always on the look-out for fresh talent.'

Sandra listened thoughtfully as he explained: 'Terry used to sing himself with Geraldo and some of the big dance bands. Now he has his own music publishing business and manages some of the best known groups in the charts. He's an old buddy of mine from way back and he'll give you an honest opinion about your chances of making it – and he won't diddle you out of your cash either unlike some other managers I could think of.'

She looked at Adrian who gave her a little smile and said: 'I completely agree with what Dickie says, but Terry won't take you on unless he's convinced you've got a career in front of you.'

'I can't ask for more than that, and I'm truly grateful to the pair of you for your advice and help,' commented Sandra and picked up an L.P. which was lying on top of the record player. 'Never mind me now, I hope you both like real music? Elaine has some fabulous records, I was playing this marvellous recording of Grieg's Piano Concerto by Konrad Kochanski. You know the opening, of course, DAH, da da dum, da da dum da da dum da da dum, dah dah dah dah dah and so on.'

'I should say so,' said Adrian wistfully. 'I had to perform the first movement at a school concert and I reckon poor old Grieg must have been turning in his grave. My parents bored the whole family silly for the next three months about my recital which turned out to be my first and last.'

'You're being far too modest,' protested Dickie and as Sandra refilled their glasses he told her: 'Adrian's a bloody good pianist – classical, jazz, pop – the lot! In fact he reminds me of the story about the fellow who's playing the piano in a pub and pretty girl comes up to him and says: "Excuse me, but do you know your flies are undone and your prick's dangling out of your trousers?" and he answers: "No, love but you hum it and I'll play it!"'

Sandra burst out into a fit of giggles and again sitting down between them, she moved her hand lightly across his thighs and teased: 'And if I unzipped your flies, would your prick dangle out of your trousers or would it salute me by standing up to attention?'

'Go and see for yourself,' answered Dickie. Sandra ran her palm over the bulge which had appeared in the impresario's lap and let out a throaty chuckle. 'My, is that a wallet in your pocket or are you just glad to see me? I suppose there's only one way to find out.'

She swung herself round to unbuckle his belt and Dickie himself ripped open the button at the top of his flies as he arched his back upwards to allow her to tug down the zip of his flies and roll his trousers down to his knees. With a sensuous smile playing about her lips, Sandra quickly yanked off his briefs and with a tiny yelp of triumph, she slid her fingers around his huge erection, gently kneading his pulsating prick in her hand.

Then without further ado, she began to masturbate him, moving her clenched fist up and down his swollen shaft. Dickie growled with delight as the gorgeous girl bent down and swirled her tongue over the mushroom helmet of his cock. When she repeated the exercise, he croaked: 'Don't do much more than that or I'll come in your hand.'

'Dear me, that would never do,' Sandra giggled and at once let go his cock and stood up to kick off her shoes and shrug off her silk blouse which fluttered to the floor to bare her thrusting uptilted breasts. But she found some difficulty in opening her designer jeans and complained: 'Damn it, what's the matter with this button – will one of you guys undo it for me?'

The two men sat mesmerised for a moment and Sandra demanded: 'Come on, one of you, how can we fuck if I can't take off these jeans?'

'It would be almost impossible,' agreed Adrian and he turned to Dickie and said politely: 'Will you help this maiden in distress, or shall I?'

'No, I'll do the honours,' replied Dickie hoarsely as he moved forward. He fell on his knees in front of Sandra who ruffled her hand through his hair as she stood over him. He looked up at her proudly jutting bosoms whilst he fumbled with the recalcitrant metal button.

'At last!' he grunted as he pushed the disc through the narrow buttonhole. Sandra congratulated him by kissing on his forehead and saying: 'Well done! Now see if you can save time by pulling down my knickers, tights and jeans together.'

Dickie duly obliged and she placed a hand on his shoulder as she daintily freed herself from the squashed-up pile of garments whilst he scrambled up and embraced the naked girl. Their lips met in a frantic tongue-waggling kiss. Hardly able to believe his good fortune, Dickie's hands roamed over her ample breasts whilst she unknotted his tie and undid the buttons of his shirt and he jiggled his feet out of his fashionable laceless Italian shoes.

As he continued to undress, Sandra wagged a reproving finger at Adrian. 'Come on, Ade, this won't do at all,' she reproached him playfully. 'Get cracking now, Dickie and I haven't a stitch on between us and you haven't even taken off your jacket.'

He smiled and shrugged: 'If you insist, but I understood that two's company—'

'And three's even more fun,' she finished as she gently pushed Dickie down again on the sofa and seated herself on his thighs.

Adrian tore off his clothes in double-quick time and when he finally yanked down his boxer shorts, Sandra reached out and grabbed hold of his rock-hard erection Then she levered herself off Dickie's lap and knelt as if in homage before the two men. Curling her fingers around their throbbing tools, she kissed each of their cocks in turn. They sighed with pleasure as Sandra tried to cram both their knobs inside her mouth simultaneously, but this proved impossible and she was forced to alternate between the two pricks, sucking first one and then the other, her lips gliding wetly over their smooth-skinned shafts as she slid her hands between their legs and cupped their balls.

'Sweetie, I still think we have a slight problem because, despite what you say, two into one doesn't go,' said Dickie breathlessly. 'Why don't you treat yourself to a ride on my cock while Adrian goes and has a nice cup of tea?'

Sandra pulled his cock out of her mouth and rejoined: 'Oh there's no need for that, though I fancy a good fuck. Ade, why don't you pop to the kitchen and see if there's some butter?'

Dickie was pleased to have Sandra to himself but was slightly mystified by this last request. But Adrian let out a crude chuckle as he heaved himself off the sofa and padded quietly out of the room. He had immediately realised what the luscious girl had in mind.

Still, it certainly did not bother the impresario, especially when, with a nimble spring to her feet, Sandra placed herself back on his lap and kissed him on the lips. Their tongues twirled together as she rubbed his twitching todger. He caressed the ample rounded globes of her breasts, rolling her pointed cherry nipples on the palms of his hands whilst she pulled his hand down into the curly patch of pussy hair at the base of her belly.

'It's time for me to ride that big thick cock of yours, Mr Segal,' she announced as she settled Dickie on his back lengthways on the sofa. 'Here we go,' she giggled as she straddled his legs and slid her fingers around his scrotum, rubbing her palm against the wrinkled pink skin as she weighed his balls in her hand.

'They're nice and heavy,' she observed judiciously. 'I hope this means you're going to shoot a huge spunky stream into my juicy little cunt.'

'I'll do my best,' he panted as Sandra moved her body upwards. Clutching his cock, she squatted over his hips until she felt the tip of his knob brush against her pussy lips. Dickie groaned in delight as she lowered herself down on her knees and, with slow deliberation, slid down upon his straining shaft until she had taken every inch inside the clinging wetness of her sticky honeypot.

'Ooooh! That's heavenly, Dickie, my cunny's full of cock!,' she gurgled. She thrilled to the feel of his palpitating prick and Dickie arched his hips upwards to meet her downwards thrusts. Her cuntal muscles contracted and expanded as they gripped his shaft whilst the nubile girl bounced up and down his rigid rod at an increasing speed, her jiggling bosoms dangling invitingly over his face as she rolled her springy buttocks from side to side.

Sandra squealed happily as a sharp series of crackling climaxes shot through her body. She flung herself savagely up and down on his quivering cock. This uninhibited fucking continued to drive the pair onwards and Dickie cupped his hands around her breasts and moved his head up to suck on Sandra's elongated rubbery titties. She threw her head back and wailed in ecstasy as she leaned forward to let the ridge of Dickie's knob rub exquisitely against her erect clitty.

They were so absorbed in their wild lovemaking that neither of them heard or saw Adrian trot back into the lounge until Sandra felt him prising apart her dimpled bum cheeks. Then a high-pitched yelp escaped from her throat when she felt his oily fingers slide into her bottom, smearing her arsehole with the chunk of butter he had scooped up from the dish on the kitchen table.

'Woooh!' she squeaked as, with her cunt still stuffed with Dickie's cock, Sandra continued to wiggle her backside whilst Adrian finished the lubrication of her back passage. 'You naughty boy, are you going to fuck my bum?'

'That's the idea,' answered Adrian cheerfully as he climbed up behind her and pressed his prick (which he had also coated with butter) in the cleft between her buttocks. She gave a tiny wail when the greasy tip of his helmet nudged against the puckered opening of her anus.

'Careful now, darling,' puffed Sandra breathlessly as Adrian slid his shaft slowly into the dark furrow of her superb bottom. She rocked to and fro in complete abandon as he filled her narrow sheath with his beefy shaft.

She was now sandwiched between the two men and their arms locked around the willing girl. She gasped loudly as Adrian and Dickie's cocks stretched and filled both her orifices, their shafts separated only by the thin membrane of the wall between her cunt and arsehole.

'Shoot your loads, you dirty rascals,' shrieked Sandra. She shuddered all over as she felt the fierce momentum of an approaching orgasm building up rapidly inside her tingling quim. She ground herself down on Dickie's tool and arched herself back to enjoy the urgent stabs from Adrian's shaft as it slithered along the greased funnel of her anal sheath.

Dickie's jerking movements quickened and his tool began to twitch as the swell of jism rose up from his balls. Through gritted teeth he panted out to Sandra that he was about to come.

'Yes, yes, go on, Dickie, I'll come too! Fill my cock with creamy jizz!' she howled. Dickie's prick pulsed uncontrollably as, for a few moments, he hovered on the verge. He lurched his hips upwards and his shaft was fully embedded inside her sopping slit as a surging gush of sperm flooded out of his knob.

'Y-e-s-s-s! Y-e-s-s-s! Y-e-s-s-s!' she shrieked and her lithe body convulsed with pleasure whilst she rode his spurting cock. Dickie closed his eyes and sighed in ecstatic bliss as she bounced up and down on him. The squeezing of Sandra's cunny milked his throbbing tool until his shrivelled shaft finally slid wetly out of her cunt.

However, the tremendous climax building up inside her had still not exploded. She urged Adrian to keep pistoning his prick in and out of her bottom. Nothing loath, he continued to bull into her, his balls slapping against the backs of her thighs. Sandra's hands flew to her pussy to rub the hard nub of her erect, fleshy clitty which had burst out of its hood and was standing out stiffly at the top of her crack. The notion that Sandra was playing with herself whilst he was fucking her arse sent fresh thrills through Adrian's mind as he slewed his shaft in and out of the tight sheath of her bottom.

'Hargh!' he spluttered as he pumped a flood of sticky seed into her glorious backside and they melted together into a magnificent simultaneous orgasm. Sandra wiggled her bum as Adrian deluged her prickling arsehole with spout after spout of jism until, with an audible 'pop', he withdrew his still semi-erect shaft and sank back momentarily on his haunches before he fell on top of her and the three of them collapsed in an exhausted sweaty heap on the sofa.

After they recovered, Adrian poured out three more large cognacs – 'for medicinal purposes' as he explained – but after sipping his drink, Dickie looked up at the clock and exclaimed: 'Fuck me, Adrian, just look at the time! I must be getting back to the office pronto.'

'What's the rush, Dickie?' Adrian asked disingenuously. 'You said you're not meeting Lennie Lieberman till five o'clock and Graham's waiting outside in the car. It won't take him more than twenty minutes at the outside to get you to wherever you have to go.'

'Yes, but God knows how many phone calls my girls have had to field,' he replied. 'I also told you that Tony Hammond's coming round to see me this afternoon.'

Sandra winked at Adrian as she quickly came to his rescue. As Dickie bent down and picked up his pants from the floor, she wrapped her fingers around his cock and began to slide her hand up and down his shaft in a gentle frigging motion. Her left hand tenderly cradled his hairy balls, rolling them back and forth until, to Dickie's own surprise, his cock started to thicken in her fist and Sandra closed her lips over his burgeoning bell-end.

'Oh my Gawd! Stop that, darling, I have to get back to work,' he muttered, but above her bobbing head, Sandra heard him moan as she began her own special sucking motion around the rim of his knob with a technique she had honed to perfection. Dickie slumped back onto the sofa, holding her head in his hands as she tickled the ultra-sensitive underside of his cock with the tip of her wet tongue.

'Phwaargh!' he groaned as Sandra gobbled deeply, sliding her mouth to and fro whilst she pumped his prick up and down with her clenched fist. She rubbed his knob on the roof of her mouth, licking and lapping on his chopper which had recovered all of its former hardness and was as stiff as a poker in her grasp.

Keeping his cock firmly inside her mouth, she climbed on top of him for a second time and sat on Dickie's face. He grabbed Sandra's soft bum cheeks in his hands and positioned her until her pouting pussy lips were directly on top of his mouth. Then he closed his eyes and kissed her quim, working his questing tongue around the musky folds of Sandra's cunt, which made the girl whimper with genuine enjoyment as she continued to suck his twitching tool.

He could taste the flow of her tangy cuntal fluid as she slowly moved her hips in tiny, controlled undulations. He eagerly licked up the love juice which was now seeping out of her cunny, matting her curly black bush with moisture.

Sandra's eyes closed and her mouth widened into a contented smile as Dickie's tongue penetrated her cunt. She shuddered all over when his lips closed over the nub of her raised-up love bud. Then it was Dickie's turn to shiver as she renewed her oral ministrations on his cock, licking his shaft right down to his balls, lapping like a beautiful sleek kitten with long, sexy strokes.

And it was Dickie Segal who came first when Sandra delicately squeezed his scrotum. With a great groan he expelled an immense spunky torrent down her throat which she gulped down with relish. Then she trembled all over as a tremendous orgasm powered through every fibre of her body and she achieved a splendid climax, drenching Dickie's face as he manfully continued to frig her engorged clitty, swallowing her pungent emission until Sandra was finally sated and she swivelled round into his waiting arms and gave him a grateful kiss.

'Relax lover, five more minutes won't make any difference,' said Sandra soothingly when Dickie tried to reach down to the carpet for his pants which were lying just out of reach.

However, when Adrian silently mouthed 'Let him go,' she hopped off the panting impresario and said: 'On the other hand, when you've gotta go, you've gotta go. Would you like to telephone your office before you leave?'

'No thanks, love, whoever wants me will have to wait till I get back,' he answered. He heaved himself up to a sitting position and rubbed his hands across his cheeks. Then he picked up his pants and as he stood up to pull them on he said to Adrian: 'So long as I've still got enough strength left, I'll see you tonight for round two, young man. To be honest, I've thoroughy enjoyed seeing you and Sandra this afternoon but I'm so knocked out that for two pins I'd cancel our arrangement this evening and go home and have an early night.'

A horrified expression passed over Adrian's face but quickly receded when Dickie added: 'On the other hand, I've already told Josephine not to wait up for me and anyhow, it would be bloody silly not to pass up an opportunity to have dinner on Rose and Griffin! So come round to my place at about eight o'clock – oh, and don't worry if you haven't brought your car into town today, Graham will drop you home after I've run my eye over your Mr Godfrey.'

'Bye then, Dickie, it was good to meet you,' said Sandra, giving him a hug and a kiss as the impresario chuckled and said: 'Goodness had very little to do with it! No, seriously though, I've got your phone number and I promise to pass it on to Terry Blacker as soon as I can get hold of him. He's in Scotland this week looking for another Lulu but I'll speak to him as soon as he gets home.'

Adrian walked downstairs with him. As he opened the door Dickie said quietly to him: 'Sandra's a lovely girl but I really hope you didn't fill her head with ideas of starring at *Sunday Night at the London Palladium* because she's got a long way to go – if she ever gets started, that is. But I meant what I said and I'll lean on Terry to do what he can for her.'

'Bless you, Dickie, I'd be very grateful if you would,' answered Adrian. 'I've never tried to lead her up the garden path for the sake of a quick screw.'

'Good, because it's not exactly uncommon in this business,

and that includes providing goodies for friends,' said Dickie meaningfully. He walked towards his car where his faithful chauffeur had been waiting patiently across the street and Adrian had the grace to blush.

As Adrian was waving goodbye to Dickie, Allan Godfrey was sitting at his dining-room table running through the material he planned to use that night. He hoped he would impress the astute impresario. Like all comedians who exhibited a cheery and confident persona on stage, in his private life Allan was prone to bouts of self-doubt and there was a frown on his face as he nervously drummed his fingers on the table.

Diana, his girl friend and part-time waitress at *La Miraggio*, sighed when she came into the room with a mug of tea which she placed at his side. 'Al, please stop brooding! There's no need – you've said yourself that the audiences have been eating out of your hand from your very first performance at the club – and I should know, I've seen it for myself every night I've worked there for the last two weeks.'

'Maybe so, but it would just be my luck to get some sodding drunk heckling me tonight,' he muttered. She sat down next to him and put her hand on his arm. 'It's unlikely, isn't it? *La Miraggio*'s a sophisticated West End night club, not some back-street dive up North.'

'I know, Di, but you never know,' he answered gloomily.

She looked at him and shook her head sadly as they sat in silence. Then Diana snapped her fingers and said: 'Look, I've a good idea. Start your act and I'll heckle you myself. I'll be as nasty as possible and do my best to come in on the punch line of your first gags just when you need to establish yourself with the audience. So pull no punches and make sure you see me off.'

Allan brightened up and said: 'Hey, that's good thinking, Carruthers. Let's have a go! Now we'll pretend you're a man because I've never come across a female heckler in my career – probably because women don't get bolshie when they've had a few. Anyhow, are you ready? Lights, music, applause.'

He stood up and bowed to his imaginary audience. 'Good evening, ladies and gentlemen, good evening—'

'It was till you came on,' called out Diana but he ignored her and continued: 'Thank you for the welcome but if applause is music to an artiste's ears then the only song I've been hearing lately is *Silent Night*. In fact Mr Calabro came up to me the other night and said "Alan, there's only one thing wrong with your act and that's that the seats face the stage."

'For those of you who don't know Angelo Calabro, he's the proud owner of this establishment. It's a nice place, a very nice place which'll look even better when it's finished. And I don't like to criticise anyone but Angelo has a very mean streak – do you know I have to put a penny in the slot every time I want to get into my dressing-room.'

'Bollocks! Get off and bring on the girls!' Diana shouted and Allan retorted: 'Still, on the other hand, Angelo can be very kind-hearted. As you just heard he's allowed someone in from the Home for the Sexually Deprived tonight. You're a big fellow too, aren't you? How tall are you, six foot two? Well, keep growing you're well on the way to being a half wit.'

Diana stifled a giggle and bellowed out: 'Why don't you piss off, shitface? You stink!'

'What a clever fellow you are, sir – I call you sir but that's only in fun – keep it up and it won't be long before you can use a potty. Still, one mustn't mock the afflicted and this loudmouth has just had a serious operation, his teeth were taken out and a new sewer put in.

'Now where was I? Oh yes, I was about to give apologies from my wife who can't be with us this evening, she's under the weather. She dropped one of her fairy cakes on her foot and it's splintered a bone. Mind, I'm not saying she's a lousy cook but Fanny Cradock pickets our oven.

'And I'm in enough trouble as it is. My regular pianist couldn't make it tonight and the only guy they could find to deputise for him is Angelo's nephew. He's a nice enough fellow but a little on the limp-wristed side. I'm not saying he's a poof but if they ever—'

'Melted him down for soap he'd be Fairy Liquid,' hooted Diana, who was beginning to enjoy her role as a drunken reveller.

Allan wisely ignored this interruption and carried on: 'Still, as I said *La Miruggio's* a lovely club. You should have seen the place I played in last month in Cardiff, like an abattoir with carpets. It was so dirty that the mice ate out.

'Not that I'll ever go back to Wales, they kept a welcome on the hillside all right, just as well because the manager wouldn't let me back into the hotel. I wouldn't mind but I'd travelled all the way to Cardiff by train and it took five hours. A lovely girl in a mini-skirt was standing on the platform when I got off. She looked at me and said: "Hello, you gorgeous man, could you tell me the way to the optician?"'

Diana cleared her throat noisily and began to chant: 'Boring, boring, boring!' and this time Allan responded by pointing a finger at her and saying: 'I'm afraid I'll have to ask you to leave if you don't stop drawing attention to yourself. I'm trying to be funny but I can't compete when they start looking at your face. Perhaps Disney will offer you a job, you make even Goofy look handsome!'

This time Diana burst out laughing and held up her hands in surrender. 'I give in, Allan,' she chuckled. 'And so will any hecklers who dare to mess with you. Not that I think anyone will even try and give you any grief.'

'Let's hope not,' he grinned, feeling much easier now that he had shown himself how easy it had been to deal with any interruptions. 'Di, I have to make tracks. Adrian Klein's office called this morning to arrange for a photographer to take some new shots of me for their publicity people. I arranged to meet him at the club at four o'clock.'

'Okay, Al, I'll see you there when I clock on at seven-thirty,' she nodded and Allan pulled out a key from his pocket and said: 'I'm taking the Wolseley as Adrian's secretary has arranged for me to leave it in the Rose and Griffin car park.'

He put on his jacket and kissed her on the cheek. 'Bye, love.

I'd love to kiss you somewhere else and then follow that up with—'

'So would I,' she rejoined with a lop-sided little smile. 'Though even if you had time, I'm afraid you'll have to wait till the end of the week. I came on this morning.'

'Oh,' said Allan flatly but Diana slid her hand down the front of his trousers and she licked her lips suggestively as she murmured: 'But that's never stopped me from looking after your cock, has it? I'll suck your shaft dry when we get back home tonight.' This promise instantly brightened him up and he grinned: 'I'll hold you to that, as the actress said to the bishop. Ta ta for now then, I'll see you at the club.'

However, as Allan drove down Bayswater Road, his nervousness began to resurface at the thought of being critically appraised by as powerful a showbiz mogul as Dickie Segal. *Perhaps I should cut out some of the more risqué material*, he muttered to himself. Indeed, he was so wrapped up in thought that he drove through a red traffic light on Piccadilly as he turned left into Berkeley Street.

Luckily for Allan, there was only a solitary pedestrian crossing the road at the time and the young man was agile enough to leap out of harm's way, but his transgression had been noted by a uniformed policewoman standing on the pavement. She stepped out into the road and raised her arm to flag him down.

What the fuck does the stupid mare want? Allan thought to himself as he pulled into the kerb and wound down the window as she approached the car. Nevertheless, the comedian managed to keep the anger out of his voice. He composed his features into an ingratiating smile as he said: 'Good afternoon, officer, what's the problem?'

She gave him a withering look of disdain. 'Good afternoon, sir. Are you telling me you seriously don't know why that gentleman had to leap out of your way when you turned the corner? You didn't just cross when the lights were changing from amber to red, you crossed them when the red light had been on for at least fifteen seconds.'

'Surely not,' exclaimed Allan with as much innocence as he could muster. 'I would never do such a thing, officer. My Uncle Sid almost lost his leg in a road accident when some fool jumped the lights. I've been driving all over the country for the last eight years and I've never even had as much as a parking ticket to my name.'

'I'm glad to hear it, but I'm afraid it doesn't excuse what you did just now,' said the policewoman drily. Allan wondered why she was looking at him so carefully as she reached into her pocket for her notebook. 'Can I see your licence, please?'

He bit his lip in frustration as he pulled out his wallet. For a fleeting moment he recalled the advice of a saloon-bar bore in Wolverhampton who advised his listeners always to keep a five-pound note folded inside the pages of the licence as an unspoken offer after being stopped by the police. However, he sensibly concluded that it wasn't worth risking a headline of COMIC TRIED TO BRIBE ME SAYS PC, for the sake of a fine and an endorsement on his licence. So he handed it to her with a deep, wordless sigh.

But to Allan's astonishment, after the policewoman had glanced down at his licence, she looked back at him with a bright expression of admiration on her face. 'I thought I recognised you, Mr Godfrey! I was with a party from the station at *La Miraggio* last Thursday night and we almost fell off our chairs, you were so funny.'

It's my lucky day, after all, Allan said to himself as he returned her smile. He mentally blessed Angelo Calabro who had let it be known that officers from West End Central would always be sure of a warm welcome and a fifty per cent discount on their bills at his establishment.

'Would you sign an autograph for me?' the policewoman was saying to him as he broke off this happy reverie. Allan looked up at her with interest and realised that he had been stopped by a young girl of no more than twenty or so who must have been one of the most attractive WPCs in the entire Metropolitan Police.

'It would be my pleasure,' said Allan with even more

sincerity than when he signed up with Rose and Griffin. He rummaged in his pocket for one of the postcard-sized prints he kept about him for whenever he met a fan.

'Damn, I don't have any photographs with me,' he went on, but then a wild idea crossed his mind and he blurted out: 'Tell you what though, I've whole stack in my dressing room. *La Miraggio*'s only up the road. Jump in and we'll be there in a minute.'

'I'd love to, but I was on the way back to the station to sign off,' she replied but Allan said eagerly: 'All right then, hop in and I'll drive you there, wait till you've clocked off and we can have a cup of tea at the club. It's no trouble, honestly. In fact I've just realised I shouldn't have even gone straight to the club because my agents have reserved a space for me in their car park in Dover Street.'

The pretty policewoman hesitated a moment and then, snapping shut her notebook, she slipped it back into her pocket. Allan had already opened the passenger door by the time the officer had walked round to the pavement. Once inside the Wolseley 1100 she took off her hat and smoothed a hand through her gleaming strawberry blonde hair. 'My name's Roz Owens,' she said in a surprisingly shy tone of voice. She held out her hand which Allan took and looked her into her large blue eyes as he replied: 'Pleased to meet you, Roz, and I'm truly sorry about going over that red light. The truth is, my mind was miles away and you don't have to tell me what a dangerous thing that is to be when you're behind the wheel of a car.'

'I hope you mean it, Allan,' she rejoined amiably. 'The worst job I've ever had to do was tell a lady that her husband had just been killed crossing Baker Street, though to be fair he just rushed out from behind a taxi and the driver who hit him didn't have a chance of stopping in time. If I'm going to be honest, even if I hadn't have recognised you, I might not have given you a ticket so long as you weren't lippy about it and genuinely apologised for what you did. Maybe it's wrong but we're human too and you would hardly credit all the paperwork we have to fill out when we pinch somebody, even if it's only a driving offence.'

'I can well believe it,' said Allan sympathetically. He executed a neat U-turn and gunned his way back to the junction where he was careful to stop on an amber light. 'See, I've learned my lesson,' he added with a smile and he and Roz chatted amicably until he drew up just short of West End Central police station in Savile Row.

'I'll be less than five minutes,' promised Roz and she kept her word. It was only five past four when Allan swung his car into the empty parking bay which had been left for him behind the Rose and Griffin building in Dover Street.

'A photographer's meeting me at *La Miraggio* to take some publicity shots,' he told her as they walked down Hay Hill to Berkeley Street. 'It shouldn't take him very long but if you're in a hurry to get home, I'll sign something for you first before he begins the shoot and we'll have tea together another time.'

'No, I've nothing to rush back for, but I'll go if you think I'll be in the way,' Roz replied. They crossed the road to the front of the club where a stocky bearded man was unloading a tripod from the back of a taxi. She pointed to him and added: 'Look, that must be your fellow over there.'

Allan waited till the man had paid off the cabbie and then tapping him on the shoulder, he asked: 'Excuse me, are you the photographer from Adrian Klein's office?'

'That's right, Melvin Clough's the name,' he answered genially. 'You must be Mr Godfrey. Can we go inside the club straightaway? Adrian's said he doesn't want me to take any outside shots.'

Allan nodded: 'Fine, let me give you a hand with that tripod,' and he led Melvin and Roz round the side of the building to the staff entrance where they were ushered through by the doorman.

They passed Mr Hobart, the friendly day manager of *La Miraggio*, in the corridor. He readily gave permission for the photographer to set up his equipment in front of the stage.

'Let me know if you need any extension leads for the lights,' he said and after thanking him, Melvin said: 'It'll take me a few minutes to get organised, folks, so this would be a good time if you fancy a cuppa.'

'Good idea, Melvin, would you like me to bring one back for you?' asked Allan.

'Thanks, mate, white and two sugars, please,' answered the photographer as he bent down and opened up the battered black case which he had brought with him. Allan placed his hand on Roz's elbow and guided her towards the kitchen.

'There's a vending machine for the staff but it's awful stuff,' said Allan. They arrived just as Judy, Mr Hobart's long-serving secretary, was switching off the electric kettle. She smiled at them and declared: 'What perfect timing, Allan! Do the same in the act tonight and you'll have Dickie Segal eating out of the palm of your hand.'

He looked at her with raised eyebrows and commented: 'Blimey, news travels fast!' Judy smiled again as she went on: 'Oh come on now, sweetheart, you know how gossip leaks through this business like water through a sieve. Anyhow, we all wish you the very best of luck. You really deserve a break into the big time.'

Then Judy turned to Roz and said: 'Have you seen him work the audience here, love? Colin, Mr Hobart that is, and I have seen hundreds of comics but Allan's definitely in the top five as far as we're concerned.

'Yes, you should seriously think about turning professional,' she added with a giggle Allan thumbed his nose at her as she poured the boiling water into a large china teapot. 'Meanwhile, you can get two more cups and saucers out of the cupboard for you and your arresting officer.'

'You're too kind,' grunted Allan and Judy blew him a kiss and said to Roz: 'What's he up for? Embezzlement, indecent exposure, blackmail or perhaps a mix of all three?'

But before Roz could answer, Allan retorted: 'Poor girl, she's to be pitied. Let's face it, if she had a brain operation it would only cost a quid and ten bob of that would be for search fees.'

'He's a fine one to talk,' she replied spiritedly. 'This man – I use the word loosely – is so ignorant that he thought the electricity bill was the Charge of the Light Brigade.'

Roz frowned as she wondered whether there was any genuine venom behind this quick-fire repartee, but the startled look on her face was soon replaced by a broad smile as Judy gave Allan the thumbs-up sign.

Allan introduced the two women to each other. 'Judy Redhouse, meet Roz Owens – and before you say another word, although Roz is off-duty, she's a fan and so all those wicked things you've been saying about me will be taken down and used in evidence against you!'

'Roz, I don't suppose you could stay for Allan's act tonight, could you? This guy Dickie Segal is one of the biggest producers in the country. Allan's going to star in one of his new West End shows if he cuts the mustard this evening.'

Roz turned to Allan and said with an evident enthusiasm: 'I'd have to go home and change, of course, but I'd love to come back later if you would like me to.'

It so happened that Allan had been surveying her rounded curves and was about to invite her to watch him from backstage when he remembered that Diana would be working at the club later on and swiftly came to his senses. 'That's very kind of you, but it's not necessary,' he said hastily. 'If I do badly I'll be in a terrible mood and if I do well then I'll be busy with Dickie and my agent and won't have any time to talk to you.

'Now let's all have a nice cup of tea,' he added and Judy opened a pack of shortbread biscuits for them. Then Allan poured another cup to give to Melvin and brought it back to the photographer who nodded his thanks as he adjusted his light meter.

'Cheers, mate,' he said to Allan. 'Let's make a start now and I'll have the tea later.' At Melvin's request, Allan posed in a variety of positions until ten minutes and two rolls of film later when he said to him: 'That's enough, isn't it? You can't need any more unless you want me to pull down my trousers and take a few snaps of my dick.'

'I don't fancy doing that, it would take too much time to blow up the print,' grinned the burly photographer. He put down the camera and after quickly swallowing down his cold tea, he asked: 'But would any of the club's chorus girls be around by any chance? I was thinking about a nice shot of you sandwiched between a couple of glamorous showgirls showing a bit of leg.'

'Who, me or the girls? Sorry, Melvin, they don't turn up till nine o'clock,' replied Allan and grinned at Roz as he said to her: 'The costumes are here though if you could persuade Roz to change into one.'

Roz looked doubtful at the idea and said apologetically: 'I don't think I could do that. It sounds great fun but my sergeant would go bananas if he saw that kind of photo of me plastered all over the place.'

'It won't be plastered all over the place,' Melvin Clough assured her. 'At best the photo might possibly appear in a newspaper or magazine once Allan's publicity people start work on him. Even then, your name wouldn't be mentioned in the caption.'

'And I take it you would send Roz a set of prints which I could sign for her,' said Allan. The photographer nodded: 'Of course, that goes without saying,' he said.

'Go on, Roz, be a pal,' added Allan persuasively. After a brief pause, she shrugged her shoulders and said: 'Okay then, why not? So long as it's guaranteed my name will never be used.'

'I give you my word,' said Melvin, placing his hand on his heart. Roz gave a short smile and drily replied: 'I've heard that one before.' She followed them to the wardrobe room. There, after surveying a selection of the gaudy outfits, they agreed a silver-spangled costume cut low to display an abundant amount of cleavage and high around the waist so as to display an equally generous quantity of thigh and backside.

'This'll also look great on you,' enthused Melvin, picking up a glittering shiny tiara which he placed on her head. Roz giggled as she looked at herself in the mirror. 'It'll make a change from wearing a uniform, I'll grant you that,' she commented. She began to unbutton her tunic as the two men left the room.

'That's a nice girl you've found there, Al,' observed the photographer as they walked back towards the stage. 'Have you known her long?'

'No, we met only about an hour ago,' answered Allan and he rapidly explained the circumstances of his meeting with the attractive young policewoman. Melvin grinned: 'They say some fellows are kinky about uniforms. In fact I heard that there's a Tory MP who pays his secretary to dress up as a traffic warden and she gives him a ticket every time he fucks her!'

'You're kidding me,' remarked Allan as they sat down at one of the tables at the side of the stage. Melvin shook his head. I can't say that traffic wardens turn me on although I had a great fuck a couple of months ago when I was invited to a preview of Dennis Le Baigue's latest collection of photographs at Disney and Bell, one of those posh Bond Street galleries just up the road from here.'

'Dennis Le Baigue? Isn't he that crazy guy who drives around London on a motorbike, stopping girls in the street and asking them to pose for him in the nude?'

'Yup, that's the guy, got some nerve, hasn't he? I've heard that he screws most of the birds he photographs,' continued Melvin blithely. 'Anyway, it was about twenty past six when I parked my car in Conduit Street and strolled round to the gallery. It was an invitation-only do but at the gallery I suddenly remembered that I'd left my invite in the glove compartment of my car, so without even pushing open the door, I turned round and walked back to get it.

'Now I was parked only a couple of hundred yards away so I couldn't have been away from the car more than five minutes at the very most, but when I turned into Conduit

Street I could see this traffic warden standing by it with his notebook in his hand writing me out a ticket.

'"Here, hold on!" I shouted but it was too late – by the time I had run up to him, he had torn the ticket from his pad and was sticking it under my windscreen wiper. I was absolutely furious and yelled at him: "For God's sake what are you up to? You don't have to use a meter after half past six. In any case I only arrived here a few minutes ago and it's not as if I'm parked on a double yellow line."

'He looked at his watch and said: "But it's not half past six yet, is it? I saw you park at exactly seventeen minutes past and it's now six twenty-four. I'm sorry, sir, but I'm only doing my job."

'"That was the Nazis' excuse," I said angrily. I know it was wrong of me but I was more than a little tempted to take a swing at him. Then all of a sudden another warden suddenly appears, only this time it's not some weedy little middle-aged runt but a well upholstered blonde in her late twenties.

'"What seems to be the trouble here?" she said crisply. Trying my best to keep my temper, I explained what had happened. She listened carefully and then took her colleague to one side, whispered something in his ear and then he turned round and walked off. Then she came back to me and said: "I'm sorry about that, sir, Eddie's only been with us for a few weeks and he hasn't settled down yet."

'"Gets his kicks out of writing tickets, does he?" I sneered but she shook her head and said: "Possibly, but between ourselves we've got this new boss who goes barmy if we don't give out a certain number of tickets every day. Eddie's worried about losing his job. Look here, I can't tear this one up but I'll have a word with the office and if you write to them I'm sure they'll cancel the charge."

'This immediately calmed me down and I thanked her for sorting things out so quickly. Well, just like you clicked with Roz, I found myself chatting away to this warden who told me her name was Maureen. When I said I was going to this preview of Dennis Le Baigue's new pictures, she said:

"Oooh, I've heard of him – isn't he the one who takes those rude photographs for *Playboy*?"

'"He would call them artistic studies," I chuckled. "But if you were shocked by his *Playboy* pictures, you had better not take a gander at his latest work, the girls bare all, and believe me, Maureen, I mean all!"

'She gave me a wink and said: "Oh, I wouldn't mind, I'm no prude," and to cut a long story short, I took her with me to have a look at Dennis's photographs and afterwards we went for a drink at a pub. Then we went out for a curry and I took Maureen back to her house in Wandsworth and she invited me inside for a nightcap.

'Maureen made us some coffee and we sat down together on the couch in her living room. "So shall I tell Dennis Le Baigue it would be worth his while to stop his bike if he ever sees you walking down Bond Street?" I teased her. "After all, naked girls have been the subject of artists for thousands of years."

'"If you like, Melvin, but I think I'd be a bit nervous though I'm not ashamed of my body," she retorted warmly. "My ex-husband used to paint a bit and I modelled for him now and then. The trouble was I soon found out I wasn't the only girl taking her clothes off for him nor the only one who the dirty bugger was shagging!"

'"Oh dear, I'm sorry," I said but Maureen shrugged her shoulders and said: "He was no loss, it wasn't as if we had any kids to worry about. I'm enjoying my freedom, although it can get lonely being on your own especially in the evenings."

'She stood up and twiddled with the control on her radio till she found some nice smoochy music before coming back to sit with me on the couch. We had a glass or two of wine as we chatted away and before long nature took its course, you might say. I wrapped my arms around her and kissed her on the lips. She opened her mouth and we sucked each other's tongues and I moved my hands down to her knees.

'As I stroked her knees she moved her legs apart and I inched my hand upwards under her skirt till I came to her bare thighs. I stopped for a moment and then explored further, running my fingers between her legs and rubbing my palm against her thin silky panties. She opened her legs wider and I cupped my hand over her quim and slid a finger under her panties and found that she was already wet. So I slipped the tip of my finger inside her cunt which tightened around it.'

He paused to pull out a new roll of film out of his bag but neither of them had noticed that Roz had left the dressing room and was standing quietly in the wings when Allan smacked his lips and said: 'Sounds as though you were on to a winner, Melvin – I must remember to leave my car in Conduit Street one evening!'

The photographer gave a hoarse laugh and went on: 'Well, I pushed her skirt up over her hips and she lifted her bum off the couch to let me yank her panties down to her ankles. Maureen pulled her lips away as she kicked off her shoes so she could wriggle them off her feet. I unbuttoned her white blouse and saw the outline of her nipples beneath her cream lace bra.

'She looked at me and said in a low voice: "Melvin, I don't want to get all worked up for nothing so, before you carry on any further, you should know that it's a house rule that, if you fuck me, you have to stay the night."

'"I wouldn't want it any other way," I answered, which made her smile. She nodded and, taking hold of my hand, she pulled me up from the couch and led the way up the stairs into her bedroom.

'There we whipped off our clothes and in no time at all we were writhing together naked on the bed. Without even saying anything to each other, we soon found ourselves wriggling into a sexy *soixante neuf*. Maureen lowered her chubby bottom onto my face whilst she cupped my balls in her hand and gobbled my knob into her mouth. Then I curled my tongue and flicked it around the rim of her wrinkled little arsehole. She squealed with pleasure and wrapped her lips tightly round my cock, plunging her head downwards to take me deep into the back of her throat.

'As Maureen sucked my cock I moved my mouth forward and began to lick her quim. Almost at once her pungent pussy juice came flowing out of her cunt and dribbled down my chin.

'"Aaaah!" she gurgled as she lifted her head and threw herself down on her back and panted: 'Fuck me, you randy sod! I want to be screwed by that fat juicy cock of yours!"

'Maureen's eyes were shining as I watched her spread her legs and run a finger between the pouting pink lips of her cunny. "Come on, Melvin, I need you," she begged. I quickly swung myself over her and she let out a deep sigh of contentment as I slid inside her crack. Her clingy cunt held my cock like a velvety wet glove. Our bodies slid together and I jerked my hips to and fro, pounding my prick in and out of her squelchy snatch at top speed.

'"Oh God, that feels wonderful . . . like fireworks exploding inside my cunt," she gasped. "Now shoot your load and we'll make it together!"

'I paused to catch my breath and then continued to fuck her, filling her snatch with my throbbing tool. Suddenly she screamed with excitement and shuddered into a tremendous climax. This set me off and the sticky cream burst out of my cock as I rubbed my shaft against the walls of her love funnel until my cock had been milked dry. I rolled off her, my chest heaving as I lay on my back gasping with exhaustion.

'It took an hour or so before I could get another hard-on so I licked out her honeypot before we fucked again. Though I say so myself, girls always tell me that I'm really good at eating pussy – perhaps it's my beard which tickles their cunnies whilst I'm on the job but they all seem to love me to bring them off with my tongue.

'Anyway, I was too tired to fuck Maureen more than one more time before I fell into a deep sleep. Frankly, I can usually do rather better than than but then after a long day's work, a few drinks and a Chicken Madras, I don't think I did too badly!'

Allan gave an appreciative *heh-heh* but then both men were startled by Roz who loudly remarked as she sauntered out onto the stage: 'No, you probably didn't. But when will you men realise that it's quality and not quantity that counts!'

'Ooops, I'm sorry, love, I didn't hear you come back,' said Melvin hastily but Roz waved away his apology. 'That's all right, I've heard much more lurid stuff like that in the canteen down at the station.

'Now where do you want Allan and me to stand for these blinking photographs?' she added.

'Right in the centre of the stage, please,' he replied. When Allan took up his position, Roz struck a coquettish position at his side, looking at him with a sexy smile as she leaned slightly forward to accentuate her ample cleavage.

'That's great, absolutely fabulous,' said Melvin as he snapped away. He took some shots of Roz on her own looking extremely voluptuous in her scanty costume.

Ten minutes later the photographer wound on the finished roll of film and thanked her again for helping out. He went on: 'Give me your address so I can send you a contact sheet and you can pick what pictures you want from it. I know Adrian Klein won't jib at paying for a few extra prints.'

He packed up his equipment and shook hands with them. 'Nice meeting you both,' he said cordially. 'And all the very best of luck for tonight! Al, go out and break a leg!'

'That wasn't a very nice thing to say to you,' frowned Roz after the photographer left them but Allan shook his head and grinned: 'No, no he didn't mean anything bad by it. Saying "break a leg" is theatrical slang for "best of luck". It's an old superstition like you're always supposed to say "the Scottish play" instead of *Macbeth*. Don't ask me why because I don't know but there it is. Mind you, if I go out and trip over my own feet, I dare say I might get a laugh out of Dickie Segal!'

'You might at that,' she agreed. They were walking back to the dressing room when she suddenly grimaced with pain and sat down sharply on a wooden chair.

'Ouch! Oh, that's really painful! I get this terrible cramp in my legs,' explained Roz as she screwed up her face and gritted her teeth. 'Ow! It comes from walking the beat since eight o'clock this morning! Allan, sorry to be a nuisance but would you be a darling and massage my calves for me?'

'Of course I will,' he answered instantly, trying to look suitably concerned. While Allan was genuinely sorry that the girl was in such discomfort, he was happy to be given this unexpected opportunity of fondling her shapely legs.

He knelt down at her feet and felt his prick begin to thicken as he rubbed her smooth bare calves. 'Ooooh, that's better,' she breathed as she twisted herself up into a more comfortable position. He carefully caressed her soft warm legs and Allan was so intent on his work that he did not notice Roz smooth her hands over her bosoms. However, his eyes widened when he looked up and saw the buxom girl was engaged in undoing the zip at the back of her costume. His cock leaped to attention as he goggled at her rounded bare breasts which jiggled so enticingly in front of him.

With a saucy look on her face Roz giggled as she stared in turn at the bulge in his trousers and passed her tongue sensuously over her top lip. 'I think you could do with a nice massage too,' she said in a husky voice. She slid down from the chair to sit on her knees next to him. Their mouths met in a fervent tongue-to-tongue encounter as Allan flung her arms around his neck and he cupped her luscious soft spheres, squeezing the creamy soft globes and making her moan with excitement as he rubbed his thumbs against her elongated nipples.

Then Roz herself tugged off her costume completely. She moaned again when he yanked off her knickers and put one hand on her moistening mound, massaging her pussy lips with his finger while, with the other, he took hold of her own warm hand and placed it firmly on the tented bulge in his trousers.

Her whole body tingled when she felt the thick, rigid rod pressing against her fingers. She caressed Allan's shaft through the thin material of his cotton trousers.

'Phwaugh!' he gurgled when Roz unzipped his flies and released his throbbing erection which sprung up through the slit of his underpants. She clutched at the hot, rock-hard column in her fist and moved her hand slowly up and down the pulsing fleshy pole whilst Allan pressed his thumb directly into her squishy cunt.

Then for a short time he withdrew his digit from Roz's pussy to stroke her pouting love lips, his fingertips playing inside her thick bush of light brown curly hair. She bucked her groin up and down against his hand to increase her pleasure. In response he slid his fingers up and down the length of her dripping crack and reinserted his thumb and two further fingers inside her, gliding them gently inside her cunt which made her clitty swell with anticipation.

'Oooh, you wicked lad,' she said breathlessly as Allan continued to grope inside her churning love tunnel with his long sensitive fingers. The heat between her thighs reached fever point when he found her tingling clitty and used his thumb to massage the vibrating little button.

'Please, Allan, please,' she whimpered, and Allan was unsure if she wanted him to fuck her or bring her off with his hand. So he compromised by removing his hand from her cunt and her fingers from around his cock before positioning himself between her thighs. For a moment he looked into her beautiful blue eyes and then buried his face inside her hirsute wet thatch and ground his mouth up against her cunt.

Roz mewed with delight as he nipped her tingling clitty with his teeth. Her orgasm began to build as he sucked on her honeypot with a growing intensity. She clutched at his head and screeched with joy as Allan flicked his tongue at speed in and out of her dripping crack until she orgasmed and a flood of cuntal juice washed over his face.

'Now you must fuck me,' she gasped. Allan clambered up and nudged the tip of his helmet into the wet folds of her pussy, rubbing it against her love lips before easing himself into her sopping sheath of her love funnel. He paused and withdrew slowly and Roz shivered with pleasure as he entered her a second time, but inserting only his knob before withdrawing again. She squirmed under him as he continued to tease her until Roz thrust her hips upwards to embed his shaft fully inside her cunt and her cunny muscles closed around his throbbing tool.

'Aaaahh!' gasped Allan as he rested on his elbows for a moment. Then he began to fuck her, pistoning his prick to and fro in short jabbing strokes.

'Deeper, deeper! I want to feel every inch of that lovely thick prick!' she hissed as she grasped hold of his bum cheeks and pulled him forward until his shaft was buried inside her tingling cunt and their pubic hairs mashed together.

'All right then, here we go!' he panted. He yelped in pained surprise when he felt her finger sliding along the cleft of his bottom and the tip of her index finger pushing gently until it gained entry to the tight puckered entrance of his arsehole.

A wild primal snarl escaped from his lips when her fingernail rasped against the tender flesh. He began to slam his shaft to and fro inside Roz's juicy quim and the aroused girl bucked and twisted as fiercely exciting spasms racked through her body. Again and again Allan plunged into her squishy wetness, sliding his quivering cock in and out of her sopping cunny in long sweeping strokes with all the energy he could muster.

'Y-e-s-s! Y-e-s-s!' Roz cried out as his buttocks rose and fell whilst he pounded away into her pussy. She screamed out in joy as a series of climactic sensations shuddered out from her pussy. The clenching muscles of her cunny gripped his throbbing tool as wave after wave of blissful delight washed over her as her body exploded into a tremendous orgasm.

Now Allan felt an awesome climax building up inside him as his balls smacked against her beautiful bum cheeks. He lunged forward one final time and, with a passionate sob, he jetted a sticky stream of spunk which splattered against the walls of her cunt as thrilling ripples of sheer bliss swept through his muscular torso.

Totally spent, he collapsed down upon her trembling body but there was to be little rest for the lusty pair because seconds later there was a sharp knock on the door and they heard Judy call out: 'Allan, are you in there? Mr Hobart wants to see you as soon as possible.'

'Be with you in a couple of minutes,' he shouted back, shaking his fist towards the sound of her voice but Judy did not deserve his wrath. For she had guessed what might be going on inside the chorus girls' dressing room but had nevertheless resisted the temptation to make any suggestive comments about why Allan had locked himself in there and the fact that his policewoman friend was nowhere to be found.

He whispered to Roz that they had to get dressed and she agreed: 'Yes, of course, Allan, but I really would love to come back here later with my flatmate and cheer you on. After all, knowing there are people on your side out in the audience should give you some extra confidence and make you forget about this important chap who you said is coming to see your performance tonight.'

This was true enough, he thought to himself. Although a vision of Diana's face quickly crossed Allan's mind, he could always explain Roz's presence to her. He wouldn't have to lie about how he met the pretty policewoman, all he had to do was to be economical with the truth if Diana pressed him about what had happened after Melvin Clough had left the club.

In any case, Allan suddenly remembered how, just before he had left the flat, Diana had told him that her period had just started, so she would be feeling very tired and might very well slip off home whilst he stayed behind at the club to discuss his future with Adrian Klein and Dickie Segal. And then perhaps there would be time for a quick fuck with Roz and possibly her flatmate afterwards . . .

So he smiled at her and said: 'Okay then, on the condition that you come as my guests. I'll tell Judy to reserve a table for two for you. Look here, you know how the guy who owns this place, Angelo Calabro, loves to keep in with the police, especially from West End Central? Now Angelo is also a partner in a minicab firm so give me your address because when I tell him who you are, he'll arrange for a car to bring you here and take you back home with his compliments.'

'Fine, what time should the driver call for us?' asked Roz. She took out a ballpoint from her tunic and quickly scribbled down her address on a scrap of paper which she handed to him.

'There's no great rush,' he answered. 'Say ten o'clock, but I hope that neither of you are on an early shift tomorrow because if all goes well I doubt if you'll be home much before two o'clock in the morning!'

Roz gave him a smacking wet kiss on his cheek as he pulled on his trousers. 'Ooh, thanks Allan! I'm sure it'll all work out for you tonight. Never mind about your Mr Segal, I know you won't find it difficult to make Frankie and me laugh our heads off.'

When Adrian Klein returned to his office from his visit to Sandra, he scanned through a pile of messages Debbie had left on his desk. Fortunately, all could safely be ignored till the next day. He was about to call Belinda Headley at the *Evening News* to check that she was still free this evening, for Adrian knew how journalists sometimes had to dig out information regardless of time and he still had to work out how to pick her up from her flat without leaving Dickie Segal's side. Then Debbie came in and informed him that Teddy Dixon wanted to see Adrian as soon as possible.

'Okay, Debs, I'll go up to him straightaway. Tell anyone who wants me that I'll call them back later,' he replied. Hoisting himself out of his chair, he smiled broadly – for the odds were that Teddy had called him to find out the state of play *vis à vis* Dickie Segal. His managing director would be well pleased with the way Adrian had kept the impresario away from rival agents with the help of Sandra Davies' pussy.

Still feeling tired after his bedroom exertions, he jogged up the stairs to Teddy Dixon's opulent office and rapped on the door. Then he raised his eyebrows when he heard Teddy's fruity voice call out: 'Adrian, if that's you outside, come on in, anyone else needn't bother!'

What the heck is he up to? wondered Adrian as he turned the doorknob and obediently trotted in – but to his bewilderment, the managing director of Rose and Griffin was nowhere to be seen. Adrian noticed that there was an open bottle of red wine and two glasses on his shining mahogany desk.

As he stood with his back to the wall, he realised that his boss must have retreated into the small private shower room which had been installed the previous year. This was immediately confirmed when the sliding black door in the wall behind the desk glided open and the slightly corpulent Teddy Dixon appeared wearing only a white towelling robe.

'There you are, old boy,' said Teddy as he wiped his face on the sleeve of his robe. 'Sit down and have a glass of wine whilst you tell me what happened with our friend Nipper Segal this afternoon. Did he take the bait?'

Adrian gave a tiny smile and replied: 'I think it's fair to say that Dickie was very impressed by what Elaine's friend had to offer. He would have stayed to audition her for the rest of the afternoon but he had a five o'clock meeting with Lennie Lieberman which I was happy enough to let him keep.'

'Lennie Lieberman, the manager of the Hurricanes? Well, those boys are no threat, Dickie could hardly bung them into his show to replace Quentin Ludgate,' shrugged Teddy as he poured Adrian a glass of wine. 'Here, you'll like this Spanish plonk, it's a gorgeous glug. That guy who wanted Sharon Saxon to front a big concert in Marbella sent me over a case of the stuff last week.'

'Don't tell me he's on about his precious vinos again,' came a sibilant female voice from behind Teddy's chair. Adrian looked up to see the tall, long-legged figure of Marlene, the managing director's private secretary, standing in the doorway of the shower-room, dressed in nothing but a short red silk kimono. However, her appearance did not startle Adrian overmuch. It was an open secret amongst the staff at Rose and Griffin that their boss was shagging Marlene although this was the first time Adrian had been given hard evidence of their liaison.

She coolly sauntered over to them and said to Teddy: 'It's almost half past four and that person-to-person call you booked to Dave Zwaig in New York will be coming through any minute now. Do you want to take it in here or on my telephone?'

He frowned and then rose to his feet. 'I'll take it in your office,' he decided. 'That'll give me the chance to run over those Australian contracts one last time before we agree his terms. You stay here and entertain Adrian and I'll tell Jennifer to put the call to Dave Zwaig through to your extension.'

Marlene smiled as Teddy hurried out and she sat down in his vacated leather chair and crossed her shapely legs.

'So all went well for you, Ade? Teddy told me your game plan and I'm not surprised that you succeeded at keeping Dickie Segal out of his office. But then why should Nipper be any different to most guys I know. The trouble is, if you open their flies their brains fall out with their cocks!'

'There's no need to be so cynical about men,' Adrian scolded her lightly but Marlene fluttered her large hazel eyes across at him and said. 'So you couldn't be diverted from your work by the prospect of some nookie, Mr Klein?'

'No, I don't think so,' he said thoughtfully but his eyebrows shot up when Marlene stood up and slid her robe off her shoulders to stand stark naked in front of him.

'Now look here, Marlene,' Adrian managed to say before his voice subsided into a strangulated gulp. The delectable naked girl skipped over to him and, plonking herself down on his lap, she kissed him squarely on the lips. Marlene was a most proficient kisser and her tongue slid directly into Adrian's mouth and shimmied around his gums and teeth, so even if he wanted to protest there was hardly a chance for him to do so.

At first he tried to resist her exciting embrace for Teddy Dixon's philosophy was very much a don't-do-as-I do, do-as-I-say affair when it came to office romances. Although he was notorious for making full use of the casting couch, only a few months ago Teddy sent round a stern note to all staff warning of the dangers of such relationships after he had opened the door of a junior agent's office to discover the young man copulating on the carpet with one of the front-desk receptionists.

His own grandfather's warning that a stiff cock had no conscience also flashed through his mind, but after Marlene had pressed her hardening nipples to his chest through the thin cotton fabric of his shirt, Adrian knew he would be unable to resist. He made one final half-hearted effort when she pulled her lips back slightly to draw breath.

However, like all the other executives at Rose and Griffin, Adrian had almost daily lustful day-dreams about bedding Teddy Dixon's gorgeous young secretary. When she kept possession of his tongue and sucked it deep into the wet warmth of her mouth, he surrendered unconditionally and slid his arms around her luscious curves.

Marlene extracted her tongue for a moment and winked at him. 'Still sure about that, are you?' she enquired softly, giving Adrian an appreciative gurgle when she felt his rigid shaft pushing up against her belly whilst she unknotted his tie. After she had helped him shuck off his shirt, Marlene slid down from his lap and pulled off his shoes.

Then Adrian stood up and yanked down his trousers and pants. Marlene grabbed hold of his cock and pulled him down to the thick pile of Teddy's carpet. Their naked bodies were quickly locked together.

Adrian lay her down on her back and cupped her rounded breasts in his hands before moving them downwards to the insides of her thighs. He kissed her erect nipples, nipping the rosy berries with his teeth. Marlene lay back and purred with contentment as he ran his fingertips through her curly brown bush and let out a tiny yelp when his long forefinger slid unerringly between between her puffy pussy lips and teased the hooded bud of her swelling clitty.

'Hoooh!' she breathed as she reached down and grasped hold of his circumcised cock, rubbing her hand up and down the fleshy shaft which leaped and bounded in her hand. Then using his prick as a handle, she pulled Adrian up on top of her and guided his domed knob directly into the clinging moist wetness of her honeypot.

Whilst he inserted his cock in her juicy quim, Adrian squeezed the nubile girl tightly against him so that her breasts were pressed against his broad chest. She felt his warm breath on her cheek as he whispered fiercely: 'Wrap your legs round my back, Marlene, and I'll take you on a ride to fuckland!'

'Yes! Yes! Go on!' she gasped, clasping her long shapely legs around him as Adrian lay quite still, savouring to the full the exquisite sensations afforded by his tool being enveloped inside Marlene's tingling cunt. Then he started to move his throbbing tool to and fro, squelching a sensual path in and out of her sopping slit. She raised her legs till her toes were pointing up to the ceiling as he pushed deeper inside her, increasing the vigour of his strokes and she wiggled her backside, working it round and round as he slammed his thick prick in and out of her love funnel.

'Yiiiieeeh! Fill me with cock, big boy!' panted Marlene, her silky brown hair whipping across her face. Adrian upped the pace and his balls slapped against her bum cheeks with each lunging thrust as he reamed out her cunt at an even greater speed.

Her creamy breasts jiggled excitedly as she surged uncontrollably underneath him and then her body began to tremble as she felt a swell of erotic ecstasy welling up inside her. When the force of her tumultuous climax shot through her body she cried out: 'Here it comes, oooh, it's so good! Cream my cunt, lover, I'm going to explode!'

Adrian inhaled a deep breath and his cock fairly vibrated as it slewed faster and faster in and out of Marlene's slit. He thrilled to the feel of her soft belly sliding against him and her slippery cunt joyfully swallowing his shaft with each pistoning plunge. His climax came upon him quickly. With an anguished cry he jetted three powerful streams of spunk into her juicy cunt before he slumped down upon her, their bodies pressed together with Marlene's cunny still clinging to his shivering shaft.

After she had milked his cock of its last droplets of sticky jism, Adrian rolled off her soft curves and lay flat on his back, his chest heaving from these thrilling if unexpected exertions as he fought to regain his breath.

However, when Marlene looked over and saw that his meaty penis was still semi-erect, she clambered to her knees and draped herself across his body, positioning Adrian's head between her thighs so that her muff of pubic curls tickled his nose and her breasts were pressed against his belly.

Then she curled her long fingers around his glistening wet cock and gave a throaty chuckle when his cock began to throb inside her clenched fist. 'M'mm, this tool looks tasty enough to eat,' she said lightly as she rubbed her hand up and down its swelling length. Her tongue darted out and swished over the purple dome of his helmet. 'Hahhh!' he gasped as in one swift gulp she sucked his shaft inside her mouth and began bobbing her head up and down, licking and lapping his throbbing shaft. Adrian shuddered as warm waves of sheer ecstasy coursed through every fibre of his body.

Those delicious ripples rapidly invigorated him and now it was Marlene's turn to shudder when he kissed her pouting pussy lips. She squeaked with delight as Adrian worked his tongue over her erect fleshy clitty and Marlene's love juice filled his mouth as he struggled to hold her steady during the electric surges of her passion.

In the meantime she sucked harder and harder on Adrian's cock, swirling her tongue around his knob. She pulled back her head and Marlene squeezed his pulsating prick in her hand as she declared: 'Ade, we're running out of time, Teddy might well come straight back with a letter for me to type after he's spoken to Dave Zwaig. So let's break up the party now because I want to have a shower before he comes back. I had just finished giving him a wank and was just about to turn on the tap when you knocked on the door.'

'I'll join you if I may,' he answered as he scrambled to his feet. Marlene chased Adrian into the shower stall where she drew the curtain and embraced him again while he turned on the tap and a warm torrent of water cascaded down upon them. He soaped her pneumatic breasts as she toyed with his stiff shaft, slapping it playfully from side to side and wiggling it like a stick. Then she turned to let the water stroke her nipples, the spray smacking her titties in such a sensitive fashion that goose-pimples appeared on her breasts.

Dropping to his knees, Adrian lathered her bum cheeks and then he made her bend forward with her arms outstretched and her hands spread against the wall. Next he unhooked the detachable nozzle from its mooring and with his free hand he pulled apart Marlene's jiggling buttocks and placed the nozzle in the cleft to let the fierce jet of water spray against the tight puckered opening of her back passage, sensuously massaging her arsehole with an intoxicating force.

Adrian chuckled as he moved the nozzle further between her thighs and twisted it round to soak her thick bush. Marlene began to tremble as she removed one hand from the wall and pulled her pussy lips apart, opening herself wider to feel the maximum force of the powerful gush of water shooting into her tingling cunt. He moved the nozzle back and forth and Marlene quivered all over when, with a careful deliberation, Adrian focussed the jet on her clitty until she shivered into a short but potent climax.

'Wooogh!' she gasped as the force of her climax sped through her crotch like molten lava from a volcano. Adrian replaced the shower-head in the fixture above their heads and reduced the stream of water to a warm trickle.

Then Marlene grasped hold of a sponge and, with a husky giggle, she lathered his cock. She looked up at Adrian as she slid one slippery hand up and down his pulsing boner and with the other she soaped his balls with soft sponge. He leaned back against the wall and clutched her shoulders as she started to fondle the smooth dome of his helmet whilst her right had pumped slowly up and down his shaft in long, slow strokes.

Adrian's eyes were now closed as he gyrated his hips to rub

his cock harder against her moving hand as he murmured: 'Marlene, you're a wicked girl. Careful though, I won't be able to stop myself from—'

'Let it go, Ade. I want you to come in my hand,' she whispered. She gently squeezed his balls as she tightened her grip on his rigid rod, clutching it firmly as it slid in and out of her grip. In no time Adrian let out a low groan and thick gobs of spunk spurted from his prick into her hand. She released his shaft and massaged the spunk onto her breasts and, when Adrian's final dribble of seed ceased, he crushed Marlene to him. They kissed with lustful passion as the water continued to cascade down upon them.

Then Marlene switched off the water and they hurriedly dried themselves with towels which Teddy had thoughtfully purchased at Selfridge's last New Year sale. Then they trotted back into Teddy's office and as they dressed themselves Marlene remarked: 'Adrian, how would you like me to pop down to *La Miraggio* tonight to cheer on Allan Godfrey? There are two old school chums of mine from Swindon staying with me this week and I know they would really enjoy Allan's act.'

'Sure, why not? The more friendly faces the better,' he answered. He could hardly refuse Marlene's offer although he was set on making his play for the gorgeous Belinda Headley and he was already faced with the problem of how to keep Tanya away from his table after she had finished her stint in the chorus line of the cabaret.

Still, there should be safety in numbers if Marlene was going to bring along two friends, Adrian consoled himself as he zipped up his trousers and went on: 'Will you book your own table or do you want me to call Angelo for you?'

'No, that's all right, I can't believe there'll be a full house on a Monday night,' she replied and Adrian nodded in agreement as he picked up his jacket from the carpet. 'Super,' he said. 'I'll see you at the club then if not before. Forgive me but I don't have time to help you clear up, I've just remembered there are two really important phone calls I must make.'

'Okay, Ade, off you go,' said Marlene, blowing him a kiss as he left.

Debbie was standing by his desk when he returned to his own more spartan quarters and she gave him a knowing look as he slumped down into his chair. 'Are you all right, boss?' she asked. 'Is it my imagination or are you out of breath from running down the stairs? You need to take more outdoor exercise.'

The manner in which she stressed the word *outdoor* made Adrian look up sharply at his secretary but she ignored his glance and continued: 'You've had a call from Belinda Headley of the *Evening News*. She says that she has to follow up a story which will probably mean she'll be a little bit late tonight, so you shouldn't bother calling round for her at her flat, she'll meet you at *La Miraggio* at about nine o'clock.'

'Excellent, that saves me a job,' commented Adrian for he could now stick to Dickie Segal like glue without asking Belinda to come to *La Miraggio* by herself in one of Angelo Calabro's minicabs.

'Fancy a cup of tea?' she asked and Adrian gave her a grunt and a thumbs-up sign as he picked up the telephone and dialled Simon Byrne's number. 'Hi there, mate,' he said after Herald Books' telephonist had put him through to his friend. 'Yup, we certainly had a great time with Jennie and Tanya last night, but I didn't call you about the girls. There's something I should have mentioned to you first thing this morning – does the idea of publishing Quentin Ludgate's autobiography turn you on? You know the sort of thing, from rags to riches all thrown away for a few mad minutes of carnal lust.'

'Christ, why didn't I think of that? It's a great idea,' said Simon excitedly. 'Mind you, he would have to spice it up a bit and name some of the showbiz shirtlifters to make sure of a good Fleet Street serialisation deal. Have you got a writer lined up to knock it out for Quentin or would you want us to hire a hack for you?'

'Well, he's scribbling it himself so we might not even need

a ghost writer, but business is business, Simon, what kind of advance can you offer?'

'Let me come back to you on that, Ade,' he answered quickly. 'Do me a favour though, I know we're mates and I wouldn't ask you to compromise your client's best interests but promise me you'll give me first refusal and top-up rights.'

Adrian was unfamiliar with literary licences and he enquired: 'I'm not sure, Simon. What would that commit me to?'

'Nothing that's not to Quentin's advantage,' Simon assured him. 'All I want is the right to put in the first bid for the book and if you decide to show it around to other publishers, you'll give me the chance to beat it – though that doesn't hold you to accepting my offer just because it would be fifty quid higher.'

'That sounds fair enough, Mr Byrne. I'll write you a note confirming this arrangement as soon as I've put down the phone,' replied Adrian.

Simon said: 'Super, I'm sure we'll work something out. So when can I tell my people we'll have a précis and a sample chapter?'

Adrian shrugged: 'I'm not too sure but I'll find out from Quentin himself later this week. Right, that's work out of the way – now will I see you tonight at *La Miraggio*? Frankly, I'd like as many people there as possible to laugh as loud as they can at Allan Godfrey's jokes.'

'I'll do my best, Ade, but I really don't know where I'll be this evening,' sighed Simon heavily. 'I'm just about to ring Jennie who I've promised to take to the films tonight. I don't suppose she would mind going to *La Miraggio* but when I made the date with Jennie I forgot that I'd already arranged to fuck Clare Norrice and that pretty young girl, Trish Jackson, who might also be bringing a friend along to the Norrice's apartment. Do you remember Trish? She's the bird I stole the other night from your lesbian lady at Rose and Griffin.'

'How could I forget?' laughed Adrian as he leaned back

in his chair. 'I'm sure Carola Watforde blames me for what happened because she snapped my head off early this morning when I asked her for some figures! Good luck Simon, I hope you manage to keep your harem happy. If I were you, I'd take them all to see Allan Godfrey perform and then make a dash for the exit as soon as the cabaret's over.'

'You're probably right,' grunted Simon. 'Unfortunately, I can't afford to splash out for a table for four or five at a posh Mayfair night club.' Then he paused and added thoughtfully: 'Still, I could always find out if Clare would stump up for the bill for my birthday treat.'

'But your birthday's not till October,' protested Adrian but Simon said: 'Well, what of it? I wouldn't ask her for another present on the day – Ade, you might very well see me tonight after all!'

'Bye, Simon,' Adrian chuckled into the phone. As he put down the receiver, Teddy Dixon strolled into his office and said: 'Adrian, I'm leaving in an hour or so and won't see you again till I get back from Down Under. Is there anything you want to talk over with me before I go?'

'I don't think so, Teddy, everything seems to be under control,' he answered. His managing director nodded his head sagely. 'Good boy, but I don't want you spending any more time with Marlene whilst I'm away. I know you fucked her this afternoon but that was only a one-off treat for sorting out Dickie Segal, all right?'

'Fine with me, Teddy, you know I wouldn't do anything naughty behind your back,' said Adrian and the managing director grinned: 'As Noel Coward said to the choirboy! Okay, my boy, I trust you. You have my itinerary, send a telegram to me in Sydney about how you got on with Dickie Segal tonight.'

Back in their flat in Hampstead Garden Suburb, Jennie and Tanya were discussing their plans for the evening ahead and were surprised to discover that they would be seeing each other later on that night. 'I wish I didn't have to work tonight, especially as Adrian's told me that he's invited a reporter from the *Evening News* to see Allan Godfrey in action,' remarked Tanya. 'And I've a sneaking suspicion that he rather fancies this girl.'

'At least you'll be able to keep an eye on him,' retorted Jennie with a troubled expression on her face. 'I'll be doing the same with Simon – we were supposed to be going to the pictures but he just rang to say that he forgot he had a prior arrangement but that I would be more than welcome to join him and his friends for a birthday dinner.'

'That's strange, Adrian never said anything to me about today being Simon's birthday,' said a puzzled Tanya. 'Still, I don't suppose it matters very much. Perhaps the boys hope to meet up at *La Miraggio* and after the cabaret come back here for another foursome frolic with us.'

'Maybe so, but why can't Simon pick me up and take me out somewhere on my own?' demanded Jennie. 'I don't fancy sharing him with anyone except you and Adrian. I won't stand for being two-timed again, and that's a fact. Remember how I had such an awful time with that pop singer I was going out with before we went to France?'

'Who, Eddie Shields, you mean? You never actually told me all the details but I won't forget how incensed you were about him.' said Tanya.

Jennie smiled ruefully. 'Oh, well I had reason to be angry and I certainly won't forgive Eddie in a hurry even if his latest record has made the charts. Would you like me to tell you exactly what happened with that rotten toe-rag?

'It all started when we went with some of his friends to Philippa's, that new club in Great Windmill Street. I could see that he fancied the redhead with big boobs behind the bar – and of course he denied it when I said in a sarky voice that the bargirl must have something going for her as I'd never seen Eddie so keen to get a round in before!

'However, he paid me a bit more attention as the evening wore on but we didn't have time for more than a kiss and a cuddle in the back seat of his friend's car because Eddie had to drive up to Leicester for a gig early the next morning. Like a fool, I was a bit worried the next day that I might have misjudged him so I thought I would give Eddie a nice surprise by turning up unannounced at his pad and stay over with him. We'd never had the chance to spend the whole night together before, because Eddie was always away on tour with the band – even though he had given me a set of keys to his flat soon after we became lovers.

I put some clothes in an overnight bag and took a bus all the way out to North Finchley. It was about ten o'clock when I arrived at his place and I reckoned he hadn't yet arrived back from Leicester, because I could see from the outside that all the lights were off.

'Anyway, I went in and opened the front door which I closed quietly behind me. Everything was dark and then I heard the sound of muffled laughter coming from the bedroom. At first I thought Eddie had come home and was listening to the radio in bed. Not wanting to frighten him, I tip-toed down the hall to peek in and see if he had already fallen asleep.'

'And was he?' asked Tanya.

Jennie shook her head and said bitterly: 'Not that you would notice! Luckily – or unluckily from his point of view – Eddie had left the bedroom door slightly ajar. From the bedside light I was given a bird's eye view of my dear boy friend and the redhead with the enormous knockers lying stark naked together on the bed. I was so shocked that I just stood there whilst I watched her ruffle his hair when he leaned over and started to suck on one of her long tawny titties whilst she giggled: "You just can't leave my melons alone, can you, you naughty boy?"

'"No, Rowena, I don't think I can," Eddie chortled as he slid his hand down into the fluffy ginger muff between her thighs and she spread her legs to make it easier for him to finger-fuck her. She wriggled like mad when Eddie slipped his fingers into her cunt and I must admit that I began to feel randy myself whilst I observed this girl Rowena take hold of his thick stiffie in her hand and start to wank his cock in her fist.

'Eddie twisted round and kissed her breasts which set her off and she gurgled: "Lovely, lovely . . . that's it, Ed, use your tongue on my tits, circle it round quickly, ooh, you're making them so hard!"

'Then she let go of his prick and muttered in his ear: "Come on, Eddie, fuck my quim with your thick prick, you dirty bugger!"

'Eddie didn't need any further persuasion. He raised himself on top of her and she grabbed hold of his cock and guided it inside her. I stood there silently, watching his arse heaving up and down as he pumped his prick in and out of her squelchy quim and I wondered how Eddie would feel if I suddenly walked in and snapped on the main bedroom light.'

She paused and gave a lop-sided little smile as Tanya asked: 'And did you? I would have been tempted to throw a jug of cold water over them!'

'Something like that did cross my mind,' admitted Jennie. 'But I decided not to make an undignified scene. For starters, it wouldn't be fair on the girl who might not even have known that Eddie and I were supposedly an item – although if I had interrupted their fucking and given Eddie a piece of my mind she would have known what kind of double-crossing rat she had between her legs! So I simply walked back to the front door which I closed as quietly as I had opened it and once I was outside I dropped Eddie's keys through the letter-box.'

'Did Eddie realise what had happened when he found the keys?'

'Well, he knew they were mine and when he called me the next day to ask why I had given them back to him, I said: "Give them to Rowena, Eddie, she needs them more than I do." Then I put down the phone and I haven't spoken to him ever since.'

'Quite right too!' exclaimed Tanya warmly. 'And if it's any consolation, it's odds-on he cheated on Rowena and she gave him the old heave-ho. Still that's all in the past, and I don't think Simon Byrne or Adrian Klein are that sort of blokes.'

* * *

Perhaps it was just as well that the two girls were unable to see what Simon was up to just as Tanya was making this generous assessment of his character. He had left his office and made his way directly to Clare Norrice's Mayfair apartment where a grey-haired maidservant ushered him in. 'Good evening, sir, Mrs Norrice is expecting you but she just telephoned to say that the meeting of the London Hospitals Aid Committee is still going on but she hopes to be home at about seven o'clock. She said you should make yourself at home until she arrives. Is there anything I can get you in the meantime?'

Simon shook his head. 'No thank you, Elizabeth, it'll give me the chance to have a good wash and brush-up.'

'Very good, sir,' she said and immediately retired to the kitchen for she was aware that Simon knew his way around the apartment. Elizabeth had her suspicions about what her mistress got up to whilst her husband was away, but the Norrices were undemanding employers and she was well paid for her discretion.

So Simon went through to the bedroom where he had fucked the fresh-faced young Trish Jackson less than forty hours before in the early hours of Sunday morning, watched by the voyeuristic Freddie Norrice through the large two way mirror on the wall. He took off his jacket and tumbled down on the soft quilt where he lay still for a couple of minutes.

Then he stripped off all his clothes and wandered naked into the en-suite bathroom. He picked up a portable electric razor lying at the side of the basin and ran it over his chin before he stepped inside the shower and turned on the water. After washing his hair and soaping himself down, Simon rinsed off the water and, wrapping himself in a large white bath towel, padded back into the bedroom where he slumped back onto the bed.

The room reminded him of the four-star hotel near Bournemouth where Herald Books held its spring and winter conferences at which Simon was called upon to give upbeat presentations of forthcoming new titles to the company's salesmen. He rarely failed to get his end away with one of the girls from head office on these occasions although when describing to Adrian the wild fucking which took place at the last conference Simon modestly suggested that it was the ambiance of a hotel room as much as his charm that helped to get the girls in the mood for some rumpy pumpy.

It's a shame Adrian couldn't have come here and had a nice refreshing shower before he left the office this evening, reflected Simon drowsily, unaware of course that his friend had already been under the shower with the lovely Marlene. Then he yawned and promptly fell fast asleep.

He was woken by a gentle shake of his shoulder. Clare Norrice stood at his side dressed in a green silk robe. 'Wake up, sleeping beauty, I'm sorry I was delayed but my charity committee had so much work to get through this afternoon that we didn't break up till half past six. Anyhow, I've followed your example and taken a shower and now I'm ready for some action!'

She slid off her robe and Simon sat up as he looked lasciviously over her enchanting nude body. Clare's breasts were large, heavy and tawny-nippled and when she lifted her arms to bunch her golden locks through a pink hair band, her bosoms rose sensuously upwards. At twenty-eight her stomach was no longer completely flat but it was smooth skinned and pure white, curving down in a classic line to her fluffy blonde muff inside which he could see her puffy pussy lips.

Simon's shaft thickened into an erection when she slid down beside him and he first slipped his left arm around her before reaching across her with his right arm to massage her elongated nipples before letting his fingers drop down to trace delicate patterns through the curls of her neatly trimmed flaxen bush.

'M'mmm, you're making my quim all wet, you devil,' she purred as the palm of Simon's left hand pressed against her bottom. When he inserted two fingers from his right hand into her squishy slit, Clare began to gyrate against it so wildly that she was soon on the brink of an orgasm. She spread her legs and thrust her hips forward as she grabbed hold of his throbbing boner and murmured: 'Well, my darling, now that we've switched on the gas, I think we should light the fire.'

She slicked her hand up and down Simon's stiff shaft and a fervent groan escaped from his lips when she bent forward and began to lick his prick, letting the tip of her tongue run round the ridge of his uncapped ruby helmet. He sank back on the pillow and sighed with pleasure as she lustily lapped on his ballsack whilst she fisted his pulsing prick.

But then, to Simon's amazement, Clare lifted her head and said pensively: 'This isn't right, you know. It's very wrong of me to suck another man's cock while my poor husband is away on business.'

He looked at her in total astonishment. 'What on earth are you talking about?' he demanded hotly. 'I don't see why you should give a damn whether Freddie minds us enjoying ourselves. God Almighty, when he's at home he actually encourages other men to fuck you – so long as he can watch, of course!'

'That may well be but I still feel guilty about being so naughty behind his back,' Clare demurred. She released his throbbing tool and he was about to ridicule this extraordinary statement when the penny suddenly dropped and he realised exactly what was behind her abrupt volte-face.

A grin slowly spread over Simon's face as he joined in her game, correctly judging what Clare wanted his role to be in the charade. In his best schoolmasterish voice, he growled: 'Yes, I suppose that's very understandable. You *have* been a very bad girl, and I think you deserve a jolly good spanking for your disgraceful conduct.'

Simon sat up and slid his legs over the side of the bed and ordered Clare to bend over his knees. Sure enough, she slithered across to stretch herself obediently over his lap. His erect todger throbbed against her belly as he ran his hand lovingly over the roundness of her delicious backside, allowing his finger to trail along the curvy cleft that separated the creamy cheeks.

Then he raised his arm and brought it down again sharply as he administered a firm smack on her peachy bottom with the palm of his hand. 'Ow!' squealed Clare as she wriggled sensuously under the force of the blow but Simon held her down firmly as he gave the cheek a second smart slap. He repeated the punishment and Clare's bum cheeks blushed a delicate shade of pink as he said sternly: 'There, that will teach you to deceive Freddie in such an underhand way!'

However, his pulsing pole was now aching for attention and he was able to mete out only two further slaps before he pulled her up. She immediately straddled him and whispered: 'Stand by to repel boarders! I'm coming aboard for a fuck!'

'You won't encounter any resistance from me,' panted Simon who moved his thighs to make her as comfortable as possible. Clare plumped herself down on his knees and guided his rampant stiffie directly into her squelchy slit, leaning forward so that her tawny titties brushed his hairy chest. In the long wall mirror Simon could see her rounded bum cheeks jiggle as she bounced up and down his quivering cock.

'Oooh! What a super fuck!' she gasped, all feigned words of guilt about deceiving her husband now forgotten as Simon jerked his hips upwards and his thick prick reamed out the innermost recesses of her juicy quim. Clare shivered all over as a series of electrically charged orgasms suddenly sparked out of her groin.

She swung herself off his throbbing chopper. It gleamed wetly at her as she squatted down in front of him and rubbed his knob against a large stalky nipple. Then Clare lifted his legs over her shoulders before she curled her fingers around his cock. She tongued the wrinkled pink skin of his scrotum and moved to the underside of his shaft before she crammed his full length into her mouth until the tip of his helmet touched the back of her throat.

'Haaagh!' he groaned when her lips slid over his shaft and her head bobbed up and down over his trembling tool. But again Clare pulled his cock from her mouth, but this time she winked at him and said: 'Your choice, lover. Shall we finish with a fuck or would you prefer to end with a sucking off?'

'Do you really have to ask?' grunted Simon and she giggled happily: 'Great! That's precisely what I want too!'

She pushed him backwards onto the quilt and then threw herself back on the bed. Parting her thighs, as Clare stretched her pouting pussy lips with her fingers to display the red chink of cunny between them.

Simon moved over her and buried his cock to the hilt inside her juicy sheath. He paused to catch his breath and let his shaft rest motionless inside her quim, throbbing out a steady rhythm against the clinging walls of her love funnel.

'Jesus, your cunt fits me like a glove,' he said in awe, and then he began to fuck her, wiggling his hips to slide his length to and fro as it remained embedded inside her tight wet quim.

But he realised that would be unable to hold back the tide of spunk which was boiling up in his balls for much longer. Their bodies moved harmoniously together as he increased the pace, driving his prick harder and harder into her creamy cunny and filling her crack with his beefy shaft.

Clare screamed out in sheer excitement as she climaxed just before the stream of jism spurted out of his cock, drenching her love funnel. Simon spent himself to the limit, riding stiffly in and out of her sticky honeypot until he was milked dry. His shaft slowly deflated into softness as he collapsed down upon her.

They lay quietly for some minutes until Clare murmured: 'Simon, that was a lovely fuck, I really enjoyed it tremendously. It's so nice to make love with a handsome young man like you.'

'Flattery will get you everywhere,' he answered with a smile. 'But you've a luscious body, Clare, and I can't believe there isn't a queue of younger guys eagerly waiting for you to bed them.'

'There's a happy thought,' she sighed. 'Without wanting to brag, I dare say I could call up a loyal band of boys who are keen enough to shag me.'

'And who could blame them?' asked Simon rhetorically, skimming his fingers through the damp thatch of blonde hair at the base of her belly. 'Do you have anyone in particular in mind?'

Clare chuckled as she leaned out and opened the drawer of the bedside table and took out a long white envelope. She passed it to Simon and said: 'Not as such, although perhaps I should try and contact the youngster who wrote me this letter. I should explain that earlier this year Freddie gave a generous amount of money for sports equipment to a youth club in a little Bedfordshire village where he grew up. We were invited there last month to watch the lads play cricket against the county Colts team and present an award to the man of the match.

'They certainly chose the right weekend for the match – it was so blazing hot that I felt uncomfortable just wearing only a thin summer dress over my bra and knickers. I mentioned to Freddie that I would have loved to go for a cool swim somewhere.

'The trouble was that I didn't bring a costume, but Freddie stroked his chin and said: "Well, that might not matter. There's quite a deep stream which runs through Lord Chambersbury's land only ten minutes walk away and I know a secluded spot where we could take a quick dip in the all-together. Wait here and I'll pop into the pavilion and cadge the loan of a couple of towels."

'He was as good as his word and quarter of an hour later we were larking around together in the water. Freddie took some photographs of me in the nude before we dried ourselves in the sunshine. As we got dressed I thought I heard the rustling of leaves in a nearby clump of bushes but as there didn't seem to be anyone around, I decided it must have been my imagination.

'Anyhow, three days later this letter arrived here for me,' concluded Clare. She pulled out a sheet of paper from the envelope and handed it to Simon. 'I think you might find it amusing.'

Simon's eyebrows shot up as he read the neatly typed missive:

Dear Mrs Norrice,
You really shouldn't have let your husband take rude pictures of you when you came to watch the cricket match last Sunday. But to be honest, I'm glad he did because I happened to see you and since then I've been having to wank at least three times a day thinking about your lovely tits and hairy pussy.

I would give anything to have a print of the photograph in which you stuck your bum cheeks out towards the camera with your legs apart. It seemed as if you were dying to be fucked doggie-style and I would have loved to have rammed my rock-hard todger into your juicy cunt and given you a good seeing-to before depositing wodges of sticky jism inside your quim.

My cock would still be stiff when I pulled it out and then I would rub honey all over your beautiful breasts and lick every drop off your big strawberry tits before you sucked my thick eight-and-three-quarter-inch prick until I spunked in your mouth and you swallowed all my creamy cum.

Please don't be offended by this day dream but you're the horniest cock-hungry lady I've ever come across in my whole life and I would love to fuck you senseless. Next time I write to you I'll try and pluck up enough courage to ask you for a date. For now though, I'll just sign off as Your Devoted Unknown Admirer

'Phew! This chap certainly has a vivid imagination,' commented Simon as he returned the letter to Clare who folded it up and replaced it in the envelope. 'Have you any idea who might have written it?'

'Not exactly, although I suspect it was one of the boys from the youth club. They were batting when Freddie and I took our dip so at the time there were nine of them off the field.'

'Yes, I see although it's possible that the culprit is an older bloke,' reflected Simon. Clare laughed as she replaced the envelope in the drawer and agreed: 'It's possible, but surely only a young lad would measure his cock to the nearest quarter of an inch! Anyhow, if he does write again I'll just tear up the letter because, although I found it amusing, it's hardly the way to win a lady, is it?'

She squeezed his cock and murmured: 'Now gird your loins, Simon, I want you to fuck me again before Trish comes round here with her friend – oh yes, and with any luck we can expect a visit from Adrian Klein.'

'By all means,' replied Simon manfully. 'But I'm afraid he's working this evening,' and he went on to explain how important a night it was going to be for his chum. 'In fact, he did ask us if we could find time to pop in and cheer on Allan Godfrey. He must make a good impression tonight if he wants to land this contract.'

Monday evenings were usually the quietest of the week at *La Miraggio* but on this particular night there was a tension in the atmosphere which Adrian felt he could cut with a knife. Dickie Segal was not in the best of moods, for the sexual shenanigans at lunchtime had tired him and the tough negotiations at his early evening meeting with the Hurricanes' manager had left the impressario with a nagging headache.

However, Dickie perked up at the arrival of Belinda Headley. The svelte blonde looked stunning in a tight-fitting black minidress and he was happy to exchange some off-the-record showbiz gossip with her.

Then Marlene appeared and Adrian invited her to sit down next to him and introduced her to his other guests. 'Thanks, Adrian, I'm on my own as my friends had made other arrangements,' she said. And then, lowering her voice to a whisper, she added: 'It looks like Dickie is very taken with your blonde bird. Shall we dance and leave them to get better acquainted?'

Backstage, Allan Godfrey looked out to see Adrian and

Marlene together and then to his surprise he found himself staring at Roz whose arms were round the neck of a burly young man as they smooched slowly around the dance-floor. *Who could she have picked up here?* he wondered silently and then he gave a little chuckle as he recalled that Roz had said her flat-mate's name was Frankie . . .

Just as well Frankie's turned out to be a bloke, I won't have any problems if Roz and Diana meet up, he muttered to himself as Diana came up and pinched his bottom. 'Don't worry, you'll knock them cold,' she said and Allan gave her a warm smile as he kissed her cheek.

An hour later it was clear that Belinda had paired off with Dickie which hardly bothered Adrian who was happy enough to squire Marlene. In the meantime Simon and Clare had arrived along with Jennie who they met in the foyer – but minus Trish, who had not made an appearance at Clare's flat by the time Allan Godfrey bounded up on the stage. They were all making a night of it together.

He began his patter with his usual brash bonhomie and then he switched to a tried and tested routine about his first love. 'It's the anniversary of the day I first met Joyce. I met her at Battersea Fun Fair in the tunnel of love . . . she was digging it. I can see her now. What a figure, thirty-four, thirty-four, thirty-four . . . she used to be a straight actress.

'I said to her what else do you do and she said: "I breed pigs." I said: 'Fancy, I always thought they did it for themselves.'

Allan looked quickly across to Adrian's table and his heart began to beat faster when he saw Dickie Segal was rocking with laughter. From then on, his act went down a storm with Dickie in particular applauding and bouncing up and down in his seat. The fact that Belinda's clever fingers were stroking the impresario's big cock under the table only helped to make the occasion one he would not forget in a hurry.

Allan finally wound up his act: 'Anyhow, ladies and gentlemen, I'm sure you can all think of better things to do than listen to me all night so I'll leave you with this parting thought – what do you get if you cross an elephant with a call-girl?

You don't know? You get a two-ton raver that does it for peanuts!'

He bounded off the stage to a roar of applause and when he returned to take a bow he saw to his delight that some of his audience – led by Simon Byrne – had risen to their feet to give him a standing ovation. Adrian glanced at Dickie Segal who was applauding enthusiastically while bending his head to listen to Belinda who was murmuring something in his ear which caused a wide smile to appear on the impresario's face.

The sweetest feeling imaginable swept through Adrian's body when Dickie returned his glance and gave him a thumbs-up sign. Clearly all he had to do now was to argue with Dickie about Allan Godfrey's wages when the brilliant young comedian made his stage debut in *West End Extra*.

Tanya would join his group later but he speculated that neither she nor Marlene would mind sharing his favours after they left the club and he could safely leave Dickie Segal, who was now practically sharing his chair with Belinda, to his own devices. All was for the best in the best of all possible worlds . . .

You don't know? You got a [illegible] the genius."

He [illegible] of [illegible] a [illegible] and when he [illegible] to take [illegible] he [illegible] to ask [illegible] that [illegible] of his audience [illegible]

[illegible]

[illegible] and [illegible] the [illegible] of the [illegible]

[illegible] for the [illegible]